Table of Contents

Preface...v

Frank Awakes as Randy..1

The Mission...7

Computer Reincarnation...13

Randy's Head Hunter..18

Renee Finds a Slave...36

Adam's a Recruiter..66

Meeting the "P" Class..74

Interviews Begin...83

An Ex-VP...106

Penny Jo's Discovery...115

Parker Departs..124

Disney Dream...134

Reunited with Miriam...147

Meeting a Mason...161

Finding a Mole..167

Becoming a Senator..175

Egyptian Mission..191

Bayh Goes for a Walk..204

PJ in Mexico...216

Treasure Hunt...231

Preface

I sat drinking my coffee and looking at the vast Atlantic Ocean from the restaurant of my hotel, Beira Mar, in Angra Do Heroismo, Azores, Portugal. It was a beautiful morning with a few white puffy clouds and lots of sun. As it also was a chilly, crisp, spring, morning, I could only imagine how cold the ocean water must be. I guessed the animals there were suited for it and didn't mind. *How incredible it must be to live in the ocean*, I thought, *to explore what we know so little about*. It is said we know more about the moon than our own oceans. My thoughts changed; I wondered what people with a terminal disease thought about in their final days. They probably tried to contemplate where they were going. What is it like? Will they remember who they once were? Will the trials of being human be gone? I recalled a poem my sister selected for my mom's funeral, entitled "God's Garden." It was about how tired our bodies get and how we suffer in this life. Then God lifts us up, takes us home, and brings us peace. I was tired. I hoped to find peace.

I looked back across the restaurant. I saw him standing there for a moment looking for me. I waved my hand.

"Good morning," I said as he approached. "How did you sleep?"

"Great. I left my window slightly open and could hear the waves. It was so nice and calming. Are you sure you want to go through with this?"

I looked directly at him.

"Definitely, I have wanted this for some time. I need this to end I can't take it anymore. I want to move on."

"What about her?" he asked. "Are you sure she wants her life to end this way?"

"We are both worn out and just want to be together without the torture of this life," I replied. "This will give us both what we want."

"Well, I will do what you requested. How long do you think it will take for you to tell me all the details?"

I replied, laughing, "I suppose that depends on how many questions you ask. I have been through so many lives, I can barely remember where it all began or who I was when I had my first memory. It's like trying to remember what your actual first memory was when you were a small child. I am not sure anyone can say they have had as long a run as I have had, as Frank, or as interesting."

"When do you think the world will be ready to evolve and learn more about this?"

"I am not sure. Evolution moves in small increments, just as slowly emotionally and spiritually as biologically. People are not ready for big changes to their beliefs. Maybe in time. Anyway, that is not my decision. Those in power always decide for the masses. Individuals never have the freedom they are led to believe they do."

He looked at me.

"Are you ready to begin? To tell your story? Do you want to start here in the restaurant or somewhere else?"

"Here is good," I said as I looked out over the ocean. "This is where it ends."

"Do you think people will believe what you have experienced, after they have heard it?"

"People always believe what they want to believe, no matter what is put in front of them. I can only tell what I know and what has happened to me, from my perspective,"

"What do you think it will be like for you, after you're gone from here?"

"Liberating," I said. "We will be able to explore a new realm. There are so many possibilities, so much to experience. I cannot imagine what it will be like. Maybe if I come back in another life I can share those sensations. It's exciting, I think, like being an infant all over again. We will have to learn how to move, how to communicate, learn about dangers, how to play, so many new things."

"Okay. Let's get started. I am anxious to begin," he replied.

Frank Awakes as Randy

I opened my eyes and looked around for a minute to see where I was. I found myself in a hospital room. A nurse stood next to my bed. She asked, "How do you feel?"

I replied, "I feel great, fantastic. Well-rested, in fact."

"You may have a headache for a while, but if it doesn't go away fairly quickly we can give you something," she said.

"Where am I?"

"You are in Washington DC at a Crystal Discovery facility to help you recover from your injuries."

"What injuries?" I asked. "I only remember being hit by a missile and pulling the ejection handles. I don't feel injured."

She smiled at me for a moment, then turned away to write on a chart. "You don't have any injuries anymore. You are young and healthy now. I'll tell Dr. Stevenson you're awake and he'll come by and explain it all to you in a moment. If you need anything, there is a buzzer next to your bed. Push it and I will come to help you. My name is Cindy."

I thought it was weird she said I was young. I turned my hands back and forth. They did look and feel different, almost like they were not mine. I was dressed in a hospital gown and could not see most of my body, but it, too, somehow felt different. I felt strong and full of energy.

The door to my room opened and a tall man in a white coat, in his forties with short-cropped hair, came in. He was a good-looking man, right out of a daytime soap opera. "Hi, I'm Dr. Stevenson. How are you doing?"

"I'm fine, doc. Never felt better."

"That's great. You have been through quite an ordeal."

"Yeah," I said. "I've read reports of other pilots punching out of an airplane and their comments were always something like they had been shot out of a cannon. All of them reported blacking out and it seemed they always had at least one serious injury. What injuries did I have?"

"Well, you were pretty messed up. The missile strike sent several pieces of shrapnel from the plane's fuselage into your body. One piece, which caused the most serious injury, punctured your large intestine and caused a major hemorrhage."

"Wow, amazing," I retorted. "I don't feel a thing now, no pain. How long was I unconscious? I don't remember any of this."

"You were evac'ed from Kandahar to Ramstein. You died there in the hospital."

I snapped my head around to look the doctor in the eyes and chuckled. "I'm sorry doctor, what did you just say? I thought I heard you say I died."

Stevenson was more insistent this time. "I did say you died."

I responded in disbelief, "Ah hmm. So how am I here talking to you?"

He explained. "Frank, remember the program you volunteered for where we installed a device to your brain to monitor your bio-medical conditions in combat? Well, that device did a lot more than what we first explained to you."

Shaking my head, mystified, I asked, "Wait, if I died, how am I here?" I looked over myself, as if to affirm I was alive.

"Frank, I know this is difficult to comprehend, but this body you have right now is not the one you used to have. It's not the same one you had when you were shot down over Afghanistan. We exchanged you after you died."

"Exchanged me…what do you mean, exchanged me?"

"You were one of the lucky ones to be selected to be part of CD," he replied. "I know it seems impossible or far-fetched, but we actually have the technological capability to connect to a human brain and download, store, and then upload a person's entire lifetime of memories into another body. This history includes everything from birth until the upload is completed. It might seem wildly impossible. However, if you break it down mathematically it's actually pretty simple. Consider the average human lifespan, which is approximately 75 years or about 657,000 hours. Of course, we sleep a third of that time, or 219,000 hours, and only dream or create memory a fraction of that time. The result is about 438,000 hours of recorded memory, of which much of this is either inconsequential or simply empty. Thus, one can see the computer-related numbers get more manageable to deal with, especially if you consider for a moment how much data Google has stored in its computers."

He continued. "When you first joined this project, the device we implanted in your brain allowed us to download all of your memory. Memories, which include all you have learned, experienced, thought about, and even dreamed. You see, Frank, memories are your identity, your personality: they make up who you are. We then took your data and stored it in our super computer — what we here at CD affectionately call Big Mac — in case you had the misfortune, as you did, of dying. We then uploaded your information into this body you now are feeling and getting used to. The body you now have is only nineteen years old."

"How can that be? I did not know we had that technology. Does any of the private sector have access to this?" I asked.

"If a private person could have the exchange procedure it would cost huge amounts of money, something probably in the realm of ten million dollars," he answered. "To more precisely answer your question, no. No private company is aware of this technology. An American governmental agency called Defense Advanced Research Projects Agency (DARPA) first acquired the technology from an MIT research team. CD took it over from DARPA for defense applications, and they control who gets to exchange and who does not. I was originally asked to become part of a test project to protect pilots, because of the vast amounts of time and money spent on your training and experience. The other aspect was simply to be part of the clinical trials to provide an evaluation of the technology."

I must have begun shaking a bit, because Dr. Stevenson reached over and put his hand on my forearm. "Frank, I know this is a lot to take in. Try to relax. You are still the same guy you were before this all happened, just biologically younger. You should have all your old memories, feelings, and the same personality you had before. You are still Frank Freiberg inside, just not on the outside, since if you were you would be dead."

I lay stunned for a few moments, then looked at the doctor's face for signs he was kidding or that maybe I was having a bad dream. He looked back at me with a blank stare for a few seconds, then got up and walked toward the door while writing in a chart he was carrying. "If you have any questions or problems, ring the nurse and I can come back. For now, try to process what I told you and do what the nurse says. You will be out of here in no time. Congratulations, Frank, you just got a new lease on life." I laid my head back and tried to think about what he just told me, but felt a bit weak and fell asleep.

When I woke up I really had to pee. I got up and went into the bathroom and relieved myself for what seemed like several minutes. I moved over to the sink to wash my hands, reluctant to look in the mirror, and when I did I almost fell to the floor. I could not believe what I was seeing — it wasn't me. It felt like me — I mean, I know who I am, I am Frank Freiberg — but it wasn't my reflection. The guy in the mirror did not look a day over eighteen: a kid, handsome enough, with a short military-style haircut, brown hair, blue eyes, over six feet tall, but not me. I was dumbfounded and kept looking in the mirror. I could feel my hands grip the sink, so I knew I was not dreaming. I felt dizzy and thought maybe the drugs they gave me were too strong and I was hallucinating. I slowly wobbled back toward the bed and thought I had better try to sleep it off.

Nurse Cindy came in as I was making my way back to the bed. "Here, let me help you. Sometimes those first few times out of bed can disrupt your equilibrium. You could pass out."

I stammered, "Yeah, I feel weird. Those must be some pretty strong drugs you have me on."

Nurse Cindy insisted, "Oh, no drugs. You are not on anything, but you may be feeling the effects of the brain procedure."

"Brain surgery? I had brain surgery?"

"Not surgery, but a procedure that took almost twelve hours," she replied.

"Wow," I said. "I feel pretty good for having had all that done."

"Dr. Stevenson said you should feel fine in a day or so," Cindy said. I realized now that I wasn't dreaming, that what the doctor had told me must be true. I must have had a strange expression on my face, because Cindy put her hand on top of mine. "A lot to take in, huh? The good news is you're not forty anymore. You're alive with a healthy nineteen-year-old body."

I looked back at her and softly said, "Yeah, I guess I am fortunate to be alive."

For me, being a forty-year-old man waking up in the body of a nineteen-year-old boy was not something easily processed. It sounded good, but things were strange. The waking up part was no different than we all do every morning after a good night's rest. You open your eyes and just like Descartes' famous statement, "I think therefore I am," you say to yourself, "I am so-and-so." You get up, go to the bathroom, look in the mirror, see yourself and con-firm. "Yes, I am indeed so-and-so," because it is the only face you remember. What was different this time was that when I got up

and went to the bathroom, I looked in the mirror and saw someone else. I felt like Frank Freiberg and had all of his knowledge and
memories, but the mirror showed the face and body of a man half
my age. Cindy walked away and I thought about the mission that
had brought me here.

The Mission

Our mission was support for "Operation Enduring Freedom" in Afghanistan, to seek and destroy Taliban and Al Qaeda terrorist camps, and fly close air support for ground troops. I found Afghanistan very similar to the simulated combat missions we flew in the mountains of Nevada, but there was a significant difference. In Nevada, no one was shooting back at us. Our commanders warned us that the terrorist groups we were targeting had shoulder-fire surface-to-air missiles, which could take down an F16. These missiles, "Stingers," were the same ones the United States secretly provided to the Afghans when they were fighting the Soviet Union. Now we were getting shot at with our own weapons.

The days we flew combat missions were very long, tedious, and exhausting, and included an hour or two of intense focus while we dropped bombs or covered ground troops with suppression fire from our machine guns. The missions would begin after a restless period of trying to sleep. We all knew we needed to be vigilant for about twelve to fourteen hours or risk being shot down. It was like the instances we've all had, when you know you have something important to accomplish the next day, something which demands your attention — an important test, a job interview, a vital presentation — and cannot fall asleep because you're overwhelmed thinking of the next day. Missions always began three hours before takeoff. We had an operational briefing for two hours, and then an hour preflight of the aircraft. The flight time from Saudi Arabia to Afghanistan was approximately three to four hours, depending on where the mission was located. We flew in formation up and back with a tanker escort, because F16s have small fuel tanks and can't make the round trip, plus combat, on one tank of fuel. Depending on the mission, dropping bombs or close air support for ground troops, we would only be in the mission area for maybe one or two hours. After we returned to base, there would be one or two hours of debriefing with maintenance and operations personnel. Thus, one mission day would be a grueling thirteen or so hours — and, trust me, there are no break rooms on an F16.

One evening while walking to Ops, I noticed an incredible night sky. It was a moonless night, and there were more stars than I had ever seen. I counted several shooting stars during my five minute walk from my barracks. I felt as if time had stopped or I was lost in meditation, amazed at how enchanting and mesmerizing the universe was and how much we did not know about it, at how small it made me feel, and how insignificant. Here I was, one person, in a small country, on a small planet, in a small solar system surrounding a small star. How could I possibly make a difference in the grand scheme of things?

I walked through the doors to the briefing room, when my commander's sharp loud voice snapped me back to reality. After all the pilots were seated, he dictated the mission to us: "Support a special operations unit on a secret mission in rugged mountainous terrain one hour south of Kandahar." This gave me goosebumps, as I sat listening attentively to his briefing. I knew this meant flying very low, at night, in mountainous terrain, firing our weapons dangerously close to our ground troops, where we would be visible to the enemy and risk the possibility of a Stinger hit.

We left immediately following the briefing. The mission was routine up to the rendezvous point with the special ops unit. A few minutes after we began to orbit the area of the mission objective, the ground units began to yell in their radios that they were under heavy fire from a position above them and were pinned down. Each pilot took his turn for a bomb-and-suppression fire run over the top of our guys to take out the opposition fighters. When it was my turn, the ops leader's voice sparked over the radio with greater intensity: the enemy was moving still closer and increasing fire on their position. He gave me the exact coordinates to hit and told me to come in fast and low for a precision strike. We used to practice these bomb runs in training back at Nellis and I loved the feeling of being extremely focused. I found the target and locked onto it with my laser to guide the ordnance to its target, and then bombs away. I was pulling into a steep climb when I heard the loud horn from my counter-measures radar and saw the flashing red light on my Primary Flight Display, indicating I had an incoming enemy missile.

I do not recall much after I felt the missile hit and I pulled my ejection handles. I do remember looking up at the same beautiful sky, that had caught my eye while I had been walking to ops only a few short hours before. It was like a trance and I began to dream. I laughed to myself for a second and thought that it sure was a good idea I had decided to become part of that new program.

One day, right after I finished undergraduate pilot training, my commander called me into his office and told me I had been selected for a program to track downed, lost, or captured pilots. It was called "Crystal Discovery." Only after I joined was I briefed on what the program entailed, or what I was told it involved. The program was twofold. First, it had a mechanism using GPS for locating military personnel in combat. The second was more secret and nebulous. I was told it was an experimental mechanism to record bio-medical activity during combat. These two mechanisms were contained in a single small unit, surgically attached to the base of my brain. Anyone looking at me would never know I had had a brain operation or the unit installed. Everyone who received this surgery was also given a special tattoo to identify them. It was of a square and compass with the letters CD in the middle. They put the tattoo on the underside of the left arm almost in the armpit, so it was usually out of normal sight, even with a shirt off.

After I ejected from the plane, I remember waking up a few times while being transported, going in and out of consciousness, first in a helicopter, then while I was being transferred into an airplane. I recall that after I arrived, a doctor said near my hospital bed, "He is not going to make it; he's hurt too badly." I wondered who he was talking about. Since I felt hurt but not dying, I figured he must be talking about someone else. Poor guy, I thought. His family and loved ones are going to miss him.

My family would be devastated if something happened to me. I was a healthy exuberant forty-year-old man, with a lovely wife, Miriam, to whom I had been married for ten years and with whom I have two beautiful children, Emma and Justin. I first met Miriam during college while I was out on a date with another girl, Judith. Miriam and Judith were roommates; we all went to Indiana University in Bloomington. I had only been on a couple of dates with Judith when we met up with Miriam at Jake's nightclub. Miriam was exotically gorgeous, nothing like I had ever seen before. She was Turkish, with olive skin, almost black eyes, and jet-black hair down to the middle of her back. And she was very tall, about five-feet-nine, and not someone I was used to seeing in southern Indiana. She was obviously athletic and she dressed very fashionably. I could not take my eyes off of her. Judith kept slapping me on the arm and telling me to stop staring at Miriam. I told her I was not staring, but admiring. We all laughed at that comment. After a few dates with the three of us hanging out together at their apartment, I realized I was more interested in Miriam than Judith. Judith also noticed I was becoming more interested in Miriam, after leaving the room on several occasions and coming back to find us engaged in heated conversations about politics or world affairs. Miriam wanted to be a history or political science teacher, and I wanted to be a pilot. Sometimes we had discussions about the possibility that I might have to serve in combat. She had ethical and moral objections to war, so there was some conflict between us. I told her that fighting was sometimes necessary to defend oneself, but she wouldn't have it.

She said there was always an alternative. We dated until after college and I finished pilot training, and then we got married. In the beginning we had fun traveling around the world. Of course we went to Turkey to visit her homeland, then Greece, Spain, Tahiti, Brazil, and Costa Rica, to name just a few. Miriam was very relaxed and comfortable to be with. Guys were always hitting on her, but she would be sweet and gentle when she turned them down. I loved this about her. She treated me like I was the only man in the world.

When Miriam got pregnant, we were so excited. Emma came out fearless and screaming to challenge the world. She was the type of baby who would not cry if she hurt herself investigating something new, like cabinet doors with springs. She wanted to explore and dis cover everything around her as she grew up, and persistently asked why questions. Even in kindergarten she had all the boys chasing her around, but she wasn't interested. She would rather read books or play with the family dog, a German Shepherd named Bender. Emma grew and became increasingly beautiful with her long dark hair, blue eyes, and tall frame even at just eight years old. Justin was born eleven months after his sister, with thick chocolate brown hair, and was as handsome as ever. Justin loved the water, especially water parks and water slides. It was great having the kids so close together in age. They were almost like twins and got along great, but they were very competitive with each other. As a family we loved to take trips together. Miriam and I wanted to expose the children to different environments and cultures. The last time I saw them, before I left on this deployment, was when they were headed out the front door, off to school with big smiles on their faces. They were used to me leaving for short periods of time, so they did not pay a lot of attention when I left. Their world was so innocent; their only care in the world was to go to school and have play dates. I did not feel it was a big risk going over to fight the war on terrorism, since I was going to be based in a safe place, Saudi Arabia, and flying an airplane against a country that did not even have an army or an air force. What could go wrong, right?

I thought, in many ways, it's a dream come true to, in a sense, be reborn and not to have to worry about dying. Psychological research indicates that the fear of death controls every aspect of our emotional lives, including down to the biological level which generates the flight or fight response. Imagine not having to worry about getting hurt, or contracting a disease, or being incapacitated when your body gets old. One could simply exchange and live a new life in a new body, maybe to correct past mistakes or regrets, and live a totally different experience, or perhaps continue a learning experience which could not be accomplished in one lifetime. The greatest thing is that you can remember all the experiences and knowledge you had from a previous life, a bit like computerized reincarnation. Imagine if Plato, Aristotle, George Washington, Isaac Newton, Einstein, Ronald Reagan, or Gary Cooper could have exchanged into younger bodies. What contributions could they have brought to the world?

Computer Reincarnation

I wanted to know more, this was all very confusing. I rang the buzzer. Cindy came in and I asked her, "Can I speak to Dr. Stevenson again?" She turned and walked back out. A few moments later he walked through the door. I asked, "Doctor, can you tell me more about this project and how all this came to be?"

"Okay, I will try. But I am not sure how much you will remember since you are sleeping a lot right now, you may forget our conversation," he replied. "Also, I am not sure how much I am authorized to tell you. Crystal Discovery was a research project led by two MIT professors, John and Sarah Keith. Their research teams discovered they could store human memory on a computer hard drive in much the same way that the brain stores memory. Computers, at their most basic level, achieve all their power by means of simple electronic switches, which are either turned on or off. The capacities of computing speed and memory have been limited in the past by how many switches could be clustered onto a circuit board or chip. Science has now produced the equivalent storage and processing ability of the human brain, in part, by use of cloud technology. This phenomenon uses the virtual world and multiple remote computers to store vast amounts of information. To give an idea of how far computing power has come in its short history, currently the fastest computer in the world processes at a rate of approximately one quadrillion or 1000 trillion floating point operations per second, or FLOPS, or the equivalent of about two million laptop computers tied together. The human brain stores information in much the same way computers do, except that instead of storing it electronically, it stores it bio-electronically, with cells (neurons) that act like electrical switches in a computer's hard-drive. In addition, there has been a revolutionary discovery in how brain cells store data or memory, which at the most basic level are not much different than NAND and NOR gates. Brain encoding for memory storage has been determined to occur in the hippocampus and amygdala parts of the brain. Scientists discovered that by connecting tiny wires from these two key parts of the brain to a tiny computer processor attached to the basal ganglia, or upper brain stem, the brain segments can transmit signals to an external computer hard drive. This is similar to the way the brain sends information to its main storage center, the cerebellum. Through this procedure, CD's computer can connect to the brain's memory and access it, like we would access our own thoughts and download them. Scientists also discovered that they could upload information from the computer back into a brain."

"That all sounds pretty technical. But it really works, huh?" I asked.

"Yes, indeed. You are living proof of our successes," he replied. "In addition, these discoveries caused an instantaneous quantum leap in human evolution. CD began to store some of the brightest minds on the planet, in the event of their untimely death. CD was a government-sponsored program, and it was not long after the discoveries that the government implemented their own ideas as to what the technology should be used for and took over the entire program. I do not know all of the ways the government is using the technology, but I do know that black operations were quickly involved. Lucky for you, it was introduced for testing on pilots. Later, more discoveries were made which enabled them to pick and choose which parts of memory to record or erase. Also, scientists found that they could upload simple information, such as books, to test the brain's ability to store and recall information uploaded via computer, rather than the normal pathways a brain uses to store information via the five senses. The brain was able to recall book information uploaded from a computer more easily and accurately than it could if it had been uploaded the slow way that humans have done it for centuries, by reading, deciphering, interpreting and storing written word or symbols. When the brain receives large amounts of data quickly, like a computer download, it stores it in the brain more efficiently than it does when the data is interpreted via our senses. This is not entirely different from the way we record or recall a traumatic event. Ask anyone who has had something unusual, different, scary, or catastrophic happen: they never forget it. Or ask someone about a book they read ten years ago and listen to what information they can retrieve about the book. Maybe they can give you a hint of the central idea of the book, but no specifics. Now books from ten years ago can be recalled and used more efficiently and effectively by the brain for direct application and thought."

Dr. Stevenson continued. "As you can imagine, the military and intelligence services went crazy thinking about what this technology meant to the world of espionage. For example, they believe they can now capture a foreign leader or researcher and download their knowledge; they would not have to interrogate them. Or they could capture a foreigner, erase their memory, and upload an American spy into the foreigner's body, and he would then be able to move undetected within the foreigner's community or government. But, I do not know all the projects and applications Uncle Sam is implementing with this new technology. You situation was somewhat easier than dealing with spies."

"Oh yeah, how's that?"

"Once you were accepted into the program, as you know, you were brought to the Institute's headquarters for the initial medical procedure to connect a small computer processor and memory device to the base of my brain. You have an implant attached to your brain now. First, it is a GPS transmitter. Second, the device continues to record all memory from the time of the first full download or backup, until they conduct another backup. Subsequent backups or exchanges can be performed wirelessly or without further surgery. The only caveat is you have to be in the same room as the computer for the exchange, since the computer equipment is unique for this application and there is only one in the world. As you can imagine, the technology is amazingly guarded. This procedure is not dissimilar from the manner in which we back up our smart phones periodically. In this way, they can upload or restore all of you if you are killed, as long as they have access to the implant and it has remained undamaged. The body need not be alive. Third, it allows them, before they wake you up from surgery, to download and store your entire brain's recorded memories. Everything from birth up to that point: all your experiences, education, emotions, everything that comprised your identity."

"Okay, I understand the premise and what you told me about how it works. Now I have a bigger question."

"Yes, I bet you do. Let me guess. Whose body are you in? Why did they give it up for you?

"Yeah. Why would anyone die for me, or anyone else?"

Dr. Stevenson slowly walked around the room for a bit, with his hand holding his chin. "This is getting into a fringe area. I am not sure what I should tell you."

"Doctor, this is my life. I think I have a right to know, I am part of this project!"

"The military and CD recruited volunteer servicemen and women from all branches. They were told they would be a part of a secret program, vital to national security. They were not told what the program entailed, only limited information about the program. We also brought in other servicemen to store their memories, like you for possible future benefit. So, basically the young volunteers were brought in so their brains or lives could be erased and their bodies harvested for use by others — those whose lives were deemed more useful, whose education and experience was of greater benefit to mankind or at least the United States. People like you, a pilot whom the government had spent enormous amounts of money on to train and who had valuable experiences which would have been lost if you had died."

"Wow," I said. "I guess I should be shocked. I am not, but I should be. How do you feel about the moral and ethical implications, Doctor?"

"Well, it makes one think about it, that's for sure," he replied. "There are major issues posed by this technological advancement. First, a moral dilemma created by this next level of human evolution. The discovery to record, store, and exchange an entire human identity from one person to another. The problem is, who would become the new host, who would be used to exchange the old identity into? Secret governmental agencies were experienced in dealing with such dilemmas. The military has an almost unlimited number of young, strong, healthy bodies at their disposal and the perfect place to hide unusual changes in personality. They could put a 'classified' label on something or someone and the knowledge would be protected. With this technology, we had basically discovered how to computerize human reincarnation."

I was quiet.

Dr. Stevenson looked at me. "If you have any more questions, let me know. I will try to answer them."

Randy's Head Hunter

Truly, the first few days I felt no different than I ever had. The exceptions were that I did not have pain in my left knee from an old football injury and that I felt more energetic than before the crash. Also, I found out over the course of time that a few of my likes and dislikes had changed. For example, I used to like sushi, especially raw salmon and tuna, and now it repulsed me. I used to prefer to drink 7UP, now I loved Coke. I used to like ice cream, now I was lactose intolerant. It seems when you are exchanged into a new body your memory and identity are all transferred, but a few things innate to that particular body are biologically based and remain intact in the host—small things like preferences. These likes and dislikes apparently are written into each person's DNA coding and cannot be changed or passed on in an exchange.

I now had to be debriefed about what had happened to me and what was about to happen to my life; the world, it seemed, had changed. I had to be constantly reminded that Captain Franklin Freiberg's body died and along with it his life had to be buried. And at the same time I had to be reminded that I was now Airman First Class Randy Edwards. My immediate task was to learn all about the life of Randy Edwards. He was only 19, which made it easier than if he had been 40, but he had a family, friends, a girl back home, a life. Now, life had changed; his life was over and my second life was just beginning.

The military, being regimented, precise, and thorough, had every subject who participated in CD fill out a lengthy personal history questionnaire. It chronicled all of your life: memories of childhood, crushes in elementary school, your first kiss, who you lost your virginity with, family trips, random parties, anything that could be remembered. At the time, I thought it was strange and wondered what it had to do with the GPS locator or biomedical device. But the military is all about collecting data and I figured they had some Ph.D. sitting somewhere analyzing all the data to figure out who made the best soldiers. As it turned out, these questionnaires were invaluable for me to learn about the person whose body I had just taken over. After all, at some point I would meet the family and friends with whom I was supposed to have grown up.

I had fun learning all about my new body. It was almost like when I was a kid and got a new toy. I literally examined every part of my new body, inch by inch, to see what I could find. I was Caucasian of northern European descent, taller than I had been before, six feet four inches, a height I had always wanted to be. I weighed 195 pounds, an almost ideal weight for my height. It was great; I did not have to worry about what I ate, I had the metabolism of a nineteen-year-old. Fortunately, Randy had just gotten over his pubescent stage and I did not have to deal with being an acne-faced kid. I had blue eyes, light brown hair, nice straight white teeth; I obviously had had orthodontics at some point. And for the important parts of a man, I was more gifted than I was before! I had tons of energy and felt all the urges, like any boy my age. It was almost as if I was a possessed male lion on the prowl with a pride of lionesses nearby who needed my immediate and undivided attention. I do not remember having such strong instinctual urges when I was nineteen. Maybe I had them but did not understand what they were or what to do with them. Well, I can tell you I do now. This is every man's dream come true: to have a young man's body with an older man's man mind! But I must always remember, like any covert spy I could not reveal too much or risk raising suspicion as to how I knew so much at such a young age.

I worked with an exchange team who were like a group of counselors and they helped me transition to my new body and life. I was assigned a personal counselor, Sara, who knew all the intimate details about my case. She was probably in her late twenties, sweet, empathetic, and considerate, and it did not hurt that she was tall, had short blonde hair and blue eyes, and was beautiful like the proverbial girl next door. She suggested I immediately break up with Randy's girlfriend back home and sever all personal contacts with Randy's former life. The military had their own plan for me and they did not want to risk having to answer any questions about ties to a previous life. I wrote a Dear Jane letter to a girl I had never met and knew little to nothing about. I kept it brief: "Dear Danielle, I am sorry, but my life has changed directions. I am not the same person I was when we met. I want you to find someone else, someone more like you. We cannot be together anymore. Please do not try to contact me, I am moving on to another assignment. All the best, Randy."

I then called Brad, one of Randy's friends from high school, worried that he would not recognize my voice and believe it was his indeed his friend, or think something was wrong. I had to try to hide the fact that someone had taken over his friend's body, that his friend was gone, and that I knew little about their relationship. As the phone rang I was a bit nervous and then he answered, "Hello?" I replied, "Hey dude, what's up? How are you?"

"Wow, I have not heard from you in a while. Are you okay? Where are you?"

I paused for a moment. "I can't tell you where I am; the military won't let us say. But, I am okay. I am going on a long mission and won't be back for a while. They told us to tell friends and family not to worry, that we will not be able to contact anyone. It's an important part of the mission." While I was talking to Brad, I had to remind myself that I was talking to him with Randy's voice, not Frank's. The words were mine, Frank's words, but the sound was Randy's voice. It was all very weird.

Brad hesitated for a moment, "Sounds hardcore, dude. Are you okay? Can you come back home for a while before you go?"

"I'm fine, couldn't be better. I broke up with Danielle, though. I thought it best she moved on. I just want to keep my head clear and focused on my job over here. We don't have any time off before we ship out."

Brad replied, "Ah, that sucks. Well, glad you called, bro. Hope it all works out for you."

"Yeah, me too. If anyone asks about me, maybe you could tell them not to worry."

"Sure, sure no prob. I will handle it for you," Brad assured me.

Randy was an only child, so he did not have to worry about other brothers or sisters. His parents were older when he was born, his mom was in her late forties and his dad was in his late fifties. His dad had died about ten years ago from pancreatic cancer. He had no living aunts or uncles or other relatives that I knew of. I concluded by saying, "Dude, I have to go. We have a limited amount of phone time. Take care of yourself." I thought for a few moments after I got off the phone with Brad. I wondered if I did go to Collierville, would I have any memories or recollections of anything there? Would I have any intuitions about people or places there, something my new body would somehow know or remember and relate to me?

Last, I had to call Randy's mom. I hated the thought of trying to tell a mother that somehow her son was okay when I actually knew he was dead.

"Hello?" she answered with a southern accent.

"Mom, how are you? It's Randy, I only have a short time to talk. We are pulling out in a few minutes. You know how the military is. I wanted to tell you not to worry. I won't be calling for a while, maybe a long while—it's all secret stuff."

She replied, "Oh honey, are you okay? Are you hurt?"

"Yeah, mom, I'm fine, I'm not hurt. I volunteered for this mission. Maybe it will help end the war sooner."

"Oh Randy, you're such a good boy, so strong. I am proud of you for what you are doing over there."

I had tears welling up in my eyes, knowing this woman would never see her son again. The son she had raised and loved. "Mom, gotta go, they're calling." The last thing I heard was, "You take care of yourself son. God will be watching. Love you." Then I hung up. I thought for bit. Man, I do not want to do that again.

I asked Sara how they picked the host person for me. She told me it was classified, but based on the needs of the military. She did say the host had been someone who had specifically volunteered for a clandestine operation and had been advised of the personal risk. The volunteers had had to meet several times with a psychologist and sign a waiver to fully express that they would be going undercover and might or might not remember who they were after they returned after an extended period of time. They preferred people who had little to no family. As per typical military style, the volunteers were not given full disclosure of the details of the project they were volunteering for, but just a broad concept that their service would be in the best interests of their country and national security.

I frequently had thoughts of guilt about the person whose body I stole, about the person who died in order that I might live. I also thought, why me? What did I have that he did not have? I felt like a thief. I felt like a little kid hiding behind something or someone so others could not see him. It was like I was wearing a mask around and people did not recognize me. It was very strange. I would wake up at night, forget for a second what had happened, and walk into the bathroom, look in the mirror, and scare the hell out of myself. I thought a few times that if I stared hard enough into my eyes, I could see my old self, the old me. But, the longer I was this new figure, in this new body, with this new appearance, I forgot what I used to look like. Sometimes when I was looking in the mirror, I wondered if Frank ever existed or if I was dreaming. If this is for real, how could this have happened? How could it be true?

THE EXCHANGE

The military wanted me to get started as soon as possible with my new assignment as an intelligence officer. Sara instructed me to get used to my new identity and body by enrolling in college and getting a bachelor's degree in strategic intelligence, with a minor in terrorism studies. I already finished one college degree in aviation management as Frank, so this would broaden my knowledge and skills. I would have no association with the military while I was attending school. She also wanted me to study and become fluent in Arabic, something neither Randy nor Frank knew anything about. This was going to be fun, like beginning a new life. It was a second chance. I was excited and felt fortunate about what had happened to me. This was an opportunity to correct and to not make the same mistakes I had made in my first life a chance to do the things I had not done before my life had ended so abruptly. I had a new lease and was not about to throw it away.

I decided to go to the University of California, Berkeley. Randy did not have the SAT scores to get into Berkeley, but CD had the clout to do just about anything, so getting me accepted was not a problem. I wanted to live in the dorms to experience Berkeley campus life. In my previous life as Frank, I had gone to ROTC at Indiana University, which had been strict so that I did had not been able to do the normal college kid thing. In ROTC every minute of every day had been planned and occupied with responsibilities and duties; there had been no personal time. Now, I could literally let my hair down, grow it long if I want, study if I want, play if I want, meet girls if I want. I was going to like this new life—what guy wouldn't die to relive his college days.

My dorm room was small and shared a toilet and shower with an adjacent dorm room. The thing I really liked was that the dorm was co-ed. I met my roommate the weekend before school started. He was pretty cool; his name was Steve and he was from Portland, Oregon. Steve had a small-town upbringing similar to mine, or to Frank's as I should say. So I thought we would get along. Steve was into old music, especially Pink Floyd. I thought I had met an old friend. The room next to us had two girls from the East Coast, Rachel from Boston and Chloe from Charlottesville, Virginia. Rachel was a blonde, short, law student with a sarcastic sense of humor, and you never knew what she was thinking; a prankster. Chloe was a tall, brunette, fashion design major, and was always dressed in expensive, right-out-of-Vogue maga-zine clothes. This was going to be quite an education for a Midwestern country boy.

Berkeley, CA has a small college town feel, but is only a few miles from downtown San Francisco, where there are lots of things to do. Both have lots of college-age girls. I was still getting used to my new skin, walking down the street getting looks and giggles from teenage girls—not something I was used to. I would look at myself to see if there was something wrong with me, or if I had spilled something on myself and did not realize it, or if my fly was open. I still remember, not that long ago, if I even smiled at a woman under thirty, she looked at me in disgust like I was a dirty old man. I forgot I was not invisible anymore with this new nineteen-year-old body. What was hard for me to do was to dress like a teenager and not a forty-year old man. I was having trouble dealing with the style of "sagging," which is how boys wear their pants down low, around their thighs, and show their color-ful boxer underwear. I never liked boxers, always preferred briefs. I guessed it is something that would grow on me.

My classes took some getting used to. It was not exactly like it was my first day of school. But, I did feel like I was in class with a bunch of high school kids. I had to hold my tongue and play the silent type in the back of the class. It did give me a lot of free time, though, as studying was not as hard as it had been the first time around. It was nice know-ing how to learn and how to manage my time. My elective classes were interesting, but the core classes were so boring that I continually skipped most of them, except for test day. My English literature class had a lot of cute girls, so I always tried to be there. One girl I liked, Isra, looked like she was middle eastern and was tall, about five feet nine inches, thin, with coal black eyes, and long jet black hair down to her shoulders always tied in a pony-tail. I wanted to talk with her, but needed more time to get used to this age group, to learn how they talk and what they talk about. I did not want her to think I was weird by talking about something which could reveal my age. It was my hope she spoke Arabic, so she could help me learn; it was one of my favorite subjects.

It was nice not have to worry about money. The government paid all my bills. Now I knew what it felt like to have rich parents, like many of the kids who go here. There were not many Berkeley brats, as I called them, who work and pay their own way through school. Many of the kids who were there were nerds and studied all the time, hoping to become the next Albert Einstein or land that seven-figure job after college at some prestigious company. When I was in school, everyone wanted the six-figure salary, but with inflation it became seven. There was even a popular rap song out, called "I want to be a billionaire." I do not even think we could count that high when I was in college.

As a freshman, life was a bit lonely, and I can tell you I did not blend in. It still felt like I was wearing a costume when I went out and that everyone saw I was a fake. Periodically I thought about Randy and how he gave up his life for his country. I was not sure if he would have done it if he had understood how I was going to be living in his body. I guess part of my motivation for doing well was that I wanted his sacrifice to mean something. I also continued to think about my family. To them I was dead, and I was told I could not go see them or talk to them. I missed them so much. I wondered how Miriam and the kids were doing, and I wanted to tell them I was alive. But, what would they think of me now? I did not look like the husband or father they knew. They might not believe it was me. Maybe it was best they simply believed I was dead. I didn't want to complicate their lives any more than necessary.

I really enjoyed my Arabic class, in part because I had a bit of a crush on the teacher's assistant, Isra. I wanted to get to know her more as she seemed quite interesting and was amazingly beautiful. I guess in some ways she reminded me of Miriam with her dark olive skin and gorgeous black hair. She told the class during introductions she was Iraqi and born in Baghdad. I finally decided to approach her, since I was getting comfortable enough to feel like I would not blow my cover—or at least my new identity, if that's what you can call it. Her family had immigrated when the first Iraq war broke out because they were afraid they would all be killed. Isra spoke Arabic at home with her parents growing up, so she was a native speaker. I enjoyed spending time with her and she offered to help me practice my language skills. Most of my courses were about the history of the Middle East, so we shared a common interest. As Frank I had been in Iraq, and although I could not tell her, it gave me some insight into her family's way of life. She wanted to do really well in school in order to later help her parents financially, because she felt they had such a hard life. Isra and I liked to take short trips together, and several times I took her to Lake Tahoe and showed her how to snow ski, something she said she had only dreamed about growing up. We also liked to go to clubs in San Francisco, as well as to nice restaurants around the Bay Area.

Isra seemed bothered one evening after dinner, "Where do you get all the money you seem to have, since you don't have a job?"

I did not want to tell her anything about my military background and how the government was paying for everything, so I said, "My parents both died in a small plane crash and left me a trust fund. I didn't tell you sooner, because I didn't want you to feel sorry for me or make things weird." Our relationship quickly became very comfortable, not like dating when I was a teenager, but more like an adult relationship or long-time friendship. She was easy to be with and I loved the comfort of her touch; it was peaceful. I felt I could talk openly with her about anything, including my thoughts and feelings, and I did not worry about the typical teenage fears boys have about girls.

On a couple of separate occasions Isra told me, "You're more mature than other boys, especially when we make love. Other boys always rush and are selfish. They just want to get off. You take your time and always make sure I'm satisfied first. You're a wonderful lover."

Isra and I spent most of our time at Berkeley together as a couple. We moved off campus together into a small apartment. She helped me discover a large community of people from the Middle East. Over time she introduced me to many of her friends and relatives, and soon they felt like the only family I had. I learned a deeper understanding of what it was like to be Muslim. For most of them they were no more Muslim than I was Catholic: I rarely practiced the faith. As Frank, I had been raised Catholic and had attended Catholic schools until I was twelve years old. But I was not religious and neither were most of these people; it was just how their parents had raised them. It seemed for many Middle East countries, not unlike the United States, that the people simply want to pass their religion onto their children more as a tradition than as a faith. I understood this, as I think a lot of Catholics only go to church on Christmas and Easter, but the rest of the time they are out doing something else on Sunday mornings, which was the way my family acted. Overall, Isra and I had a quiet understanding that once I finished at Berkeley, I would be headed off around the world to parts unknown and that our time together would be over. She never focused on our relationship ending, but rather on having a good time and enjoying every day as much as we could. I think that from her early childhood experiences and what she witnessed, she realized that life could end at any time and that each moment should be enjoyed and cherished. I loved her for that.

College life went by quite quickly. I remember two weeks after graduation Isra took me to the airport to fly to Washington, DC. I had told her I had been offered a job at the United Nations. It was very difficult to leave; we were both crying at the airport. Our time together seemed to have passed so quickly, almost in the blink of an eye. I wondered if I would ever see her again. It ripped my heart apart, since we shared something very special together. I will never forget the look in her dark brown eyes as we parted for the last time. She was an amazing person, and I will never forget her.

Within days I was back in the military, like I had never left, even though three years had gone by. Only now I was wearing a different uniform on a different body. I thought about the many eras of our lives—from childhood, through the teens, twenties, thirties, and forties—and how we are different people throughout each period. Most of the time our appearance changes significantly in each phase. I believe I have evolved so much through each part of my life, and now lives. I have to constantly remind myself that I am no longer in Frank's body, but in Randy's. When I look out of "my" eyes, I see the same things I have always seen. When I think, I think the same things I have always thought. I am me; I am an amalgamation of my memories and experiences. I have read that our minds cannot discern between a memory of what we have dreamed and a memory of an actual event that has occurred to us; it is coded and logged into our brain in much the same way. So, when we recall the event, sometimes we cannot recall if it actually happened or if it was just a dream. For me, life is even more complicated to sort out, between dreams, Frank's life, and now Randy's life too. At times, I feel I live in a world, wondering if it is all a dream.

I went to army OCS (Officer Candidate School) to become an officer, and they promoted me to Captain after I graduated since I had previous experience as an enlisted soldier and my other untold previous military experience. After graduation, I went on to combat training with the Army Rangers Special Operations Forces in Fort Benning, GA. When I finished all my basic military training, I was to work as an intelligence officer and had a base of operation out of Dubai, UAE. Dubai is a city much like Las Vegas, only in the Middle East. It looks and feels like an American city with money apparent everywhere—lots of glitz. Dubai was where I got to look, listen, and learn, as well as improve my Arabic. In the beginning, I just waited for my orders to come in from Washington DC, NSA headquarters. I would spend my days in cafés all around the city, reading the local newspapers and surfing the internet for open source intelligence. "Open source intelligence" is just a different way of saying that I read about the happenings around the Middle East, without secretly spying on someone or someplace. Out here, there are lots of people from all over the world transiting through the financial and transportation system, on their way to one place or another. So, at one time or another, a lot of not-so-nice people pass through Dubai on their way to not-so-nice places, to do not-so-nice things.

Finally, after a lot of waiting, I received my orders via encrypted email. The mission was to find and obtain any and all information about the leading terrorist in the area, Adam Gadahn. Gadahn was an American who had turned terrorist and was believed to be in Yemen, a neighbor to the south of Dubai and Saudi Arabia. I was ordered to go to Yemen, target Gadahn, and call in Special Ops to render him out of the country. A few days after receiving my initial orders, I flew into Yemen's capital, Sana'a, and met an operative who took me to a small hotel on the outskirts of the city. Sana'a is like some parts of Detroit, simply lawless, where there is no authority but the locals who run the streets. I had to grow a beard and let my hair grow long before I went there. One thing you did not want to do in this region is to stick out, and a blond and blue-eyed guy has CIA written all over him. I used tanning cream to darken my skin, colored my hair and beard black, and wore dark brown contact lenses. I had perfected my Arabic so as to not be detected as an American.

I stayed in my hotel room for weeks on end, just watching the street and people for patterns and routine. I ordered room service and did not walk outside, except after dark. Night was when Yemen came alive, because the daytime temperatures could reach nearly 120 degrees Fahrenheit. I sent my daily email check-in requirement back to Langley to my coordinator and reviewed any reports or news he sent me. My coordinator was someone I had never met before. I had talked with him on the phone a couple of times to get intelligence briefings. He went by the code named Khufu; I laughed when he first told me. I said to him when he told me his name, "Khufu, after the king who built the Great Pyramid? That's random, not exactly discreet is it?" He replied, "Yes, but you probably won't forget it, will you!" We both laughed and I never forgot it. After a couple of weeks in the hotel, I got out and began to wander through the cafés and restaurants, trying to get a lay of the land. I met a few people and started some friendships. I felt like a fish out of water. It was similar to when I first woke up in Randy's body; I felt like I was in a strange place and did not know who the players were. Imagine being on a different planet with alien people everywhere and you are trying to hide among them. I felt as though everyone looked at me like I was green and from Mars.

I decided my cover was to be an American student attending the world-famous Sana'a Language Institute for Arabic Studies. The Institute was known for its links to the terrorist organization Al Qaeda, the organization Gadahn was working for in Yemen. In the past, other Americans and westerners who wanted to join Al Qaeda came here and were inducted through connections at the Sana'a Institute. I hoped the same would happen to me. It would be easier if they contacted me, instead of me trying to contact them. When I was out meeting people I would subtly let them know I was sympathetic to the radical Muslim cause and then waited and hoped for the best. The best scenario was that I would be taken in to the organization and given an assignment, and hopefully in the process I would locate Gadahn. Then I could notify Special Ops to come in and take him out.

I had only been at the Institute for less than a month when they contacted me. One night I was sleeping in my dorm room when I woke up to the door flying open and several people rushing in around me. Someone threw a hood over my head, and then I was taken away in a car. I was driven for a couple of hours over very bumpy terrain; it was obviously off-road. I should have been desperately afraid, but I wasn't. I had a sense of calm, because I knew back home they would track me with the GPS installed in my brain. It was then I realized just how ridiculous this whole mission was. Langley never expected me to come out here and find Gadahn. Rather, I was to stumble around until his people found me and took me to him; I was bait. I was the newest CIA weapon, which could be tracked but not exactly killed. Meaning, they could kill this body, but Washington could quickly transfer my identity into another body, so my training and experience would be preserved. I got to thinking with this hood over my head and could only imagine what was going to come next. The only question I had was: how much torture would I have to endure before Special Ops came to get me? It was kind of weird. When you do not have to worry about dying it removes a lot of fear. Fear of death could be a worry, especially when you are captured by terrorists who have a bad habit of cutting people's heads off! Strangely, I felt a sense of calm about the possibility of dying.

I thought further about what it would be like to not have to worry about death. Would people be more adventurous? Or if people could live many lives, how would they want to spend each life? I think we would have to change marriage vows and licenses to read something like, until this body dies or this life is over, or for a certain time frame. What would happen to the way we interpret life and living? What about money? Would we continue to carry our bank accounts and retirements into our next life? How would the banks know who their clients were, if they changed bodies? Maybe it would be better if when we changed bodies we could keep the same name, which would keep things less complicated. I can see for now why it is better that this technology is kept away from the public and in the hands of only a few people. But, there I was in Yemen as a human experiment, sacrificial lamb, and human tape recorder, and locator beacon.

We arrived at our destination and I was taken inside a tent. It was very quiet outside and I did not hear any sounds of the city. They took my hood off and I saw several men around me. One man about forty, with a long dark but graying beard, who wore a dirty white robe with a tall turban, tried to talk to me in broken English. I told him in Arabic that it was okay if he spoke to me in his native tongue.

He then asked me, "Why are you in Yemen?"

I answered him, "I came to improve my Arabic and to join Al Qaeda. To fight against the west."

Another man, who appeared to be the leader, a huge guy, about six feet six, two hundred and sixty pounds, asked me, "Are you a spy? Do you work for the CIA?"

"No no, I am no spy!" I quickly and adamantly responded.

"Why do you color your hair and wear brown contacts to cover your blue eyes, if you are not a spy?" the apparent leader asked me.

I again quickly and fervently responded to him, "I did not want people to think I was an American." I then changed my tone, to calm and submissive-like and asked the leader, "I want to join and serve Gadahn."

"How do you know Gadahn?" he immediately questioned.

"Everyone knows he is the most powerful man in Yemen," I answered. The leader-looking guy stopped talking and walked outside the tent and did not come back. The next guy to come in the tent was wearing a very long machete at his side, like something you would see in *Lawrence of Arabia*, with a long curved blade. The guy seemed angry, pacing around and snorting almost as if he was a mad bull. Blade, I'll call him.

Blade sternly instructed, "We make a video of you. You will confess you are spy and work for the CIA."

I professed to him over and over, "I'm not a spy!"

Someone punched me on the side of the head. I never saw it coming; it made me dizzy. I then felt a rope go around my neck from behind, and someone choked me. Two other men grabbed my arms and made me stand while another one kicked me in my groin, which sent a pain shooting through my body like I had never felt. My knees buckled and I must have blacked out, because I felt my face on the floor of the tent when I awoke and started to move. I was again hoisted to my feet by my arms and Blade stood in front of me and punched me in my chest. It took my breath away. He then punched me in the jaw and I blacked out. I awoke again.

Blade continued to yell at me, "Confess! Confess or we will chop off your hands."

"I do not know what you are talking about!" I screamed.

Blade calmly said, "I will give you time to think." And the other men put a bag over my head. One of them tied my hands behind my back, tied my feet together, and then pulled my knees up to my chest and tied a rope around my entire body, very tightly. I could barely breathe. It felt like time stood still. I seemed to be able to remember every part of my life in vivid detail. *My life*, I laughed to myself, which life? This one as Randy, or before as Frank? It is weird, but I know I am, or feel like I have always been Frank. Randy seems like just someone I was for a while. Maybe the way an undercover officer feels after being deep undercover for several years. I reflected back on the first time I saw Miriam and the softness of her lips and the scent of her skin when we first kissed, and then thought about waving goodbye to her for the last time. I remember the day I got married like it happened yesterday. We had an outdoor wedding in a park with a lake. I was so excited and nervous to actually see Miriam in her wedding gown. She looked so beautiful, with her olive skin against her bright white dress. I recalled when I first saw her walking toward me as the ceremony began; I could not take my eyes off her. There could have been an earthquake or tornado, and I do not think I would have remembered either; all I saw was her, glowing and smiling. It was one of the best days of my life. I can still the smell of aroma of my children, right after they were born when I held them in my arms; the smell only new born babies have. Or when I left and saw them for the last time, running off to school. I can still feel the intense force from the seat of my F16 when I pulled the ejection handles. I actually recall being shot out of my plane and hearing the air rush by and the chute deploy. It is all recorded in my brain, like some sort of movie. Life is strange, a continuous recording of events, as time and memories never stop.

It felt like two days went by before they untied me and again stood me up. One of the men yelled at me—I could not tell which— "Tell us you are a spy and we stop your pain!"

Desperately I again told them, "I do not know what you want me to say. My name is Randy Edwards. I am an American. But I hate America and promise to wage holy jihad against the west."

Blade came back into the tent. The same two men who had grabbed me before yanked me by my arms and held them across a table. I watched as Blade raised his machete high above his head, then swung it down very rapidly. I was in disbelief as my two hands separated from my wrists. It was a surreal experience, like watching a scene from a horror movie, looking and seeing my wrists without hands. I tried to move my fingers, but nothing happened. Somehow I felt like I could still feel my hands. I felt no pain, as the shock must have been too much for my body to absorb. I simply stared at Blade.

He yelled at me, "Are you a spy? Tell the camera."

I moved my head side to side to indicate no. I watched him again raise his machete high over his head and off to one side. As if in slow motion I watched it move down toward me. I first felt the blade as it touched the side of my neck and cut through the muscle, tendons, arteries, and finally my spinal cord. I could feel my head separate from my body. I watched through my own eyes, as if somehow I had a videotape inside my head, as my head fell to the ground and rolled on the tent floor, my body still standing for a few seconds before it collapsed into a heap. For a few seconds I could still see everything that was going on around me, and then it went black.

What I did not know was how intensely Washington's Special Ops was tracking my every position. They fully understood that if they put live bait in such a hostile zone, I most certainly would be picked up by someone they were interested in. And the best part of it was, they were not risking someone's real life. I could always be exchanged if I was killed; they would just need to retrieve the hardware from my brain, which was easier in this instance since they only had to transport a head, not an entire body. Special Ops used my GPS tracking device to find the grave where the kidnappers buried me in the sand out in the middle of nowhere, miles from the city center. Yemen is indeed a very dangerous part of the world. It is similar to what the United States was during the days of the wild west. Still today they have not found or killed Gadahn. I read where a judge in Yemen has issued a warrant for his arrest, dead or alive.

Renee Finds a Slave

Here I was again, back at CD headquarters. But this time I had an idea of what was happening and had happened to me. I felt great, no pain, but something was definitely different; my body felt different. They had me strapped down to a gurney for the duration of the exchange, which takes about twenty-four hours with CD's super computer.

Sara was again there and introduced me to myself. "Welcome back. We were lucky to have found you and your hardware intact. You are a little different this time, though."

"Really. Why is that?" I asked in a high-pitched voice.

"You are now a young woman, Renee Wunderlich,"

"WHAT! A WOMAN?"

Sara put her hand on my forearm to try to calm me. "Easy, try to relax a bit. Take a few breaths. Command has a special mission for you—one they thought you would be best to handle. No one has ever had a gender exchange."

I tried to relax. *A woman,* I thought. What was that going to be like? I liked women, but I'd never wanted to be one. Miriam had commented one time when we were arguing, "You should try being a woman sometime—maybe you would have a better appreciation for how difficult it is, trying to please men and society." I guess I could refuse and tell them to exchange me into a man's body. Or maybe I could try this. Part of me wondered what it would be like to feel what a woman felt—kind of sexy and perverse, I wasn't sure which. Special mission, what was that about? Okay, I thought, I would see where this goes.

The idea that someone else controlled who I would be in my next life or if there even would be a next life and that I did not get to decide was a difficult, mind-boggling moral and ethical issue. However, I guess I am fortunate in knowing that at least I have a chance to be someone else, if some person somewhere decides so. I still do not even know who makes these decisions. Is it completely random? How many other people are in a similar situation? Why don't I get to make the choice? I have always been told since the first day of basic training that the military needs come first. I am at the military's disposal, a human guinea pig. But, I do feel lucky to be alive and to have the knowledge of what is happening to me.

I thought about how difficult it would be to actually pick a body to exchange into. How would I decide? Who would I want to be: man, woman, tall, short, fat, skinny? There were lots of choices to think about. Would I want to be everything I hadn't been in my previous life? What would most people want? If you were short, would you want to be tall? If you were black, would you want to be white? If you were German, maybe you would want the experience of being a Jew. Or if you were a man then possibly you would want to be a woman. The possibilities are seemingly endless—just walk down any street in a big city and look around to see how many choices there are. I wonder what would happen to society if we all could exchange when we got old and our bodies began to fail, or if we contracted a terminal disease. If all this were possible, you no longer could have a preconceived notion about someone based on their looks. You would truly have to talk to someone to learn their history and background before developing an opinion. Would certain prejudices, like racial, gender, or age, lessen or go away? People could truly get a sense of what it would be like to walk in another person's shoes, and see life from a different perspective.

Renee was a twenty-two year old U.S. Air Force Senior Airman, five-foot-three inches tall and 110 pounds, with short blonde hair and blue eyes. Renee's father was a USAF pilot who had been killed in a training accident. Her mother, an alcoholic, had been killed in a car accident while driving drunk. Renee had joined the military to separate herself from her past and had volunteered for CD, maybe in the hope of erasing her tragic past.

Renee was a unique opportunity for me, not only as an undercover intelligence officer, but also as a man inside a beautiful woman's body. I was going to get to experience every man's dream. What was it like to be a woman? The biggest challenge for me was going to be not acting like a typical man, in a petite woman's body. My new assignment was to be attached to an international task force investigating human trafficking. It was cooperation between the military and law enforcement. I did not require as much transition time after this exchange with Renee's body as I had with Randy's. I understood a lot of the dimensions and problems of taking over a new body with the same mind. However, it was indeed very strange to look at myself in the mirror. It was sort of a turn-on to see myself—so bizarre. I did not know how I was going to act like a woman.

After I was released from CD, Sara told me to take some time to assimilate to my new body. I decided to go to Miami to relax and have some fun. This was going to be a much more difficult assignment than I could have ever imagined. I needed to learn everything about being a young woman—from how to fix my hair, and how to put on makeup and paint my fingernails and toenails, to how to dress and how to act around men and other women. It's almost like going back to school again. I am now a forty-four-year old man, with two lives behind me, two college degrees, killed twice, and now in the body of a beautiful young woman. This was going to take some getting used to.

When I arrived in Miami I got a suite at the Hyatt Towers hotel. I wanted to stay somewhere centrally located to all the city life. My next order of business was to find a female friend. Someone who could teach me how to be a woman. I would tell her I just got out of the military and therefore knew nothing about fashion. The military picked up the tab for all of my expenses, so money was no object.

But finding a girl friend, only as a friend, was something I had never done. I decided to go on Craigslist when I first arrived to and post an advertisement for platonic friends, new to area. I soon got an email from another girl who had just moved to Miami from Boston. We met for coffee and I liked her right away. Gwen was a tall, dark-haired girl, well-educated, from Boston College, who had moved to Miami to become a fashion designer; perfect. What better way to learn how to be a woman than from someone in fashion? I told Gwen I was newly out of the military and was trying to figure out what to do next. She told me I could stay at her place if I wanted, but I told her the military had a program to take care of soldiers when they get out, which was why I had the hotel room. I said I had to pay extra for the suite, but that I had figured it would be worth it.

I shared with Gwen that I knew nothing of fashion and had been wearing nothing but military uniforms for the last four years. So we went on a shopping spree in Miami which was expectedly fun. It was the strangest thing, going in women's restrooms and dressing rooms, and I was weirdly self-conscious about my new body. I was petite, with small breasts and a small butt. Gwen helped me find a cool bikini which showed off my body. When I was alone, I ran my hands all over my body. I thought it would feel like Frank's hands on Renee's body, but it was not like that. It was almost like the fact that you cannot tickle yourself; it was different touching my own body. I liked touching my own body, running my hands over my newly-found breasts and exploring what it felt like to touch myself in places where as a man I recalled it brought pleasure to a woman. Strangely, my mind felt like that of a lesbian because I was still attracted to women. However, I also had heterosexual urges in that my body was attracted to men. It was a very gender-confusing time.

My first night out on the town in Miami with Gwen was exciting and we went to a lot of clubs. But I felt very reserved and did not know how to act. I did not know if I should act like Frank in a woman's body or try to act like how I think Renee would have acted, or a combination of both. Or if should I take on a whole new personality. In the end, I tried to be who I was, a culmination of all of my personalities and life experiences, or in my case "lives experiences." I noticed Gwen was a bit protective of me when guys approached us in the clubs or on the street. I think she sensed I did not have a lot of experience in dealing with guys. She kept telling me that all the guys were checking me out and hitting on me. The strange thing for me was that I could, too. I had one guy buy me a drink; he was kind of cute and sat next to me in a bar, and then he put his hand gently on my thigh. I did not mind him doing that—he was cute and flirty— but then I noticed my nipples stiffen and my inner thighs become warm. I realized I was turned on by this young man. Gwen and I bar-hopped for most of the night and then returned to my hotel.

Back in the hotel room, Gwen and I laid down on one bed and laughed about the night of teasing men. Gwen said to me, "All men ever want to do is feel you up or get in your pants for a one night stand."

I laughed and replied, "Boys will be boys."

Gwen took off her outer clothes and plopped next to me, "You want to watch some TV before we fall asleep? I'm still wound-up."

"Sure." It was a hot, muggy Florida night, and we had opened the windows instead of turning on the air conditioner. I took off my clothes, except for a cute pair of panties we had bought earlier in the day, and laid back down on the bed.

Gwen laid next to me. "You have a great body. You are so small and petite. I am too tall and feel awkward."

"No, you are so tall and beautiful— not awkward. You are elegant, and you move like a runway model." Gwen smiled at me and softly ran her fingertips across my stomach and between my breasts. I did not feel embarrassed or uncomfortable. It felt so natural, both as a young woman and as a man. We fell asleep with the TV still on.

The next day when Gwen went down to the pool I contacted my handler, Khufu, back in Washington and told him about her. He told me to stay put and build a relationship with Gwen. The task force thought they could use us as a pair. They wanted us to act as bait in a sting operation for the slave trade industry in Miami. Organized crime was using modeling agencies as a ruse to find and lure young women, and then kidnap and exploit them. Khufu had arranged for Gwen and me to get hired by a local modeling agency. I did not tell Gwen what was happening. She thought it was all on the up and up and that we were going to be America's next top models or something.

The agency sent Gwen on a couple of real modeling gigs for magazine print advertisements. Gwen had no idea what she was getting herself involved in; the modeling industry is full of nasty people who prey on young, beautiful girls. The agency told me we were going to be set up on a modeling assignment with lots of other models on a huge yacht for some rich Latin men. The Latin men were representing agencies from all over the world. We would be flown by helicopter from Miami out to the yacht for an all night gig. When we arrived at the yacht we were given our own cabin. The closets were full of clothes, gowns, and bikinis they wanted us to wear throughout the evening. We were first going to have a runway show; after that we were to mingle in our other outfits for most of the night. The Latin agency representatives would contact our agency representatives later to inform us if we were hired or not.

There were a lot men from many different countries on the yacht. I could hear Spanish, French, Arabic, Thai, Portuguese, and English from the ones I could recognize. This was no small operation. The night was a lot of fun. Gwen and I stayed glued together; we both felt a bit isolated out on this boat since it was not like we could just say we were leaving and get a cab home. Later in the evening, a dark-skinned man speaking a language I could not recognize approached Gwen and told her he had a proposition for her. He told her he represented an agency from the country of Brunei and left her his business card.

"It sounds like a great opportunity to build your budding model career." I said.

"I'm afraid of going alone," Gwen said in a low tone. "Would you go with me? I will only go if you go with me."

"I'll think about it and tell you later." I answered.

Excitedly Gwen said, "The guy from the Brunei agency told us we could let him know within a week!"

The helicopter brought us back to Miami and we returned to our hotel. Gwen was nervously excited about the idea of going on such a fantastic trip to Brunei. I contacted Khufu told him what had happened. He told me to talk to Gwen and get the Brunei company to take us both. Washington thought they were a good lead as they had some girls go missing from a similar type of offer. I told Gwen, "I'll go with you. But, tell the agency guy he has to take us both or you will not go."

She called back the Brunei representative; he quickly agreed and was enthusiastic after he found out I was the "little blonde." Two days later we received a FedEx with a portfolio about the agency and two First Class tickets to Brunei, as well as contact information when we arrived.

A week later, we left Miami on Cathay Pacific Airlines for Brunei. Gwen was both nervous and excited. I was anxious for Gwen; we had grown close in a short period of time. I felt guilty about not telling her everything I knew about this so-called Modeling Agency. But I was not sure—maybe it was legit. Maybe it would be exactly what she wanted for her career. Besides I couldn't have told her about what I was doing, since I did not have authorization to do that. And if I did who knows what she would have done—probably blown the entire operation. I did, however, consider her a friend and confidant someone who had taught me about being a young woman. I contemplated on the flight how nice it would be someday to teach my daughter Emma and to talk to her like Gwen had done for me. I laughed at my own thoughts and tried to imagine myself both as a man and a woman talking to Emma. I wavered which would be better for her, and which would be better to be me, as a man or a woman discussing life's issues and questions. I thought for a few minutes about Emma and what she must be going through in her life right now, almost a teenager. She needs her dad, I thought, even though she has her mom and plenty of other girlfriends to talk to. I missed her.

I also thought about these different lives I had lived and how they had allowed me to grow emotionally. I thought about how different I was because of all my experiences. I believed I was a better person, more fulfilled, happier, smarter, wiser, and more intelligent. What I questioned was that I wasn't sure if after having lived three lives, I understood any more about life's meaning than I had during or at the end of my first life. It bothered me that I was simply making the same mistakes over and over and selfishly taking as much as I could, and had stolen the potential from two people, who might have done something amazing with their lives. I am sure they had had dreams and desires for themselves.

I looked out the window of the airplane and stared across the many clouds and thought back to Frank. It was nice just to close my eyes and daydream about a less complicated, stress-free, freedom-filled time of my life. I had grown up in Northeastern rural Indiana, in a small town named Huntertown. My family had six kids; I was the youngest. We moved from the suburbs when I was ten to a horse ranch to raise and show Appaloosa horses. Over the years on the ranch we had many horses, but my favorite was Frito Bar. Frito was my best friend; we used to spend summer days exploring open fields, dense woods, and riding with friends. On cold winter afternoons after school we would sleep together on his stall floor. Frito would lie down completely flat and I would curl up under his neck to stay warm; he would never move or try to get up until after I did, so he would not hurt me. I thrived in the open spaces and freedom of the countryside.

A couple of years after my family moved to the country, I began to working on a neighbor's farm. It had a large crop and livestock operation, with lots of work. A friend I met at school and I began working at the farm at the same time. I thought it was great how people in the country seemed to help each other out and were more friendly than people in the suburbs. My dad grew up on a farm and he told me that people in the country had to help each other out because since neighbors were few and far between, you had to rely on each other to survive. The people of rural Indiana taught me strong values, like how to be a good neighbor, and how to be honest, trustworthy, and helpful whenever I could. It seemed everyone helped each other back then, and we had lots of parties and gatherings after the work was done. I loved to drive tractors and be around the animals on the farm—a big change from the suburbs—and for a young boy it was fantastic.

My father was a police officer for the county sheriff's department, my mother a stay-at-home mom. I cannot imagine trying to manage six kids, with food, school, horses, and the teenage years...how is that possible? I would rather attempt to fly a fighter jet at mach 1.5 at 300 feet over mountainous terrain, with someone trying to shoot me down, than negotiate with six children with very different personalities and opinions. I was the youngest, which I liked, because my older siblings always broke new ground for whatever I had to do later, like school, bedtimes, curfews, getting in trouble, and getting grounded. It was nice for me because my parents were less strict by the time I was older, with a been-there-done-that attitude.

When I was fifteen, I followed a bit in my father's footsteps and became a police cadet for the sheriff's department he worked for. I liked being a police cadet, especially at such a young age. Cadets had full and open access to the inner workings of the sheriff's department. We could intern in any area we liked, from the jail to riding-along on patrol, to crowd and traffic control at large public events, to helping serve civil papers, to the 911 communications center. This gave kids the opportunity to help the community and learn about police work to discover if that was something they really wanted to pursue when they got older. I loved to ride patrol and spent many weekend nights over my junior and senior years of high school riding-along with the police officers during the graveyard shift. The graveyard shift was most exciting because all the officers on the shift had police dog partners. I rode along with many different officers and I got to know many of the dogs and their very different personalities. Sometimes I would assist when the dogs and their handlers went to training by playing the bad guy who would get tracked, chased, sniffed out from under boxes or in cars and ultimately bitten — the dog's reward. Of course, I always wore a large protective sleeve, so as not to get hurt.

It was my plan when I turned 21 years old to become a police officer with the same sheriff's department my father worked for. However, I did have a yearning to leave Indiana and explore the world. My family did not have a lot of money, so going to college was not an option they could afford. I decided to enlist in the United States Air Force, so that way I could travel the world and have the military pay for my college. My second passion in life, besides police work, was airplanes. I, like many boys, wanted to fly fighter jets and I seemed to be good at operating machinery. I found out I first had to become an officer in the military, which meant I had to finish four years of college. So I became very focused, not like in high school, and went to Indiana University while I was doing my air force job, which was working on the electronic systems of the famous B52 bomber. I chose this job because it got me near airplanes and how they worked.

I finished college and was accepted to the OCS (Officer Candidate School) and pilot program in the Air Force. I found pilot training invigorating and extremely exciting. When we got out of the first phase and into our assigned aircraft, the heat got turned up. I was assigned to the F16 fighter, a small but extremely agile airplane. I remember thinking the first time I was flying at mach 1.5 at 300 feet above the mountains of Nevada that this was insane and a dream come true. I could not stop smiling for days after that flight. Then, a fateful day for all of America happened: September 11, 2001. I, like other Americans, felt a sense of anger and patriotism after the attacks and wanted to do my part to make sure it did not happen again. My father taught me protection of one's family and neighbors and so I felt that personal freedom was worth any sacrifice.

The plane hit a bit of turbulence and jarred me back to reality—or at least this one. As I sipped on my cold drink, the bumps subsided and I began to drift into thought again. I had doubt if I should be doing all this, defying what seems natural: death. What would we really gain from living longer? I think we should somehow make the world we live in better or benefit mankind in meaningful ways. Also, what should we attempt to learn if we live longer lives, even if it was in multiple bodies? I hope we would be more like Albert Einstein and Thomas Edison and other great thinkers or inventors, and conquer basic problems of human existence. First, the easy things, like hunger, energy needs for all, no wars. I am not religious, but what if I am angering God or messing with his plan? Or maybe this is God's plan, maybe this is what he intended us to do, by being more than we could in one life. Wouldn't it be great if we could see and correct the mistakes of past lifetimes and evolve into more intellectual, peaceful beings, right? Beings who could learn to move away from this planet and travel to other parts of the universe. Or would we all simply spend more time being selfish, abusing our body, and turning our brains into vegetables by watching reality television? Much of the time there seems to be something we are all missing in our lives, something we are struggling to reach, achieve, discover, learn, or understand. I always wanted to spend more time with my family, exploring the world together, either traveling to foreign lands or simply playing together, maybe on a houseboat on some remote lake, or learning something completely new and different. We all simply seem to just want more time, but our bodies have an expiration date.

I think it would change how we think and perceive life, if we removed the fear of dying or at least prolonged it for an extended period of time. We all remember how we felt when we were young and took risks: we were fearless, we were not afraid of or even thought of the consequences of being seriously hurt or dying. What if we could extrapolate this youthful exuberance over many centuries? How would that feel and what more could we learn? We could rise to new levels of achievement if we did not have to worry about getting physically hurt, losing a limb, losing our eyesight, or dying. We could take our limits a bit further and possibly find a deeper understanding of life. We might learn more of what it means to be human and simply be happy or content with each moment we live. If we live ten lifetimes or only part of one, where do we derive contentment? I guess it is different for each of us, what makes us at peace with ourselves, since not everyone wants to be a Bach, an Aristotle, or the President of the United States. Some of us just want to enjoy our time with those close to us with those things we like doing, from eating, drinking, laughing, to playing sports. There is no right or wrong—never has been. Not all of us on this earth are supposed to achieve enlightenment. It's simply enough for some of us just to enjoy a peaceful moment in the middle of our chaotic lives.

Are our bodies the important parts of this life, or is it our minds, our thoughts and ideas, our memories and experiences? What gives us our identity and our will to live, and brings us peace and happiness? I don't think it is really a moral problem to exchange bodies or if we had clones, to use clones. How much would we really change if we could exchange bodies with another? We are still the same person on the inside. What if we could be a Chinese laborer in one lifetime, an African tribe woman in another, a rich powerful CEO in the next—or a doctor, a politician, a homeless person, a handicapped man, a blind woman, a prostitute or a priest? I think for most people not a lot would change: the exterior would, but the interior would remain the same. However, I do not believe that we would live to be better individuals. In fact, people might get worse if they knew they were just going into another body when they died. By living only one life and having the fear of the unknown on the other side of life—death, that is, and God's judgment—I think we strive to be better people and care more for ourselves and for others. My dad used to tell me about my car or for example, "You'd better take care of it: it has to last you a long time. I'm not buying you another one." Some people do not want to learn answers to age-old questions. To them it is not important to learn if there really is a God or if the big bang was the beginning of the universe, or if there is life on other planets. Many people have to concentrate on where their next meal is coming from and how they are going to pay for it. Some would say that having multiple lives would be simply postponing our fear of dying.

The rich and powerful say that what humanity needs to do is to save only the good people: the intelligent, educated people and the influential people. I think of what has happened to me; I was only saved because I am part of the U.S. military and a human lab rat, a valuable asset. The military machine does not care about my thoughts or feelings, my emotions, or my eternal being. I am just a mission to them to save money and provide a good return on investment. I'm just a test case to learn what it is like to make the exchanges so others do not have to take the risks. Who makes these moral decisions anyway? Is it a special board of people, or one man or woman's decision? Right now, someone is playing God or controller of the universe, by deciding who must give up their lives so that others may live. I want to know who that is.

I will never forget when I was growing up in high school and in one of my classes we discussed the philosophical question of the sinking ship. The question was: who should survive if a ship sinks and there is only one raft for a small number of people? Who decides who shall live and who shall die? Who are of most value to survival, and how do we—or even should we—place a value on human life? There are times, it seems, when those kinds of decisions have to be made, but how do we do that? Is it like the health care issue: panels to decide who gets certain treatments and who does not? Different people come up with different solutions for what works for them, emotionally and spiritually. All life is precious; we all want to determine our own destiny and not give up until we have some sort of reassurance as to what is to become of us. The problem is that such reassurance will never come. I believe that what is most compelling in the human spirit is the will and determination to survive, to continue to struggle for what we do not know; it is our holy grail. I do not think the volunteers for this project would have given up their bodies so easily if they would have known the outcome.

The plane finally began its descent into Brunei's capital city, Bandar Seri Begawan. It was beautiful and modern. Brunei is on the north coast of Borneo and on the southern edge of the South China Sea, so it's warm and tropical. The weather did not seem much different than in Miami. We were taken to the Empire Hotel, a glorious palatial resort, where Gwen and I both got our own rooms. Gwen was very excited to be there and started to relax with her surroundings, while I was getting increasingly nervous. Gwen said so enthusiastically, "Oh my God, I have never seen such riches—this is crazy. I love it." I, on the other hand, wondered what we were going to have to do to earn such accommodations. Typically, entry-level models do not make enough money to support this kind of lifestyle. Gwen did not appear to consider or comprehend this concept.

Our agency coordinator, Juan Bautista, met us at the hotel and said, "You have a few days to rest up from the jet lag before you have a fashion show. There will be a mixer very similar to what you experienced on the yacht in the Caribbean. During the party, you two need to mingle with the men who are coming from all over the world. These men are very rich and represent large fashion design companies."

Later at the show, most of them men would not talk to us. However, they definitely kept their eyes on us; it was all a bit creepy.

Juan said to Gwen, "There is a man from Paris who wants to meet you privately."

She asked, "Where is he?"

Juan replied, "I will take you to him."

They went off and left me in a main ballroom. Before we left for the party that night, as a gift, I gave Gwen a gold toe-ring with a tiny pendant. Khufu sent me the ring and told me to give it to her so they could track her. It had a GPS locator device in it. Khufu told me that task force agents had followed us to Brunei. I did not know how many of them there were, where they stayed, or if they would try to contact me.

Gwen came back from her meeting and said, "Renee, he offered me a job and a contract at his modeling agency in Paris. And he said he would pay me double what these guys are offering us." She was so excited. A question that entered my mind was that no one had even made us any offers yet. This all seemed a bit strange and unorthodox. "Renee, I do not want to go anywhere without you. I asked him to take you, but he said the offer was just for me. I don't know what to do."

"It's okay. You should take the offer," I said. "I will find something else or just have a good time and go back home. What was the name of the modeling agency? What was this guy's name?"

Gwen replied, "I have never heard of the company—New Vision Modeling or something like that. His name was Pierre. He was so nice. He was an older guy, about fifty, I guess, with a graying beard. It all seemed on the up-and-up." Gwen then lowered her head a bit and slowly replied, "Let's sleep on it and make our decision tomorrow."

I said, "That seems like a great idea."

THE EXCHANGE

The next morning I tried to call Gwen's room but there was no answer. I went later in the morning and knocked on her door; still there was no answer. This did not seem like something Gwen would do; she would not go anywhere without telling me. I called the front desk and asked where Gwen was and they told me she had checked out early that morning. I called Juan and he told me that Gwen had accepted the offer to go to Paris and had signed with the modeling agency. I needed to tell Khufu what had happened. When I tried to use my room phone, the hotel operator said there was a problem getting outside lines and that it would be a while before they were fixed. I decided to leave the hotel and try to find a telephone. I had a bad feeling of what might happen next and wanted to try to find out what had happened to Gwen. As soon as I stepped out of my room into the hallway, I was stopped by two husky, dark-skinned men wearing blue suits. They told me that Juan wanted to meet me at different hotel. I told them I did not want to meet him now and they said I must go. I knew it would be futile to try to resist them. Therein lies a problem, being an agent alone in a strange country, with little knowledge of the language, people, or geography. What are you going to do if things go wrong? I figured I would go along with it and try to find out more about Gwen and how to find her. I hoped she still had on the GPS device and that Ops was tracking her. I would try to find a phone to call Khufu. I still needed to gain more intelligence on this operation and did not want to seem uncooperative—at least not yet.

I was taken by car on a scenic road along the coastline; it was beautiful. I stared out the window for a bit at the ocean. Back before this mission had started and while I was still acclimating to Renee, I had told Sara I did not want to work for the military any longer, if something else happened to me. I told her I wanted a chance at a normal life, a predictable one without danger, so I could raise my family. I wanted to stop these exchanges and have time to adjust to a new body, long-term. I needed time to consider all that had happened to me and wanted time to let it soak in before any more exchanges took place.

We arrived at a large estate that had a guarded front gate and was surrounded by high concrete walls with fencing on top. I did not think
the compound was unusual, as it seemed common in some parts of the
world for the security of wealthy people.

I met Juan inside and he told me, "An agency from Brazil really
liked you and wants to offer you a job."

"I'm not interested. I want to talk to Gwen. Where is she?"

"It's not possible to talk to Gwen, she is on her way to Paris," He
indignantly replied. "The Brazilian offer is a good one; You should
take it."

"I do not want to go to Brazil. I want to go with Gwen."

"You should be a little more grateful for what we have done for
you. Now, come with me."

I followed him into a hotel-like room, which had bars on the windows. "Wait here and I will make arrangements for you."

The room's only door strangely had a lock from the outside, which
he bolted when he left. So I had little choice but to stay put.

In the middle of the night, I was taken to the airport and forced to
board a private jet. Again, I saw no point in resisting because I wanted
to understand how this was all going to play out. I had no idea where
they were taking me. There were two other girls in the plane with me.
I tried to talk to them, but another man in a suit turned around and
said with a heavy middle-eastern accent, "No talking during the flight."
I do not think they could speak English, because they looked Russian
or Eastern European. One was a very tall, thin, gorgeous blonde. The
other one was also tall and thin, but a brunette with a short bob haircut; both were in their early twenties. I slept for most of the flight and
lost track of time. I think we were airborne for at least twelve hours,
because it was dark when we took off, and then it got light out and
then dark again when we landed. I had no idea where in the world we
were but it seemed as though we flew southeast by the way the sun-
rise was off the nose of the airplane and then set behind us. The other

girls and I were taken in a stretch limousine to an estate about an hour outside the large city where we landed. All three of us were escorted to our rooms.

When I arrived at my room, the escort opened the door to let me in and said, "I am going to lock the door, so there is no reason to try to go anywhere."

I replied in a friendly tone with a smile, "Your English is very good. Where did you learn? What's your native language?"

He looked at me and replied with half a smile, "I learned in primary school; English was a required course. Portuguese is my first language. Now go in. We are not supposed to talk to the girls."

"Sorry, I don't want to get you in trouble."

I walked in and the door quickly closed behind me; I heard the latch lock. I tried to get settled and hoped the task force had enough time to locate me. I realized there were only two countries in the world who primarily spoke Portuguese; Portugal and Brazil. My guess was that this is Brazil. I needed to get out of this room and learn more about this operation.

The next day a man called and introduced himself as Che. "I am going to be your manager for your stay here. There is going to be an important client coming to see you for dinner at six. Please choose one of the many new evening gowns picked out for you in your closet. Later this afternoon some people will come up and help you get ready."

"What about food? Can I go somewhere to get something to eat?"

"There is a menu on the desk. You can order anything you like and it will be brought up to you."

I ordered some food, which was amazingly good. About 4:00 pm there was a knock at the door: a makeup artist and hair designer had come to help me get ready. This was a first-class operation. I felt like the model I was supposed to be getting ready for her big gala event. The hair designer, who was a beautiful, olive-skinned woman in her mid-thirties, wore her dark hair in a ponytail. She introduced herself.

"My name is Jen, I will be fixing your hair. Do you want to wear it up or down?"

"What do you think? This sounds formal, so maybe up?"

"Yes, I think up would be best."

The other woman spoke when Jen finished. "I'm Polina, I will help you with your makeup. Please sit over here in the chair." Whereas Jen appeared to be a local Brazilian, Polina had a different accent and my estimation was Russian or eastern bloc. They were very business-like, and this obviously was not the first day on the job for either of them.

"How long have you two been working here?"

Polina interrupted, "No time for talk, please sit."

Polina and Jen finished in about an hour, then left. I went to my closet and picked out, long dark blue velvet gown, with shimmering gold decoration all over it. I picked what I thought would look beautiful on a woman—not hard for a man. At about five minutes before six there was a knock at the door and it opened. A man was there to escort me to dinner. I discovered after I walked into his room that our dinner was to be in the client's private suite. When I walked in, the apparent client was standing next to a window. He was a Latin-looking man much taller than me, chubby, with a short, slightly graying beard. After a brief introduction, my escort took my hand and raised it high above my head and guided me around the room like a peacock showing off its feathers. My escort took me to an adjacent room, which had a beautiful candlelit dinner waiting.

He sat me down and said, "Mr. Gutierrez does not speak English." The escort walked away back toward the door. The Latin man came into the room where I was sitting and reached out for my hand; I thought he was going to kiss it. He was not a handsome man, but not completely ugly either. He took my hand and pulled me to my feet, and then tried to kiss me. I turned my head and abruptly pulled away. He reached out again for my hand, with a bit more force this time, and led me over toward the bed which was only a few feet away, next to the dining area. He stopped and let go of my hand and walked back over and sat down at the dinner table. I did not know what to do. The Latin man looked over at the man who escorted me to his room and they spoke briefly in what I believe was Portuguese.

The escort then walked toward me and said, "He wants you to slowly take off your clothes."

I looked at the Latin man, "I am not taking off my clothes. That is not why I am here."

The escort raised his voice, "Please Madam, take off your clothes. Mr. Gutierrez insists."

"NO. I am not taking off my clothes." I was not sure how far this was going to go, so I just stood there, a bit unsure what to do next.

My escort walked up next to me and whispered close to my face, "If you do not take off your clothes, there is going to be a big problem. Please do as you are told!"

"No, I will not. I am not doing this."

All the while, my Latin suitor sat there at the dinner table with a grin on his face. My escort walked over and picked up the phone. He spoke in Portuguese for a bit and then walked back over to the door and stood there. I thought, I'm not going to be a call girl for this guy. I waited to see what was going to happen next. I felt a bit like a matador waiting to see what the bull was going to do. Within a couple of minutes, four men came into the room and grabbed me. Each man grabbed one of my arms and legs, and then they lifted me up onto the bed and held me there. They tied my arms and legs to the bedposts. One of the guys took out a knife and ripped open my beautiful evening gown.

I screamed at them over and over, "Stop! Stop! Don't do this!" One guard, with a long handlebar moustache, slapped me so hard across my face that I bit the inside of my cheek. I couldn't believe this was happening to me. I have only been a woman for a short time and now I was getting raped. Me—a pilot, an intelligence officer, a man—and yet here I was, a woman unable to defend myself. There was nothing I could do and I knew it; I had a brief flashback to the tent in Yemen when I was being held and beaten before I lost my head. I could not believe I was going to be raped for my first sexual experience as a woman. I was completely exposed and vulnerable, my dress cut up the middle, with only my bra and panties on. The four men laughed at me and then left the room. The pudgy Latin man undressed and I could see his small penis was erect.

The Latin man had obviously paid for me. He had to climb onto the side of the high bed to get up to me and he had a huge smile on his face, like he was about to feast on a roast pig. He ripped at my already torn dress and underwear and pushed his face between my legs, licking me hard, like I needed a tongue bath or he was trying to take something off my skin. He forced one of his fingers inside me and I felt something tear or rip; a shooting hot pain ran through me. The fat pig of a man was panting like he had run the 100-yard dash as he got on top of me. I felt his penis push inside me—fortunately it felt smaller than his finger. It was over quickly. He moaned, then rolled off of me. I thought it would be over and that they would come in and untie me. I wondered lying there how long it would be before the task force would rescue me. What was taking them so long?

My mind drifted for a minute or so as my rapist got dressed. I thought about growing up in Indiana and riding Frito on a hot summer day. And I thought about Miriam: I wondered what she was doing and how she was getting along without me, and if she had found someone else and gotten remarried. I missed her. I missed lying next to her in the morning. When we first woke up we would always reach across and stroke each other's face, like a good morning greeting rather than saying a word. I heard the door close and looked over in that direction.

The fat Latin man had left, but the four guards had come back in and closed the door. They all had wild looks on their faces and were talking in Portuguese. I began to get a bit worried and nervous when

I saw them all starting to undress. The one with the handlebar moustache got on the bed and forced his limp penis in my mouth, forcing me to gag on it. I thought I was going to vomit. Another guard, one with a big belly and a disgusting body odor, climbed on the bed and on top of me, thrusting in me while he grabbed and pulled at my breasts. One of them started slapping my face, so I could not see anymore. I could not keep my eyes open. Someone grabbed my mouth and pulled it open, while another straddled my chest and forced his penis in; thrusting back and forth until I was covered in his fluid. I felt like I was back in the desert in Yemen. I wished I was back in the desert in Yemen. I know they would not have treated me like this. These sub-human pigs were like wild animals. I was in disbelief and shock at all that had happened to me. I reflected for a second back to when I accepted this mission and realized something like this could happen. I just figured it would not happen to me. Here I was again, waiting and dependent on my comrades to rescue me. I wanted to drop a round in each one of these guy's heads.

I lost track of time. I started to dream and think of my life, my lives. I've had so many great experiences and traveled so far, and have met so many wonderful people. I needed to keep my wits about me and learn about this operation so other young girls would not have to go through what I just went through. The men untied me and left but I remained motionless on the bed. I laid there for what felt like a long time, then finally got up and went to the shower. I did not turn the light on to the bathroom, as I did not want to see my reflection in the mirror. I wanted to chalk this up as a bad dream, a nightmare. Maybe I should have just submitted to their demands; it probably would have all gone much easier then. If I let Frank's ego get in the way, it could jeopardize this mission. I sat in the dark shower for what must have been an hour.

I heard someone come into the bathroom, and a man's voice yelled at me: "Get dressed and I will take you back to your room." I got out of the shower and saw the man was dressed in a blue suit. He escorted me back to my room. I thought to myself that these guys are like storm troopers. Before he closed and locked the door, he scolded me, "Be more friendly to the customers next time or more bad things will happen to you."

I laid on my bed. I thought about what had happened, all the way back to when I had first woken up as a woman. I had felt anxious about how I was going to handle it and what it was going to be like. It had taken me a while, but I had begun to feel more comfortable and had even thought it would be a great opportunity as a human being and a man to discover what it was like to be a woman. I had thought about the possibilities of learning about various things from girl talk, having a period and PMS, sex, my feminine feelings, relationships, and pregnancy. But I had no thoughts about being raped. I had never thought of how women feel being vulnerable and afraid of men. I almost never felt afraid as a man, especially of other men. I thought about Gwen and hoped nothing similar had happened to her. I hoped not, but feared as much. I woke up later and found a note under my door. The note instructed me to be ready for another client tomorrow evening. I immediately began to wonder where the task force was and how long before there would be a rescue. I needed to try to get out of this room so I could get more details about this place. I wanted to know how many other women were being held here, who was doing it, where they were coming from, and how I was going to get them out of here.

There were not many options for escape. The windows had bars bolted to the building, the door was locked with a deadbolt, and I had no tools. I could only wait and hope that acting as bait with my tracking device would provide enough intel for a rescue of all of us. The next afternoon came and I began to get ready for my "date." I thought that if I cooperated more, maybe I would get an opportunity to learn more about this operation. Jen and Polina came back about four o'clock to do my hair and makeup; they both told me not to fight. At six I was taken to the lobby area and paraded in front of an older man, probably in his sixties. This man was much bigger than my previous suitor, maybe six feet four, so overpowering him did not seem like an option. I wondered for a moment how these guys could be with someone who does not want to be with them? Maybe they thought in their twisted, chauvinistic minds that the girls somehow desired them. Or was this some sort of animalistic behavior where they felt they were holding their prey. I saw my date smile at the guard who was escorting me, who then walked me over and sat me down next to this guy.

The man put out a cigar he was smoking and in a soft low voice said, "Hello. I am Juarez. What is your name?"

"Renee," I answered.

"Would you like to have dinner with me, Renee?"

"Yes, I would be delighted."

He smiled at me and said, "Marvelous." My guard smiled and walked away as we got up to walk toward a dining room next to the lobby. Juarez was a gentlemen and pulled my chair out for me so I could sit down at the table. His English was quite good, with only a small Spanish accent.

"Where are you from? I love your accent."

"I was born in a small village a few hundred kilometers south of Buenos Aires. My father owned a large cattle ranch, and I lived there until I went to college in Buenos Aires. What about you? Where are you from?"

"I am from a small town outside of Washington DC—Chantilly, Virginia."

"Well, you are a very beautiful woman." Juarez stated admiringly. "How long have you been here?"

"Where is 'here' exactly?"

"You are in Brazil, about two hours west of Campinas. It is kind of resort area for wealthy Brazilian businessmen. I was invited here because I do a lot of business with Brazil. I still raise cattle."

"I have only been here a week or so—I'm not sure with the time change. I was in Brunei, and then came here. I wish I could see your cattle ranch. I love wide-open spaces. Do you have a lot of horses on your ranch?"

"Yes, we do. You should come and ride someday." He seemed like a genuine man, who just enjoyed life. He probably had not had to work very hard in his life and had built on what his father had given him. He was not an unattractive man for his age; his skin was not dark and leathery like you would expect from a cattle rancher. But I am sure he did not spend a lot of time in his life handling cattle or riding horses.

Juarez ordered dinner for us both, which was an amazing five-course meal. I had one of the best prepared steaks I had ever eaten. I had always heard that Brazilians really know how to cook meat. We sat back after our dinner and drank red wine. I sipped mine while Juarez drank several glasses, I wanted to keep my wits about me and learn as much as I could. I asked him, "Have you ever been here before?"

"Yes, I have been a couple of times. This place is kind of exclusive and you can only be invited here. I have a few associates who work in the restaurant business and they arrange to come here after we settle contracts for my beef. It's like a gift or business token."

"Have you ever taken a girl away from here, or has anyone ever married a girl from here?"

"I have not, and not that I am aware of. But, I am not that familiar. They seem pretty quiet about where the girls come from. I assume they hire the girls from all over the world."

"Well, I have heard that some of the girls here are not hired, and they are forced against their will to be here," I whispered.

"Kidnapped, you mean? I don't think that is true. Probably just girl talk, I would not worry if I were you. These guys all seem very nice here."

I innocently replied, "Maybe you could take me back to your cattle ranch. I would love to see it. I have never been to Argentina."

He looked intently at me. "Well, we'll see. Are you finished, would you like to finish your wine up in my room?"

I knew that was not much of a question; it was already assumed. "Sure, I would love to."

We went to his room, a large suite with a fireplace which was already lit. I asked Juarez, "Would you like more wine?"

"Yes, yes that would be great. Maybe you could do a nice strip tease for me in front of the fire. I want to see that beautiful little body of yours. I love blonde American women."

"Wow, you don't mess around, do you?" I laughed. Then so did he.

"I am an old man, I don't waste time like I did when I was young."

I watched him down another glass of wine, so I poured him another. I thought maybe he would pass out before I would have to do anything with him. I danced a bit in front of the fire and slowly took off my shoes, then my gown. I could see he was getting aroused and had a small bulge in his pants. I did not even think at that point he could get an erection with as much wine as he had drunk and given how old he was. So I told him, "Undress and lay on the bed. Watch me dance." I continued to dance slowly in front of the fireplace and slowly took off my bra and panties, as erotically as I could imagine. I told him, "Stroke yourself. It excites me to see a man do that." So he did. I hoped he would get himself off and that that would be it. I then asked him, "Can I stay here tonight with you?"

He smiled a huge grin, "Yes, of course. If you like." He reached his arms out to have me come over to him.

"Please go slow, I am nervous." I was still very sore from being raped and did not want to tell him.

He pulled me on top of him and guided himself inside me.

It hurt but I tried not to show it.

It was over quickly and he let out a low groan. He rolled his head back and his eyes closed as if he was pleased and ready to go to sleep. He said, "Can you get the light? Let's go to sleep." Then he rolled over and was snoring within a minute.

I thought this would be a good time to try to find out how many girls were here and who some of them were. I had noticed when I first came in the room that there were no bars or locks on the windows. I looked out the window and over the open expanse with a large pool area, tennis courts, and beautiful gardens. I wondered if I went out the window I could walk around and get a better lay of the land, and gather intelligence. Juarez's room was on the first floor with French doors leading out to a patio area behind his room. I did not want to be seen by anyone and had to wait a few minutes for some men to pass by the area. I walked out and headed for a dark area around some trees to hide and get a look around. When I got there I looked back at the hotel; it was large, six floors, and maybe 300 rooms. There must be a lot of girls here. There were many rooms with their lights still on and I imagined there were many girls doing things they did not want to. I wanted to blow the cover on this place. I wondered how long it would take before the team would get here. I needed to try to make a call to Khufu.

I started to walk back to Juarez's room when a guy who must have been a guard approached me. "You are not supposed to be out here alone. Where is your date?"

"He fell asleep so I went for a walk."

"What is his name or room number?"

"I don't recall the room number but his name is Juarez and he's from Argentina," I answered. The guard grabbed me by my arm and escorted me to the lobby.

Che was standing in the lobby when we arrived.

"What were you doing outside? Trying to escape? I assure you, you cannot! Where is Juarez?"

I quickly responded, "I was not trying to escape. Juarez went to sleep so I went for a walk."

Che scolded me, "You are not to be alone. We will check with

Juarez. Take her back to her room." With that, the guard escorted me back to my room and locked the door.

I got undressed and wanted to take a shower. I put the water on as hot as I could take it and sat on the shower floor and let the water rain down on my head. I wondered how many other girls were here going through this same ordeal. How many women were submitting to this slavery all over the world in situations like this? How could we, how could I, stop this madness? I felt a bit helpless as the huge multi-national problem seemed so overwhelming. I again thought back to Emma. I wondered how I could help her or teach her to never be taken in by such deception. I imagined how big she must be and what she now looked like. Sadly, I could not conjure a new image, only the last time I saw her as she left for school. I finished my shower and went to bed.

The next morning at about eight-thirty, while I was still asleep and in bed, the door flew open and about six guards burst into my room. Che was the last one through the doorway,

"Did you really think you could get away with killing him? What did you do to him how? Did you kill him?"

"I did not kill anyone. Who do you think I killed?"

"Juarez is dead. We found him dead in his bed this morning."

"I did not kill him! He fell asleep last night right after we had sex."

Che announced, "Oh, is that why you tried to escape and run away? Take her! The guards rushed around me. I could see in their faces that they were not happy with me. To hell with them—I was not there to make their lives easier. They dragged me out of my room. One guard said, "You will be sorry for being a problem." I did not give his threat too much credence. They made me walk outside in a back courtyard area. There were many girls already seated in chairs, almost like a wedding was going to take place. I estimated that there were thirty girls seated, waiting for something. I was led past all the seated girls, which I again thought was weird. Next, I saw what they were waiting for. In front of all the girls was a large tree, and thrown around one of the limbs was a hangman's rope.

I remembered thinking that I could not believe what was about to happen to me. I was going to be executed again! What happened to Juarez? Did he die of a heart attack, or of a Viagra OD, or did they kill him and want to blame it on me? Was this a dream?

One of the guards in the front spoke in English, like a judge addressing a courtroom. He said, "This is what happens to you when you do not comply with our wishes and then kill someone!" With that said, they led me over to the rope and put the noose around my neck. They did not put a hood over my head; I was glad. I looked out at the surroundings. It was a beautiful day, clear blue sky, trees swaying in the wind, very green, green grass. I could see only about half of the girls were watching or looking at me; the other half were looking down in their laps, and some were crying. Strangely, I felt more sorry for them than I did for myself. I wished I could have helped them. The rope was itchy on my neck but not very tight; it was thick, maybe three-quarter of an inch in diameter.

I have always been amazed at how one person could kill another. I can understand our need to kill animals to eat. I can understand the instinct to survive when our bellies are empty. But, I completely do not understand how one person cannot realize the pain and torture of killing another. Or maybe it is simply ignorance. No one knows what it is like to die; no one has reported back with any degree of certainty or with evidence of what it is like. Maybe murderers do not realize what they are doing, maybe they do not feel they are taking something from someone? Or maybe they feel like it is returning something to a store with no consequences? Death is such a big question, such a big unknown, so scary to us all. What happens to us when our bodies die, what happens to our personalities, our identities?

I heard one man yell at another, and then I felt the rope go tight and my body start to be pulled off the ground. I was not in any pain.

THE EXCHANGE

I never felt like I had an out of body experience and never felt like I went into a tunnel. It was over in a fraction of a second. After I felt a sharp sensation on my neck, time seemed to stop. I have had many dreams of dying, but this was not like any of them: things just went blank.

Adam's a Recruiter

I woke up back at CD headquarters. This time I did not want to move or open my own eyes. I felt like a human guinea pig going to slaughter over and over again. I could not even think anymore; my mind just seemed to hurt. I was lost in a maze and did not know who I was, where I was, or if I was in a dream. I thought I had been in a terrible accident or had had a stroke as Frank and was trapped in my own mind, unable to move, lost in my own thoughts. I recalled reading about a French editor who had a stroke and was basically trapped in his own body, unable to communicate with the outside world. He could feel, he could think, but he was locked up in his own mind, and could not move a muscle. I empathized with that editor. I was so confused and disoriented. I wondered what had happened to Gwen.

Sara was there with two other men. She said they were there to debrief the mission. I think they could tell, from how quiet I was and reluctant to provide any feedback, that something was not quite right with me. I did not have the same enthusiasm as when I had awakened the previous times in a new body. I began to scan the outline of my latest body; a man, probably in his mid-twenties. Carefully I got up and walked over to the mirror to examine my new reflection…me, another me. The person who looked back at me was handsome, with a heavy five o'clock shadow, dark brown eyes, dark brown wavy hair, about six-feet-one tall, thin, almost too thin. I did not want to stare at him anymore. It had happened all over again and I wanted it to stop.

The excitement I had had in the beginning, after Frank died and I found new life in Randy's body, was all gone. The concept of being exchanged and given a second chance in the beginning had sounded great. But this way could not be the best path to discover the magnificence of such an evolutionary breakthrough. I wanted to think about the great things we could do with such an amazing accomplishment for mankind. We could learn so many more things with it, like getting several college degrees or learning things no man could ever learn before, because of the several lifetimes needed to accomplish complete research. Today many occupational fields need people who are multi-disciplinary in order to understand the complexities of a question. How great would it be to have people with such extensive backgrounds? Humanity could benefit from individuals who have spent multiple lifetimes in several diverse fields of study and could reap great rewards by solving complex social, scientific, and philosophical questions. Instead, we are chained to the same age-old sins of humanity: lust, envy, gluttony, sloth, wrath, pride, and greed.

I looked at the men for what seemed like a long time. They did not question, only looked back as if to give me time to process my new awakening. Then I asked, "What are you going to do with me now? What happened to Gwen?"

One man, taller than the other, spoke first. "My name is Samuel Malcolm. I was part of your special ops team while you were working as Renee. Gwen is fine; we found her in Jordan. She was smuggled there by the fake company from Brunei. We were able to shut down their trafficking operation. She kept asking about you. We finally told her you were killed in Brazil."

"What happened to the Brazil operation?" I asked.

Sam replied, "We called in the Brazilian military to help us shut them down. They apparently had had your compound under surveillance for a long time because of the number of crime bosses who frequented it. But they had no legal reason, until you, to enter the property. You were the lynchpin for the rescue of 45 young girls from 15 different countries. We now have leads in many countries to follow up on. Job well done, Captain!"

I looked at Sam. " 'Captain'—I have not heard that in a while. Is that who I am?"

Sam insisted, "Sorry, Sir, I did not know exactly how to address you."

I apologized, "That's okay. I do not know who I am either."

I walked over to the window and gazed out at the landscape and thought for a bit about what were they going to do with me next. Maybe shoot me into outer space and see if I pop like some over-cooked piece of food in a microwave oven, or use me as a live test dummy in some car crash experiment, or maybe test a long-range bullet on how fast it kills a human being. I felt emotionally exhausted; my mind was spinning and I couldn't stop it. I needed a rest. I just wanted to lie on some beach and enjoy the warmth of the sand and sun on my body—a body that most people would want to protect and preserve, rather than see how fast they could destroy it. It would be nice to talk with someone who understood what I was feeling. I felt so alone. I wondered if there were other people like me out in the world, if there were other exchangers who had had such a hard time staying alive. I would have to keep my eyes open for other people with the same tattoo as mine.

I looked at Sara. "Who am I now?"

She replied, "Adam River. Your father was not a nice person and had a rap sheet a couple of feet long, which included murder. He died in a prison fight when you were four years old. Your mother was a drug addict and prostitute. She apparently spent most of her life half-unconscious in a drunken, doped-up stupor. When you were six years old, you were found by police after you called 911 from a hotel where they found your mother dead from a heroin overdose. You were in and out of foster care most of your early life. A wealthy foster family finally placed Adam in an ROTC boarding school near the southern California coastal town of Oceanside. It seemed you learned to work through your past by swimming. You competed in swimming events your entire time in boarding school. It's noted in your file that Adam's classmates were worried because you used to go for open water swims far offshore to test yourself against death. Apparently the surf's very dangerous there, with steep cliffs, a rocky coastline, and a large number of great white sharks. Your friends commented that Adam liked the risk of ocean swims, daring the sharks and the sea to try to kill him. As you can tell, Adam's body is in great shape."

Sara continued, "Emotionally, Adam had a lot of difficulty recovering from his terrible childhood. For many years he used to wake up at night screaming in fear because he was alone. Dorm attendants reported he would often sleep under his bed, rather than on top. Adam told therapists that he got used to sleeping under his bed because he did not want to watch his mom have scx with the many strange men she would invite into their room. While Adam was at ROTC he did not socialize well with the other boys. However, he became very protective of the girls. He apparently associated the girls with kindness and the boys with violence. His therapists said this was a result of the time he had spent with his mother, witnessing her beaten up by men coming in to have sex with her. It was not until Adam was nearly fourteen that he began to put some of his fears behind him. Adam became an ideal candidate for the Air Force Academy, and after graduation volunteered for CD as a Second Lieutenant. CD was actually a good deal for someone like him. They both got something valuable: he received freedom from his pain and we got his healthy young body."

Sam, his partner Bill, and I spent the next several hours going over the details from my last mission. I guess CD realized— maybe Sara told them— that I needed time for this transition, and maybe even a lifetime, to recover and understand all that had happened to me. I had not signed up for this; I had thought I was simply getting a GPS and bio-medical monitoring device. Of course, given the choice of living or dying and being non-existent right now, I would have chosen life.

I asked Sara, "Who makes the decisions about who I am and who I am going to be next?"

She replied, "Dr. James Colone, the director of CD, makes those decisions, as far as I know. I told him about your case and he arranged for the new assignment. I am sure he must be in contact with someone else, maybe the Defense department, but I don't know for sure. I suggested to him an administrative position for you rather than a field position. He suggested a 'recruiter' position and I agreed."

I quickly retorted, "When do I get to make those decisions about my own life?"

Sara looked away and slowly responded, "You will have to ask Dr. Colone about that."

And so I was made a recruiter for the Global Peace Institute. My job was to place graduating students into an international peace program; at least that's the façade it was given. The GPI was a school with a unique approach in that they only accept under-privileged children with little hope for a promising future. However, the GPI had a dark side and operated more like a farm than an institute of learning. As a recruiter I was someone who was less than truthful to the students and told the outside world exactly what CD wanted them to know. The children from the GPI, upon graduation, were taken to Washington, DC, where their minds were erased and their bodies were taken over by candidates selected by CD.

GPI is comprised of several schools, one of which is located in Big Sur, California, a tiny coastal town hidden in the cliffs of the gorgeous Los Padres National Forest. Big Sur is approximately 120 miles south of San Francisco and 250 miles north of Los Angeles. Its only access is the Pacific Coast Highway, also known as Highway 1, just south of the distinguished cities of Carmel and Monterey. Not unlike these two famous cities, Big Sur spends a good portion of the year shrouded in coastal fog with average temperatures in the mid-60 degree range. The location of the Institute was chosen for its spectacular scenery and because it was far from the influence and distractions of mainstream society.

THE EXCHANGE

GPI's small student population is discreetly and carefully screened by its staff. The goal, established by its founders, is to provide a nurturing school and living environment that addresses the special needs of abused or foster children, or children left for adoption with no known parental ties. These students are the ones society has arguably abandoned. The students are provided with everything necessary to succeed in growing up with strong bodies and minds, and to serve the greater good of the world. The serene setting is designed to allow the children to thrive outside of mainstream culture. The Institute does not teach the same standardized curriculum as public schools, which the founders believed to be ineffective in teaching society how to cope without war and violence. The students are taught that they will be the emissaries of peace to future generations, and be part of an effort to rid the world of war and of military machines which waste valuable resources for the sole purpose of destruction.

The children bond quickly because of their common backgrounds, and they embrace each other and the faculty as family. There are no televisions, Internet, cell phones, or other electronic distractions allowed on the campus. The children are encouraged to focus on building themselves to be the leaders of tomorrow. The school's population is intentionally developed to be representative of global society with the enrollment of as many ethnicities as possible. The ethnic selection process is also believed to be the beginning stage of helping the students understand that they are all human beings of equal value in a global society and that ethnic and cultural biases should be removed. GPI's ethnic diversity is a model for the students to realize how all people contribute to the world.

Students are set to graduate and leave the institution on their eighteenth birthday. A few months prior to their eighteenth birthday they rank locations and programs around the globe they desire to attend, and potential institutions do the same. The selection process is secret. After all is completed a computer printout shows which institutions matched with students and where they will be attending. The number one matched institution follows up with a personal one-on-one interview by a representative from the program's host country. The students and interviewers meet for one week before the final selections are made. Early on the children are taught to realize how important their placements are and to understand that while at GPI they must strive to achieve their greatest physical and intellectual potential. Once chosen they are not allowed to contact anyone at their selected Institute until they arrive. After they leave GPI they cannot contact any of their friends or previous students. The severing of emotional ties from their past is meant to help them transition to their new lives, as any contact with the past is believed by staff psychologists to be detrimental to their maturation and personal development. This is a very difficult adjustment for all the students leading up to graduation, but the students are also excited about the lives ahead of them.

After being given this assignment I decided to take the train across country instead of flying, as I usually do, to slow down a bit, relax, think, and take in the beauty of the landscape. I had my own sleeper unit, so that I could be alone and no one would disturb me, as well as so that I could sleep whenever I wanted; one week of peace and contemplation. On the first day I settled into my tiny cabin, which seemed like a closet with a fold-down bed. The train was named after its destination, "The San Francisco Zephyr." I was amazed by how quickly the concrete jungle of Washington, DC turned into the lush, green rolling hills of Virginia. There were many very expensive horse farms dotting the hillside of western Virginia and I was reminded of the carefree days of my childhood. I recalled the distant days of long ago when my only decisions after waking up on a hot, humid summer day was where to go riding and which horse to ride. My mind kept drifting back to the children of GPI. I was not sure how I felt about their futures. They all seemed to have horrific childhoods with many resulting psychological problems. I let myself believe it was in their best interests to have their minds erased of their pasts. I also felt that they were like me and had not been given a choice.

When the students first arrive at the institute they all get to choose a new name. This is meant to assist them with getting over their difficult family history, as well as to help to do away with any ethnic or cultural biases a name may have and thereby establish more neutrality. The choice of name, in part, was based on the year the student would turn sixteen. This year's graduates are the sixteenth class of GPI, and the letter "P" is the sixteenth letter of the alphabet. Thus the students got to choose any name beginning with the letter P. This year's six graduates will all turn eighteen within one month of each other: Parker, Piper, Phoebe, Payton, Pierce, and Penny Jo or PJ.

My train ride was almost finished as I crossed over the Sierra Nevada Mountains through the small town of Truckee, California near Lake Tahoe. I knew I would soon meet the new crop of students who I would basically lure to their demise. This was supposed to be an easy job, one which was stress-free. But I couldn't do this job with a clear conscience. I couldn't believe that I was helping my country promote freedom or democracy. I did not imagine that this was helping someone or some part of the world survive. What I did think was that I was helping someone who happened to be wealthy and got rich from living off of other people's work. I didn't know all the details about what was happening, either to these young people or about the people are who are taking over their bodies. I might feel a bit better if I knew that at least some of these exchanges were going to be made for those who would become great contributors to mankind, or if some were great minds, which were destined to do great work, and which needed to be continued. I wonder what Plato, Socrates, or other great minds could have accomplished, if their lives could have been extended through to another lifetime or two in other bodies.

Meeting the "P" Class

I was sent to the Global Peace Institute to meet the graduating class in person and act as a liaison during the selection process. The prevarication that the interviewers are from renowned peace institutions is simply a way to motivate the kids to keep their bodies healthy and give them a goal to strive for. GPI is more like an athletic college than a learning institution, but academics are also good for exercising the brain to keep it healthy. It is difficult to comprehend, coming here and looking at the body who you will soon inhabit, while you are still someone else. Imagine the chance to choose who you want to be in the next life or at least what you will look like. I never got the chance; the decision was always made for me with the apparent greater good of the military and national security in mind.

I had already become acquainted with the class intimately on paper. I had read thick dossiers on each student, including every small detail of their lives: where they were born, what their real names were, and an extensive background on what had happened to them throughout their lives before coming to the Institute, including where their parents and relatives, if any, were located. In one way I felt almost like I was meeting death row inmates. These kids did not deserve what happened to them when they were small children. They just happened to be born to the wrong people, at the wrong time, in the wrong place. Now, without their consent, they were going to have their lives, their memories, their identities erased. On the other hand, their painful past problems would be gone. CD was playing god and matchmaker. Some people who believe in reincarnation believe our spirits spend time in a place called "life between lives," where one contemplates past lives and past lessons learned, and what a future life should be about to continue on a path toward enlightenment. This is a choice, according to reincarnation believers; the entity or spirit gets to decide, which is an extremely life-altering, intimate, personal decision, wrought with potential and peril. CD interrupts a natural process and allows outsiders to make these decisions for someone else. The so-called interviewers are the fortunate ones.

I could not stop thinking about all that has happened to me. I remembered lying in bed with my wife like it happened yesterday. I remembered being so thankful that someone was looking out for me and put me in a new body after I was killed in combat. After my first exchange I did not feel exploited and I did not feel this process was only for the rich and powerful. I thought in some small way I was contributing to the greater good of mankind and humanity. I thought it would be such a magnificent experience to have the opportunity to live life again to correct my mistakes and to do the things I did not have a chance to do the first time around. I really did not think there would be any downside. I didn't think about the soldiers who gave up their identities and their lives for their country—identities and lives I was taking over. I thought it was their choice, their free will, even though they did not have the full truth.

I do think that there are, in some cases, great opportunities with this technology to save something valuable by saving someone who has made or will make significant to society or mankind. How many have exchanged, I don't know, since CD closely guards all the statistics as secret; maybe no one person really knows. I do not think this technology should be used for political gain, blackmail, or to further the wealth and power of any one country. It definitely should not be used as a cost-saving mechanism, just because it is too expensive to train new pilots, intelligence officers, or covert operators. I feel torn between happiness to be alive and sadness for those whose lives were lost.

I wondered about these young people whose potential the world will never know. They have the ideas, feelings, and excitement that it seems only young people have. With every new generation of people, there are new genres of music, of art, and of literature, as well as changes in styles of thinking and ideas about the future. These could all be lost if we lose our youth. What about young love—that sweet, innocent feeling we all had with our first crush, our first kiss, our first love—will all those feelings be lost? I enjoy watching young couples gaze into each other's eyes so lovingly, so admiringly, so intently, knowing their hearts are pounding with anticipation and wonder. It reminds me of days gone by. I feel like I have lost forever the feelings of the first of anything. I would love to feel again, to feel stimulated and passionate. Yes, I have lived several lives, but what have I gained—and at what cost? I feel lost in this world, in my world.

I met all the students in a small library, very close to the cliffs of Big Sur. I could hear the surf slamming against the rocks hundreds of feet below. The students all looked at me like I had the holy grail tucked in my back pocket. I saw such enthusiasm in their faces, almost like I could touch their wounded hearts and minds; I felt the anticipation they had to start a new life and leave the old memories, the torture, and the pain behind them. They were a beautiful group of young people, fantastic physical specimens of the human race. I was reminded, looking at them, of the many insane people or groups throughout history who had wanted to start a "super race" of people to make the world a better place.

Parker, the class president, stood up first to greet me as I walked in and shook my hand. He was Caucasian, tall, strong, a very pleasant boy and considered handsome by most standards, also very polite and cordial. He spent most of his spare time training in karate. He then introduced the others in his class.

"This is Payton." He was a dark-skinned black man with a well-defined jaw and cheekbones, rugged-looking, with a short buzz-cut and a strong handshake, who was sitting between Phoebe and Piper.

He waved his hand and said "Hello" without getting up. He loved to stay fit by running and hiking the trails of the Los Padres forest.

"And this is Piper." She was a gorgeous, pale-skinned, petite Chinese gymnast with tiny features and shiny, shoulder-length black hair. She was five-feet-one inches tall. Piper gently shook my hand and looked into my eyes only briefly and said, "Hello" before sitting back down.

"This is Phoebe."

I said, "Hello, Phoebe." She was an olive-skinned East Indian, beautiful by anyone's standards, average height, with enchanting black eyes. She loved to play tennis. "Hello, Adam, nice to meet you." When we said hello to each other, Phoebe looked confidently into my eyes as if trying to gaze into my soul, to look beyond my superficial body. It was unsettling. Phoebe seemed unafraid of anything; why would she fear anything after what she has been through?

Parker introduced Pierce next, a Latin boy with brownish-black hair, dark eyes, and a suave grin. "This is Pierce." He looked at me and nodded. Pierce was a soccer jock, the kind that all fathers feared and mothers hid their daughters from. I was sure he could enchant about any woman he chose.

Finally, Parker turned to Penny Jo. She was an exotic mix of Caucasian and Asian, with light brown curly hair and light eyes; she was tall and muscular, as one would expect of a competitive swimmer. Penny was looking out the window at the ocean while the others were introduced, but before Parker said her name she turned her head and looked at me intensely and directly, and said, "PJ, nice to meet you. When is the bus leaving to get us out of here?"

I replied, "Don't you like it here?"

PJ quickly answered, "No. It is like living in a psychiatric wilderness hospital in the middle of nowhere. Everyone here is bent."

"I will do my best to find you a good match as soon as possible," I said. PJ did not seem like the sweet, soft-spoken girl I had read about in her records. I actually did not expect her to say anything when we met. She was strikingly exotic and beautiful. Her skin was a soft white, she had a smile with large, perfectly straight teeth, and she was about five-feet-nine inches tall. There was something about PJ that took me off guard. The others were quiet and polite; they obviously wanted to make a good impression so they would get the placement they wanted. They all appeared to be hiding behind a mask of pain, torment, question, and doubt, or maybe it was because I knew what they had all been through in their lives. PJ was different. She did not seem to care if she made a good impression or not. She was direct and to the point, and seemed to say what the others were really thinking. I turned and moved to stand in front of the whole class. I told them that interviewers from around the world would begin arriving in a few days and that they were not to worry, that I was there to help in any way I could, and wanted to speak with them each individually to answer any questions they might have.

I went to my room that night and could not fall asleep. I felt like I was leading these kids off the edge of a cliff. I wondered what they would think if I told them the truth. I thought that some of them might still go through with this program and rid themselves of their painful pasts and then not have to worry about their futures; a painless suicide, in effect.

The next morning I took a walk around the Institute. There are few places in the world as beautiful and tranquil as Big Sur. The property had hot tubs etched into the cliffs, which descend down toward the water and are fed by natural hot springs. I sat alone in one of the hot tubs and was amazed at how calm and peaceful I was. Looking out, I could not see any aspect of humanity: no buildings, no people. Sitting on the edge of the cliffs in the tubs, you had the perspective of a sea gull gliding about on the updrafts, which blew in from the west across the vast, open ocean. I thought about how many human lifetimes had gone by to create such an amazing picture of beauty. The cliffs were created and changed every day by the constant wind and pounding surf, in a natural way, unimpeded by man's intrusions. Maybe human life should be left to the same natural forces. Maybe we should stop trying to interfere with this process. I was lost for a few minutes with my thoughts.

PJ's voice broke the sound of the surf beating against the rocks below. "Do you mind if I join you?"

I looked up and saw her standing next to my hot tub, dressed in a light blue bikini with white stripes running across it. Her hair draped over her shoulders and was being tossed about in the wind. She was shivering from the cold, misty air, so I said, "Of course. Hurry and get in. It is so cold in the wind here." Big Sur, being on the California coast where the cold ocean water flows south from Alaska, has an average annual temperature in the sixty-degree range, and a lot of fog. This is the same reason why San Francisco stays so cold in the summer: ocean-induced fog. PJ had a demure, inquisitive expression on her face. She would not look directly at me. She seemed reserved and shy compared to her bit of an outburst yesterday about wanting to leave.

"What is it like in other countries? Will I be okay?" she asked. She seemed so young, so innocent, and so emotionally frail and vulnerable. She continued, "I'm sorry, I hardly remember what you said yesterday at our meeting. I was kind of zoned out."

"I have never been out of the US," I told her. "I have only talked with people who have. But there are many different places in the world and each one has its own beauty, uniqueness, and interesting aspects. You should be excited about the adventure of discovering each and every one of them." I always had to remind myself not to step out of character; Adam was a young man with little experience in the world. This position at CD was supposed to be his first major job. As much as I wanted to I could not tell her of all my experiences through the lives I had lived to calm her fears. I looked back at her. "Where do you think you might like to go?

"I would like to go somewhere peaceful, where no one wants to hurt one another, where everyone simply minds their own business. I have read about the monasteries of Tibet and India, where everyone walks around quietly without talking or touching each other. It sounds nice."

"Do people here bother you by talking or touching too much?"

"No, not here, but I am afraid that in a strange country people will just come up to you."

"Don't worry. Most people and places I have heard of are quite safe. It is not normal for people to do such things."

PJ got quiet and gazed off toward the vast open ocean below us. I looked at her and thought about her life. The doctors never really explored the extent of her past before she was brought to GPI. CD did not want to make the effort to treat the children's psychic issues, because they knew that at some point their tortuous histories would be erased and replaced.

PJ's circumstances even before she was born had not been promising. Her father had been killed in Iraq when her mom was still pregnant with her. He had been a handsome, tall, blond-haired, blue-eyed, rugged athletic-type guy whose job in the US Air Force had been Para-Rescue 46th Expeditionary Rescue Squadron. Para-rescue guys are nicknamed "PJ's" and it is their job to rescue downed pilots behind enemy lines; they are similar to the Navy Seals. Her father had been killed during such a rescue mission. Her mom had been a young, beautiful, Filipino girl, like so many other military wives, who had had trouble coping with the loss of her husband. She had turned to drugs before PJ, who had been named Tiffany Andrew before she came to GPI, was born. Tiffany was born prematurely: unhealthy, with crack cocaine syndrome, irritable, and highly sensitive to noises. Tiffany's condition only added to her mom's depression and stress level. She was put up for adoption shortly after she was born. Of course it was not easy to find parents for a "crack" baby, so Tiffany had been in and out of foster homes until CD had found her.

When Tiffany was only five years old her foster mother had taken her into a hospital emergency room for a rash. The doctors found that the rash was from her diapers not being changed immediately after she had soiled them. In fact, it seemed the parents were keeping her in the same diaper for days at a time, and that the urine and feces were causing open sores and an infection. The doctors also discovered that she was being sexually molested. No one was ever been arrested because they could not pinpoint exactly who had been doing it, but she was removed from that home. When she was nine years old, she ran away from her foster home and was caught a few of months later after the police stopped a car driven by, it was later determined, a convicted sex offender. Apparently, this guy had picked up Tiffany when she had been wandering alone near her elementary school after she had run away. She had fled because her foster father had been sexually assaulting her, and was picked up by a predator who made her perform oral sex on him from fear he would either kill her or make go back to her foster home. She did not have any good choices. The police knew right away when they stopped this fifty-seven-year old convict that he should not have had a nine-year-old little girl with him. The police interviewed Tiffany and found that out the convict and her foster-father had been sexually abusing her. Subsequently they were both arrested and convicted.

Tiffany did not want to go back to a foster home: in fact, she did not want to leave the police station. She was placed in a boarding school where she lived for two years. She ran away several times and lived with homeless people in parks, and performed sex acts for protection, food, and shelter. Tiffany once again was picked up by the police as a runaway and put in a custodial environment where she could not run away. This is when CD found her and offered her a position at GPI. This promised Tiffany a new life, a new name, and a fresh start, as well as education, food, shelter, and a future. In exchange, all

Tiffany had to do was to choose a sport in which she could immerse herself and be excited about as therapy and to keep her body healthy. In addition, GPI would provide her with a full scholarship to a foreign peace institution when she graduated. It all sounded great, right? Except for the part about losing her life, her identity, and having her body stolen from her.

I felt so badly for this beautiful, young girl who should have had a bright vibrant future ahead of her, full of dreams, anticipation, and wonder. I thought that maybe, in some way, it was a good thing for her. She would not have to live with the memories of such an awful childhood or the fact that she had no parents to help her through life's challenges.

I told PJ, "I will do everything I can to make sure you find a great place to go and that you will be happy."

PJ looked at me with a blank, empty gaze, emotionless, as if she did not believe me and could not trust me, or was waiting for me to take advantage of her in some way and said, "Thank you."

I thought about how all anyone had ever done was exploit her and how I was doing it too. PJ had never done anything to deserve this.

Interviews Begin

I picked up the first interviewer to arrive at Monterey's small airport, only thirty minutes north of Big Sur. He was sponsored by the CIA and had been born in the Democratic Republic of the Congo (DRC). His name was Habimana or Habi. He had been a political officer in the government before an opposition group had forced him to flee. Habi had been living in exile in neighboring Burundi when the CIA met him and began grooming him for return to the DRC, to infiltrate and spy within the existing government. The US wanted an insider to sway decisions in favor of US foreign policy. The DRC is the fourth most populated country in Africa, and its number one industry is mining. It has the richest cobalt reserves in the world, but is also rich in other natural minerals, such as diamonds, copper, and rare tantalum. The DRC is centrally located in the African continent, making it strategic for easy access to other African countries. Additionally, the US government wanted to create an elite military force in the Congo to fight proxy wars and to protect the Congo's mineral mining operations on behalf of the USA. The land in the DRC is also rich for agriculture production, which is good for importing agricultural technology such as farm and irrigation equipment. The US currently has little influence in the region, but wants to establish a major presence and dominance to control the mineral assets.

The problem the CIA faced after years of preparation was that Habi had contracted AIDS from a migrant prostitute and was not expected to live much longer. The CIA introduced him to CD so they could try to find him a suitable body to exchange with. After CD searched their database, Payton from GPI seemed like a perfect candidate. Payton was Congolese, but had been born in a refugee camp in Uganda. Payton's family and relatives had survived the great civil wars of the recent past by escaping to Uganda before he was born. The living conditions in the refugee camp were abominable; there was little food, and what water could be found was never clean and was full of parasites. Most children in the camp never lived to see their fifth birthday. Payton was lucky; he was sold as a slave to a coffee plantation owner. The plantations there used child labor to help with coffee crop, which is difficult to grow and harvest due to the mountainous terrain where it grows best. Payton used to be routinely whipped, like most of the other children, when they did not perform up to work standards. He still has scars on his back and chest from when he was beaten.

Payton was rescued in Uganda by an aid worker from the International Coffee Growers Association (ICGA). At the time, there were American companies that were getting pressured from their consumers not to have their coffee beans tainted with the blood and sweat of child or slave labor, so the ICGA established a presence in the region. At the age of eight, Payton was brought to the United States and put in an orphanage outside of Philadelphia. As you can imagine, he felt isolated. He did not know anyone, did not speak English, and had no idea where he was or how he was supposed to act. All he knew was that he was glad to have food, shelter, and not be beaten every day. But it was not long before the other children at the orphanage began to be mean to him. They made fun of him, stole his things, and beat him up every time he went to the bathroom. Payton avoided going to the bathroom, pooping and peeing in his pants, so as not to get beaten up. The other kids called him "Stinky" because he smelled so bad. After about a year, Payton was transferred to foster parents in Wisconsin, but he did not fit in there either and hated the cold weather. He frequently ran away, and his foster father would beat him after he was caught. Payton finally got away for good when he hooked up with a street gang of drug dealers called the Crips. It was not long before the police started seeing Payton on a regular basis.

After numerous arrests for small-time drug charges, Payton was arrested for aggravated assault. The gang had an initiation ritual, in which every new member had to either seriously injure or kill a random person to prove their worth and dedication to the gang. Payton was sent to a juvenile detention center where CD found him and set him up for rehabilitation. CD was willing to do whatever it took to get him to the age of eighteen, when his body could be harvested.

Payton was actually excited and energetic about coming to GPI. He settled in quickly, which was remarkable, because it was so different than anything he had experienced. He had a beautiful environment to live in, his own room, great food, and teachers who were compassionate. Moreover, Payton got to use his gifted athletic body to run in the nearby mountains and compete in track and field competitions. Payton thrived at GPI and looked forward to returning to Africa to help solve some of the problems there. What he did not know was that he would indeed be returning—but only his body, not his mind.

Habi was an interesting person and spoke of being from African aristocratic heritage. Anyone could see his AIDS was clearly taking a toll on his body. He once said to me, "I can't wait to get back to the DRC to rid the country of the people who took it over. The CIA promised me money and all the resources I need to get me into a politically influential position." I thought he was arrogant and had an attitude of entitlement. It seemed as though he wanted a dictator-type government. It was apparent to me that the US was simply going to replace one bad guy with another. I thought the DRC would be better off getting the real Payton after he finished college, rather than this guy with his vengeance-style beliefs.

Payton and Habi had several meetings over the course of the next several days. When I took them both to the airport for their trip to the east coast and CD headquarters, you would have thought they had both won a big lottery. I know Habi felt that way for a reason, but Payton did not know what his future really held. I felt helpless and like a Judas. I kept wondering what these kids would say or do if they knew the truth.

My job here was to make sure the interviewers had transportation to the Institute and found their accommodations, make introductions to the students, and answer any questions from the students and the interviewers about the process. Two more interviewers arrived by car from San Francisco; Alberte, an oil-rich tycoon from Brazil, and Sing, a Taiwanese politician. They were interested in Pierce and Piper, respectively. Alberte was from San Paulo and heir to the national oil company, Petrobras. He was seventy-seven years old. He was simply going to buy his new body from CD, with the additional contractual conditions that he would sign a lucrative oil contract with the US. It was easy to see that CD and the United States government were not going to give away this technology, or use it solely for the good of humanity. Rather, the way I saw it, it was more about indulgence, protectionism, deceit, and benefit for only the US. I guessed it would be no different if another country had come across the same technology first; they would be monopolizing it in the same way. But then, I probably would not have been involved and would be dead and buried. The same old story seems to ring true throughout history: only the rich and powerful have access to the latest and greatest.

Alberte was a relatively uneducated man, the eldest of seven sons. I would imagine he had never had to work a day in his life. I am sure he had servants, all the food he ever wanted, access to the best schools— a life most Brazilians would only dream about and that some would kill for. I wondered what he was going to do with his life in his new body. Was he going to simply continue with the status quo and proceed with the same history and politics that have been going on in Brazil for centuries? Or would he somehow realize that his new personal lease on life could be interpreted as an opportunity for him to make significant changes for lots of other people, at least in Brazil? In my experience, I have found it to be the case that when something is handed over to someone and they do not work for it or understand its meaning, they do not appreciate it for its true worth or use it to the extent of its true value.

Alberte was of average height; about five feet six and a bit overweight. I do not think that either exercise or moderation were things he knew much about. Of course, he would only smoke the most expensive Cuban cigars. Pierce, on the other hand, was a perfect example of a Latin soccer player, and took great care of his body. He was six feet one inches tall, thin, with little body fat, and when his shirt was off one could see an amazing six-pack set of abdominal muscles. Pierce had long, wavy, chocolate brown-to-black hair, bushy eyebrows, dark brown eyes, dark skin, and a devilishly handsome smile.

There was little information about Pierce other than that he had been found at the age of four at the edge of the road next to a grape vineyard in Sonoma, California. A passerby called the police when they drove by and saw him sitting alone. Pierce was believed to have been left behind by his migrant parents after the grape harvest. They probably felt that he would have a better future in America than if he went back to Mexico or traveled about the US looking for work on a daily basis. Pierce was put in a local group home and given the name Carlos Ruiz, named by the home father. Pierce was lucky to some extent, more so than Payton, in that there were other boys at the home who spoke Spanish. But the home had five boys and five girls, and none of them was closely supervised. He went to a local school outside Sonoma which was more like daycare than an academic environment.

It was not long before Carlos was getting in trouble at school, had joined a gang and was wearing gang colors to show his dedication to his new brotherhood. He was constantly reminded by his group home father that he had been abandoned by his natural parents because he was a bad boy. This always bothered Carlos, as he did not know why his parents left him behind. His group home parents said that sometimes they would see Carlos sitting alongside the road, in the same place the police had said they had found him when he was four. Maybe he thought that somehow his real parents would come back for him and recognize him and want him back. At the age of 12, the leader of Carlos's new family, the gang "Nuestra," told him he had to prove he was a life-long member by killing a member of a rival gang. The Nuestras drove Carlos to Sacramento, California, into the heart of the territory of the black gang, the Bloods. There they saw a teenage boy wearing the red colors of the Bloods; he was standing alone outside a Baskin-Robbins eating an ice cream cone. Carlos very purposefully and deliberately walked right up behind the boy, put a .38 pistol to the back of his head and shot him dead. Carlos knew what it felt like to be left behind by his family, and he did not want it happening again. He desperately wanted a family who wanted him and would take care of him. There were many witnesses to the shooting. Carlos and the other gang members in the car with him were arrested only a short distance away, after they crashed their car into a tree trying to get away.

The news of the shooting by such a young boy made the front page of the local paper, *The Sacramento Bee*. CD personnel were always in search of new talent; they saw the news article and went through their channels to get Carlos. After his conviction and sentencing, Carlos was transferred to a federal youth prison in Virginia, where CD first contacted him about their program. He was harder to convince than most others about the program, because he had never known anyone other than his gang member friends. CD told Carlos that this was an opportunity to help other boys and girls just like him who had had a terrible beginning in life, and this was a chance for him to try to change their futures. CD had Carlos transferred to GPI where they treated him better than he had ever been treated before, and they never mentioned his past again.

Once enrolled and living at GPI, Carlos changed his name to Pierce. Pierce thrived in his new surroundings, since he did not have to worry about where his next meal was coming from, or who he was going to have to kill next. He also began to play his favorite sport, soccer, which before now he could only watch on television. He thrived playing soccer and began to mentor other students at the Institute. After a few years, Pierce grew to be respected and admired around the campus.

I felt again like this was another tragedy in the making. Pierce had had such a terrible life but had been able to turn it around—but of course this had only happened because of the help of CD and GPI. It seemed to me that Pierce should have the opportunity to try to help himself in his own way, through his own choices in life, like the rest of us, and that he should not have his life taken from him. Only Pierce could know what ideas he could create or what could happen with his life. He had seen both sides of the track and knew what life was like with care, patience, love, and attention. Furthermore, he had witnessed what a life free of violence and negativity could do for one's personal humanity. But he was never going to get the chance to live his own life to its conclusion, with the many winding roads in between. It was going to be taken from him. He was going to be robbed of his youth, his opportunities, and his innocence. Maybe this was the price he had to pay for killing the young boy at Baskin-Robbins: a life for a life.

Alberte met with Pierce and told him he would be going to a renowned peace institute in Rio de Janeiro. Pierce was told he would be working in a program with young homeless boys. This program excited Pierce and he enthusiastically got ready to leave. It was sad to watch all the students get together and have a farewell party. Pierce was very popular, especially with the girls. There were many students and faculty crying while everyone said their goodbyes. The teachers at the institute had no idea of the future that lay ahead for these kids.

Sing had a lot of questions for me about what it felt like to be exchanged and to wake up in a new body. I am not sure, but believe I was one of a small number of people who had experienced the cross-gender exchange. Sing was particularly interested in my feelings about being in a woman's body, but still thinking like a man. He kept asking me if it really felt like being a woman and if I had the same sexual desires a woman would have, and not those of a man. I told him it was a strange mix of emotions, that I definitely had had the desires of a woman's body, but that they had been tempered with the memories of being a man. Sing insisted he wanted to be a woman and to feel like a woman in every way. He asked me repeatedly if I had gotten sexually aroused and if I climaxed like any other woman without any problems. I explained that I did not have that much experience, as I was a woman only for a short time, but that I was sure he would have all the sensations and emotions he desired. He seemed a bit perverse in his thinking about the whole process. He was supposed to be exchanged for the purpose of being a spy for the Taiwanese government against the Chinese. He was more focused about the sex change; I think maybe he secretly wanted to be a woman in this life as well.

Sing was a small man, seventy-six years old, about five feet four inches tall and of small stature, almost frail. He had black glasses and always wore a black suit, black dress shoes, white shirt and tie. Sing had probably never physically exercised a day in his life. His exchange with Piper was going to be a huge change for him. I could not imagine him doing cartwheels, back-flips, or vaulting. For a cover, he was going to work at a gymnastics school in mainland China, all the while gathering intelligence for the Taiwanese. I imagined that the US and Taiwanese government had worked out some kind of deal to pay for the CD's exchange process. They were probably going to share intelligence, or some American arms company was going to get some lucrative weapons contract, and the US government would compensate CD. The deal was definitely not without significant strings attached, I'm sure.

During a break I wanted to check in on PJ. Her interviewer was scheduled to arrive in another week and she seemed nervous about the entire process. She was the last one scheduled to leave, and I think seeing her classmates leave was causing her more anxiety. I went to her cabin to try to find her. Each of the students shared a cabin with one other student; each cabin had a kitchenette, bathroom, one bedroom with two twin beds, and a living room area. The cabins were like small log homes and blended perfectly in the magnificent forest setting. I knocked on PJ's cabin door and her roommate, Sariah, a thirteen-year-old Persian girl, answered the door. "Hi Sariah, do you know where PJ is?"

Sariah replied, " PJ's in bed. She has been sleeping a lot lately. I think she's nervous about leaving the GPI and is depressed. I think it would be a good idea if I talked with her."

"I think you're right. Do you mind if I come in and see her?" I asked.

"No, go ahead. I was just leaving," Sariah answered.

I went into the cabin and over to PJ's bedroom door, which was open. I saw her lying asleep on the bed. She was such a beautiful girl, sweet and innocent. She probably had never ever harmed anyone. She was wearing a pair of black mini-shorts and a white tank top, no shoes or socks; she had both of her hands tucked under her cheek, like she was praying, with her head resting on them. I noticed what a flawless body she had and found myself wanting to touch her creamy white skin, which looked like something out of a fashion magazine. I was strangely aroused—the young man part of me coming out—but at the same time the older part of me wanted to protect her. I thought for a second about how long it had been since I had been with a woman. My life had taken so many twists and turns these past few years that I had forgotten what it was like to hold someone, to care about someone, to love someone. I wanted to hold this girl and let her know that someone could care about her. To help her understand that not all people are bad.

I remembered back to a time when I was Frank during the last few days before I went off to college. I was very nervous about what life had in store for me. I recalled thinking about how many people I was going to meet during my life and with whom I was going to fall in love. I also wondered if I was going to be successful or a failure and end up homeless or in a job I hated. What was I going to do for a living? Would I die young, or as an old man? I worried I was going to miss my family and my friends and felt homesick before I left. I felt like I was starting a new life and leaving the old one behind, yet I was excited about what the world had in store for me. It is a difficult time in a teenager's life, full of wonder and excitement, yet surrounded by fear and trepidation. So I understood what she must be feeling. The only place PJ had ever felt safe and protected in her life was GPI.

God, I would have loved to just pick her up and carry her away to a place where we both could live and not have to worry about who was going to take advantage of us next. I would love to watch her grow up, to laugh and play, to fall in love, and most of all to learn to be happy. I think we can only have those special feelings just once—the ones like we felt before our first dance, our first kiss, and our first love. I would never have those feelings again, no matter how many bodies or lifetimes I live. I was too old and too experienced to feel like a young teenager again back when my heart raced so fast I thought it was going to pop out of my chest. I missed that aching in my heart when I wondered if someone special cared about me. I remembered the pure torture and worry, but I recalled how wonderful it felt to dream and fantasize about what the possibilities could be. I recalled wondering about what it would be like to touch for the first time, or kiss, or laugh with someone you cared about and hope they cared the same for you. Those teenage years are so awkward, when we are growing into bodies which are changing so rapidly. It seems our thoughts, opinions, and emotions change just as rapidly and we do not know how to control them. One minute we may feel out of control, and then jubilant and excited the next, and then scared and wanting to hide.

I saw PJ opened her eyes without moving her head. She looked straight at me standing in the doorway. "Hi, Mr. River," she said. "What are you doing here?"

"Please PJ, I am no Mister, just Adam," I said. "I am not much older than you."

"How old are you?"

"I am twenty-three years old."

"Really." PJ jokingly replied. "You seem older."

I chuckled, "Yeah, I have been told that before. How are you doing?"

"I am worried about what life is going to be like when I leave here," PJ answered. "Where am I going to go? What am I going to be doing? I have never been out of the country before and I have read stories of young girls being kidnapped and sold, even tortured and killed."

"No one is going to hurt you. I will watch out for you," I reassured her. After I said that, PJ came over and wrapped her arms around me, hugging me like I had not been hugged in a very long time. I did not want her to let go. I could feel the warmth of her breath on my chest and I could smell the fragrance of her strawberry-scented shampoo in her hair. I ran my hands up and down her arms slowly to comfort her and felt how soft and smooth her skin was. Her hips were pressed to mine and it was as if I could feel all of her. I closed my eyes for a moment, not wanting the feeling to go away. We went into the living room and sat down on a futon couch, after starting a fire in the fireplace. I felt like a teenage boy alone for the first time with his girl.

PJ asked, "What were you like when you were my age?"

"When I was your age I worked as an intern at the headquarters for Crystal Discovery," I replied. "That is the home office for all the Institutions which are under their control. I basically did odd jobs until I got this position. Crystal Discovery has always taken good care of me. They've always had a big focus to take good care of my body, to work out, to eat healthy, and to not take any big risks."

"Yeah it's really weird, they are so freakin' anal about taking care of yourself," PJ quickly responded. "I just want to go on a candy binge sometimes and veg out on a warm beach somewhere with no work-outs—just fun and relaxation!"

We both sighed and said, "That would be nice." We laughed, as if we were reading each other's minds. We sat quietly and watched the fire. I think we both reflected on our lives and took comfort in being with each other, knowing that one did not want to hurt the other. PJ looked at me and said, "Could I lay my head on your lap?"

I smiled at her and said, "Of course, come here." I held her on the couch with my arms around her body and her head on my chest. It was great being in front of the warm fire. I could hear the sound of the waves in the background crashing against the rocks.

Just as we were getting relaxed and my mind was beginning to drift to a faraway place, Sariah unexpectedly opened the front door. We both sat up quickly. She stuttered, "Oh, sorry, I didn't know…Ah, I just wanted to see if you wanted to go to dinner, PJ."

PJ awkwardly answered, "Ah, sure. That's cool."

"I should be getting back to some of my work anyway," I said. "PJ, if you want to talk again, come see me—or better yet I will come back and see if you have any more questions before your interviewer arrives."

I left and headed back to my cabin. I went to bed that night and could not fall asleep. I could not stop thinking about PJ. I felt like I was betraying her. There was an indescribable connection with her, what kind I couldn't be exactly sure, but something. Maybe I just did not want to see her hurt again. But going to CD and exchanging was not really going to hurt her; she would actually be set free from her past. I thought about my own children, especially my daughter, Emma, who was almost the same age. I wondered what they looked like and what they were doing in their lives. I missed them so much and hoped someday I would see them again. I couldn't tell if I was protective or attracted to PJ, as a forty-six-year-old father figure or as a twenty-three-year-old boy. But whatever the feeling, I was happy with it.

The next morning I went to check on Piper to see if she had any concerns about her placement.

She told me, "I do not like Mr. Sing. He's weird. He is always staring at me. He said, 'I want to see how strong your body is.' So he ran his hands all over my arms and down my legs. Then he said, 'You are very strong, but soft,' with a creepy smirk." With a sound of fear in her voice, Piper said, "I do not want to ever travel alone with this guy."

"I will find someone to go with you on your trip back east to Crystal Discovery's headquarters," I told her. "You have to stop there before going to your host country. After that, you will be traveling with a group, so that should help."

Piper continued, "He was asking me all kinds of weird questions about my body and even if I had ever been with a boy sexually. He is such an EMO!"

I said, "Well, we'll get you a chaperone over to the east coast, and everything will be okay. Then you will be going onto Mainland China to work at the gymnastics school in an exchange program to promote peace between China and Taiwan." Piper seemed to get a bit excited and forget about Sing after I told her that. I felt like I was an intelligence officer again; the lies just rolled off my tongue with the utmost of ease. I knew I was lying to her, but I could not tell her the truth. Piper had had a hard enough life. I did not want to make things any harder.

Piper was this great girl who had been dealt a bad card when her life began. Her parents both died while illegally trying to make it into the United States. Piper was just a baby when her parents bought passage from a smuggler on a freight ship traveling from Hong Kong to San Francisco. The smuggler had crammed thirty-five Chinese people into a forty-foot container, with little food and water, and two fifty-five gallon drums for toilets. The journey had taken about three weeks and several of the people had died along the way from severe seasickness, dehydration, and hyperthermia. When the port authorities found the container, Piper was taken to a group home in Oakland. She never was placed into foster care, but rather was moved from group home to group home until CD found her at age seven. She was a perfect candidate for GPI because her family was untraceable. Piper was extremely shy when she arrived and she spoke little. She really loved gymnastics, as it seemed she loved the solitude of being and training alone.

I stood and watched as Piper and Pierce, with Alberte and Sing, drove off, headed to San Francisco International airport, for the trip of their lives. I assigned an assistant teacher to escort the four of them on their trip back to CD. I did not want any of those four getting lost or into trouble before the exchange took place. After that, they would all be someone else's responsibility and I would have fulfilled my duties. I felt an awful feeling in the pit of my stomach, like I was doing something wrong or committing an atrocity.

The next interviewer arrived with her own entourage; her name was Mumtaz. She was of East Indian royalty, and was a descendant of the queen who was entombed in the Taj Mahal. Mumtaz was eighty-six years old and dying of lung cancer. Her husband was one of the richest and most influential men in all of India, which is saying a lot by today's standards. India's wealthy class has increased dramatically in recent years with the internet boom, outsourcing, and their rise in the global community. India and the United States have been partners in many ways over the years and many deals have been made to trade this for that, as the wheels of politics spin their web. I am sure the United States is gaining something significant from India for this small token favor for one of India's elite. I noticed the other day in the *New York Times* that India was trying to gain a seat on the United Nations Security Council and the United States supported them. I would not be surprised if this was a diplomatic gesture, which would provide the United States with another partner on the UNSC for future decisions it may want passed.

Mumtaz refused to stay at GPI during her visit: her liaison told me that the accommodations were not up to her standards. She also refused to talk to me personally, but rather had her staff indicate to me her wishes. I saw her dressed with only the finest garments and jewelry. I was not sure of her level of intelligence or education, but she was definitely full of herself and the pomp. It did not seem like she cared at all about Phoebe. She asked that Phoebe wear different Indian traditional dresses and parade in front of her. I told Phoebe that she was very lucky, that she had been selected to work in the most prestigious peace institution in all of India, and that it was important to her interviewer that she be able to look and dress the part since she would be traveling with Indian royalty. Phoebe, while she did not like to parade in front of Mumtaz, liked the idea of dressing up and working with such high-level Indian royalty.

I was torn when it came to Phoebe. On one hand, I felt that this poor young girl would never have had a chance back in India and would probably have lived a miserable, difficult life. On the other hand, Phoebe was so sweet and beautiful, and had been rescued by us, and it was too bad that she now did not have a chance to determine her own life. Instead, powerful and rich people were exploiting her, taking her life, and using her body. It did not appear much different in some ways from the life she had had as a slave prostitute back in India. But, at least in this circumstance, her mind wouldn't be there and her body would be taken care of much better.

According to reports about Phoebe, she had been born near the city of Bikaner, India, not far from the Pakistan border in an agricultural area. Her given name was Chaaya, which means "shadow" in Hindu. Her parents named her this because she was of no use to them, only a shadow of a boy child they wanted. She was born into a large family, but since she was a girl she could not help her parents with the farm as much as a boy could have. At the age of six Phoebe was sold to a rug manufacturer just outside the capital city of New Delhi. Child slavery is not uncommon in India. Rug manufacturers operate under the premise of training schools, where they supposedly teach individuals, who happen to be all girls, how to make fine Indian tapestry; they are actually sweat factories. The companies pay the families for their children and call it a scholarship. The children then have to work twelve hours a day or more to pay back the scholarship, and to pay for a place to sleep and food to eat. Ultimately, the children are never able to pay back the manufacturer and are indentured servants for the rest of their lives.

Phoebe was not a good worker and was constantly beaten with a stick by her managers. She liked telling stories while she and the other girls were supposed to be working. The girls at the school really liked her and they became her new family. All of them slept in an area above their tapestry machines and were only given food to eat when they were at work. Their lives were comprised of two rooms and they never went out to play like other young girls do all over the world. They only laughed when their manager stepped out of the room and Chaaya made fun of the manager by calling him a goat! One time the manager caught her making fun of him, so he took his stick and hit her so hard it broke her arm. He refused to take her to a doctor or let her stop working. The manager simply covered her badly swollen and bruised arm with an old piece of dirty cloth. Yet Chaaya was expected to work as fast as the other girls or risk getting beaten again. She used to show her injured arm to tourists who commonly went through the school to see how the rugs were made. She would tell the tourists in broken English that her arm got caught in the machine and had been broken. The tourists obviously would feel bad for her and put money in her tip cup next to her tapestry machine. The money in the tip cup was supposed to be for each student making rugs, but the greedy managers would always steal the money, saying it was theirs and not the girls'.

As Chaaya grew older, she was quickly noticed for how beautiful she was— much prettier than all the other girls. One day, one of the managers told Chaaya she was not working hard enough and had to be taught a lesson. He took her in a back room and raped her. She screamed, but no one was there to help her except the other girls who were deathly afraid of the managers. Chaaya was ten years old when that happened the first time, having already worked at the school making rugs and tapestries for four years. The manager who raped her was afraid she would tell one of the other managers and that he would be fired or beaten himself, as they were not to touch the girls. He told the school owner that Chaaya was slow, but that she was very pretty and might be worth more sold off as a prostitute. The owner, who was fat, a sign of wealth in India, went to see Chaaya and indeed thought she would be worth more sold than she would be as a rug maker. He took Chaaya to his office, where he made her parade around naked so he could see what she looked like. The school owner knew she would be worth a lot of money as a virgin, so he did not want to rape her, but instead made her perform oral sex on him.

Chaaya was sold to the owner of a trucking company, in much the same way she was sold to the tapestry school. She was expected to work for the trucking company to pay back her debt—the debt the owner paid the school for her. Her job was to "entertain" the truck drivers— who also worked very long hours, sometimes spending months away from home on the road to try to make a living for their families—by having sex with them at truck stops somewhere out in the middle of nowhere along trucking routes. The truck stops would have rows of girls like Chaaya working out of their living quarters, which consisted of no more than sheets of plywood for walls and roofs. If the girls did not work and get money for sex, then they would not have money for food and would be beaten. So the girls had incentive to make money for food, for clothing, and for luxury items like toothpaste and soap. Chaaya had long, beautiful, black hair which she loved to comb, and would buy oil to make it look shiny to entice the truckers.

Chaaya told investigators who worked for the International Coalition Against Trafficking in Women (CATW) during one of their routine checks that she was not that unhappy. She said she had her own place to live, and that she got to choose her own food, and which truckers she would allow into her hut as clients. She went on to tell them she even could decide for herself if she did not want to work on a particular day if she did not feel well or during menstruation, but on those days she could buy no food. So, she had to plan ahead for a day off by saving bits of food from previous days. The problem with girls brought up like this is that they do not know any better. All she knew was that it was better than working in the slave-like conditions at the tapestry school. Chaaya had been at the truck stop for two years. She was now twelve.

A day after the CATW worker met with her, Chaaya's owner came to her and asked if she would like to go work in another country where she could make more money and pay off her debt. This was actually a ploy to get her excited about leaving before he got caught and arrested. It turned out that because Chaaya was so beautiful and young, he already easily sold her to a company out of Dubai to work in one of their prostitution houses. She was transported by bus to southern India and then shipped out on a boat to Dubai. Once in Dubai her circumstances, however, would not be much different, just a slight change in her scenery.

When her ship arrived in Dubai, local authorities were waiting to apprehend the boat's crew and take Chaaya and other trafficked girls into protective custody. What happened was that an alert CATW worker had realized that Chaaya would be moved immediately after they conducted their inspection, because she was so young. Her owner knew they would report him to the Indian authorities. The same situation had happened in the past, so this time CATW was ready for it and put Chaaya under surveillance once they left. Since these girls were part of an international crime operation, the United Nations had arranged for various countries to take the girls and give them political asylum. In addition, they were all placed in foster care programs and enrolled in schools for their academic education. CD had a representative who knew about the UN program and offered her a position at GPI. Chaaya, or Phoebe, had been at GPI ever since and was now on her way back to India. How ironic.

Now, the only graduates left were Parker and PJ. It seemed to me that the two best were left for last. I received a call from CD headquarters informing me that the interviewer for Parker would not be coming to GPI. Instead, I was to meet him at his home in Wyoming, which was weird because I had not been told of this in advance; it was a new development. Apparently, there had been a last minute change regarding the person with whom Parker had been matched. Thus, I had to go meet the potential client and talk him through the process. I met with Parker and PJ together and told them, "I have to leave for a few days. Parker's interview has been delayed. There has been a last-minute change and I have to meet a guy for company business. Don't worry. Just relax until I get back, if that's possible." Parker took it right in stride, however PJ was outwardly nervous about me leaving. I took PJ aside and dismissed Parker.

I told PJ, "I want to see you before I leave so we can talk about anything that's bothering you. Meet me early tomorrow and we can go for a hike up in the mountains. I will pack a lunch and we'll be able to spend the day out in the forest."

PJ replied, "That's a wonderful idea. Let's get out of here. Staying around here only makes me sad."

We met up the next day and began to hike into the gorgeous Los Padres National Forest. There are many hiking trails there, but I wanted to go where no one else was going. I wanted to get away from people. I told her, "I found a cool trail on the internet called Buzzard's Roost. It's supposed to have spectacular views from the cliffs of the coast. Maybe we can stay long enough to watch the sunset."

She got excited about that. "Sounds amazing."

We hiked for the first hour almost in total silence. I think both of us were contemplating what the future might hold. Then PJ broke the silence. "Do you think I will ever see you again after I leave here?"

I replied, "I am not sure, but I know you can never predict the future. I don't like to use the word never. Maybe we will bump into each other walking down the street in Paris someday."

PJ smiled. "I hope so, the world seems so lonely and cold to me. There are so many people, but it seems everyone is just doing their own thing and does not give the time of day to anyone else."

I agreed with her but said, "Not everyone is like that. Most people walk with their head up and a big smile, and enjoy being part of life. Besides, I am not like that. I care. I care about you."

PJ looked directly at me as we continued to walk up the steep narrow trail. She had a big smile on her face, her light brown hair was pulled back in a ponytail, and a few beads of sweat were on her forehead. It was a beautiful day, the sun was out, the fog was gone, and the temperature was around 75 degrees. We continued our hike and PJ asked me many questions about my childhood, growing up, college, and falling in love. I had to reply to her from what I had learned about Adam. The rest I took from the various lives I have lived. One thing PJ seemed to focus in on was being a parent and if I wanted to have children. She blurted out, "I want to have children someday and I want to be the best mom ever! I want to share everything with my kids, everything I never had. But I want to wait until I find the right guy who loves me and when I can love: two people dedicated to each other." She spoke even louder, as if I did not hear her or perhaps to make a point. "You know what I mean?"

"Yeah, I know what you mean," I replied. "But it is hard to find. How will you know? How will you be sure when you meet him?"

"When he tells me he is willing to give up his life to save mine."

I listened to what PJ had just said; it would not leave my head. I cared so much for this beautiful girl, and yet in a short while she was going to unknowingly give up her life and I was not going to do anything about it. I was simply going to stand by and let it happen because it was my job, because that's the way life is, because that was what had happened to me. What was I supposed to do? Steal her away and hide her from CD? CD is a powerful, far-reaching organization with ties to many people, some of whom are very bad.

"Hey, are you listening to me? Or did you get us lost?"

"No, I did not get us lost," I said, "It is a marked trail. I heard what you said and was thinking about it. To die for someone is a big thing. Would you give up your life so someone else could live?"

"Not right now, I am not in love. I want to live my own life. I know things were not great for me as a kid, but I got to come to this great place and met lots of nice people here. I think my life is only going to get better. When I get to my new job abroad, I think I will learn a lot and grow up. Then I will find out what kind of guy I really want to be with."

After about two and a half hours we reached the top, called Pfieffer Ridge, where we could see for miles and miles up and down the coast and maybe for a couple of hundred miles out to sea. We sat close to each other, our bodies touching at the hip as we ate the lunch I brought. At one point PJ wrapped her arm around mine and laid her head on my shoulder as she chewed on her sandwich. I did not want this moment to end. I did not want to leave the protection of this beautiful place. I did not want to hand this beautiful girl over to her death squad. PJ reached over with her other hand and poked me in the ribs to tickle me. I twisted fast and fell backwards, grabbing her. We laughed and laid back in the soft brown grass, both of us looking up at the sky. PJ in a serious tone asked me, "Will you come and get me if I call you? If I tell you I need help?"

I raised myself up on one elbow next to her and said, "I will come for you wherever you are, no matter what it takes. I will find you."

PJ reached up with her right hand and gently stroked my face. "I trust you."

After those words I felt like I had just been stabbed in the heart. What kind of a person had I become? Who was I? I couldn't do this. How could I stop it? I pulled PJ in front of me and sat up, then wrapped my arms and legs around her. We cuddled and both gazed out over the vastness in front of us. I said, "Maybe we could go live on a tropical island somewhere, where no one will find us. We could eat fruit and catch fish. We could have a bunch of kids and start our own tribe."

She laughed. "Uh, I don't want a tribe. How many kids do you think I should have, twelve or something? Besides, how do I know you would make a good king of the tribe? Have you ever run a tribe before or even caught a fish?"

"Nah, maybe I should read a few books on survival first." I said, "How do I know you will be a good cook and strong enough to find firewood and fight off animals?"

"Ha, I am very strong when I want to be. I have a tough side and I can do anything I put my mind to. I have a soft side and a strong side, a good side and a bad side. So you'd better not get on my bad side." She looked away for a moment and then back at me, "I can do whatever it takes to protect my family. I am a survivor."

I looked away from her gaze. "Yes, unfortunately, we all have to struggle to survive at one point or another in our lives." We spent the last hour before sunset talking about our dreams of the future. I felt like we both simply wanted peace and love in our lives, and to not have other human beings take that away from us.

"What do you think love is?"

I paused for a few moments then replied, looking deep into her warm caramel-colored eyes, "Love is giving, not taking, not expecting anything in return; it is a gift. When someone asks you, 'Do you love me?' they are expecting something from you and it's not healthy. It's a sign of dependency. It's no different than if someone asked, 'Are you going to buy me a gift today?' It is inappropriate." I continued, "It's funny. Kids and animals seem to give love unconditionally from the moment they are born. Why do adult humans act the way they do?"

"Greed, lust, envy, hate."

"Yeah," I said and nodded in agreement. I told PJ, "We should head back and use as much of the sunlight as we can to get down off the mountain. The trails will be dark soon." It only took us about ninety minutes to get back. I walked her to her cabin to say goodnight. We stood at the front door in silence for a minute or so. I broke the quiet. "I will be gone for a few days. But when I get back we can talk some more. I do not expect your interviewer here for another week or so. Don't worry; everything will be all right. Trust me. Hang out with Parker and enjoy the last of your time here in such beautiful place." I wrote down my cell phone number and gave it to her. "Call me if you need anything or if you simply want to talk. I would enjoy hearing your voice." I smiled and hugged her, then slowly and softly kissed her on the cheek. She looked directly back into my eyes and grinned widely without saying word. I walked back to my room.

An Ex-VP

I had a lot of trouble sleeping that night. I kept tossing, turning, and just lying there with my eyes open and my mind racing. I thought to myself, I cannot let this go on any further. This is not right. This is an unlawful government conspiracy and I need to blow the whistle. But how can I and not risk my own life? The CIA is a very secretive, powerful, and far-reaching organization, outside the view of not only the American public, but also the near-sighted Congressional watchdogs who are charged with maintaining overview. CD is simply an arm of the CIA and the military, and I am evidence of that. There must be a way to get PJ and Parker out of here before they have their lives and memories taken away. I must figure it out over the next couple of days. Maybe I could tell Parker's interviewer that Parker's body is no good, that he is impotent and cannot get an erection or something similar to dissuade him, or at least to buy me some time to think this through.

The next morning I drove to the San Francisco airport and took a flight to Casper, Wyoming. I still did not know who the interviewer was or why I was coming here and he was not coming to GPI. I did not even know who I was supposed to meet when I arrived. I was told that some representative was going to contact me when I got off the plane. As soon as I cleared security at the airport, a man in a dark suit approached me and identified himself as US Secret Service. He said he would escort me to the person I was supposed to contact about the exchange. This was all very weird and made me nervous. I knew enough about the Secret Service to go along with the process and did not ask questions. Sooner or later I would learn what this was all about. The agent and I drove out of the city for about an hour, without talking, into the beautiful scenic countryside. Wyoming is one of my favorite places in the world, so peaceful and serene and amazingly picturesque. Finally we pulled into a long driveway, which I could see led us to a large ranch tucked up against a mountain range.

The house we pulled up to was like a southern plantation home, white with columns in front and a circular driveway. I thought to myself, whoever this guy is he obviously has a lot of money and is important to the government. I was led through the front door and there in the living room was a man in a wheelchair with his back to me. He said to the agents in the room, "Boys, you want to leave us alone now." He then quickly spun the wheelchair around and extended his hand: "Dick Cheney, glad to meet you. Please have a seat." It took me a second to catch my breath. I could not believe it was Vice President Cheney. My mind raced and I wondered how much he knew about me or CD. I had to assume he knew everything, of course, with his positions and status within the government. Looking at him I could tell that something was physically wrong with him. I knew he had heart problems a few years ago and had to be hospitalized, but I had not heard anything recently about him.

I sat down and listened to Vice President Cheney as he began by telling me about myself. He said, "Adam, I have read your complete file, from when you were born as Frank Freiberg, to being shot down, to your exchanges, to Yemen and Brazil, and up to now. You have had an amazing career and there is no one else with your diverse background and credentials, and you should be recognized for your courage and bravery. As you can see, I am in a bit of a pickle right now. My doctors tell me my heart is deteriorating on a daily basis. I could die at any moment."

I thought to myself, well, old Ironman Cheney is not looking so intimidating right now. I had never met him before, but I had heard stories that he used to yell at people so loudly their hair would blow back. Now, he appeared as a declawed cat waiting to get its ass kicked. His head hung kind of low, like he was having trouble holding it up.

He went on to say, "I have already been through the initial process and have had the device attached to my brain. They have downloaded my Identity Memory History. Now I am just waiting for a suitable donor to exchange with."

The donor exchangers are not exactly informed they are "donating" themselves. Donation implies a voluntary, worthwhile act of giving, like a charity. I do not think the kids at GPI were giving themselves up to charity. It seemed liked a play on words common to a politician.

He added, "It was my intent to take longer to search for a body, but my heart's failing faster than they anticipated. I can't chance waiting any longer. So, Adam, I understand you have met Parker at the GPI?"

I answered, "Yes, I have. He is a nice, strong, handsome, young man. He is in great shape and has taken good care of himself. Have you read his bio?"

He parried indignantly, "Yes I have. He has no next of kin. So there should be no family problems. I am not sure what I will do after this exchange or what my role in the future will be. It is important that I won't be recognized. I do not want to have a lot of explaining to do."

"I think Parker could be a suitable candidate for you and he is available immediately," I replied. There shouldn't be any questions asked. It should be fairly seamless. However, Parker was expecting to meet his interviewer. I could tell him his position would be initially in Washington, DC and that he will meet his interviewer there before he transitions to his overseas assignment. The students are all told they are going abroad to work at an International Peace Institute somewhere in the world."

Cheney said, "Adam, you will be one of only a handful of people in the world who will know I have been exchanged. This will require a higher level of security than you have already been working with. I wanted to personally meet you and discuss all of this. You will have a great responsibility laid upon your shoulders by knowing this."

I responded as if I was back in the military and he was my commander, "Yes Sir, I understand fully and you can rest assured I will not do anything to compromise this responsibility."

Cheney instructed me, "You must never reveal to anyone this privileged information. It is in the interest of national security."

"I understand, Sir." I responded like I was receiving a direct order from a commanding officer. I understood why people shook in his presence. This guy was like a Rottweiler. I thought if I tried to deceive him about Parker he would have caught it immediately. I am not sure what I could have done at that point to help save Parker.

VP Cheney's demeanor then changed. He softened his expression. "So, what has it been like to go through these exchanges? What does it feel like? Can you explain any problems I might have? Do you have your complete memory? Are you really yourself in another body?" He seemed very interested to hear what I had to say. I was taken aback and did not know exactly how to respond. I thought, what exactly did he want to hear?

I became a bit detached. "Yes, Sir, it is true, you retain everything of your previous self, except you are in a new body. I do not remember being hurt or feeling pain before the exchanges; it is almost like remembering a dream. You may experience something much different due to your current health. Strangely enough, I have never met with anyone else who has exchanged to learn what it was like for them. I only have my own experiences. For instance, I remember that when I woke up from the first exchange, I felt very energetic, revved up, and ready to go. I would imagine that for you, especially with your heart condition, it will be like you stepped back in time to seventy years ago."

Cheney's eyes opened wide and his face lit up. "Wow," he said. "It's simply amazing how far we have come in my lifetime. Are there any problems or side effects I should be aware of?"

I told the former Vice President, "The biggest thing you have to worry about are not the physical issues, since they seem to take care of themselves, but the possibility of meeting someone who knows the person whose body you are now residing in. Yet you will not recognize them or know what they are talking about. That's one thing that worried me a bit in the beginning. There is also the problem that you have to get used to, which is that you are no longer seventy years old: you will be sixteen again. So you will have to act sixteen when it is appropriate. And for you more than me, it's been a while since we were sixteen. If you do not have any grandchildren to coach you, it could be a difficult transition. As far as physical issues, the only thing I can think of are that small preferences might be different for you after the exchange—for example personal preferences, likes and dislikes. It seems that those things that are biologically rooted in the body's DNA do not change, even when a new identity is exchanged into a body."

The VP laughed and said, "Like what? Maybe I will like going to the theater, instead of hunting?"

I laughed as well and replied, "Yes, that is a possibility, depending on what your host or, in your case, what Parker liked."

The VP said with a smile, "Well, maybe I need to look at Parker's bio again and review his likes and dislikes!"

"Maybe, Sir," I acknowledged.

The former Vice President seemed to be satisfied for the moment. He relaxed back in his wheelchair as if to contemplate his future. Then he spoke to me again, looking intently at me. "Son, have you ever heard of the Masons?"

"I beg your pardon, Sir?"

"Have you ever heard of the Masons, the Free Masons?"

"Yes Sir, of course, but I have never known a Free Mason."

"Well, you have now. I am a Mason and have been one for many many years. It's a great organization of men, with a good cause and a proud history. You should think about joining. Most of the great leaders throughout American history have been Masons, and many of our Presidents, such as George Washington, Andrew Jackson, Teddy Roosevelt, FDR, Gerald Ford, George Bush senior and George Bush junior. There have been approximately sixteen US Presidents and about 90% of all the US Supreme Court Justices who were Masons. It is a worthwhile endeavor and we are sworn to the enrichment of all humanity."

"I did not know that, Sir. I will look into it," I said, slightly stunned. I wondered why in the hell was he telling me this. What the fuck have the Free Masons got to do with this job, this exchange, or me? This guy is a pompous ass. I can imagine him walking around with his Mason hat on, barking orders. This was all a bit surreal.

Mr. Cheney went on: "The Masons are an important part of hu man history. They are everywhere, in virtually every major society in the world. Like the 'All Seeing Eye' on the dollar bill, they have eyes and ears everywhere and their loyalty is unwavering. There has never been a Mason who has wanted to quit the organization." Cheney began strolling his wheelchair toward the front door to show me out. The last thing he said as I was leaving was, "I will have a Mason contact you when you return to Washington and give you more information about joining."

"Thank you very much, Sir," I replied. And with a handshake I left the former 46th Vice President of the United States sitting in a wheel-chair, half alive, in the living room of his house. I sat quietly during the car ride back to the hotel in Casper. I was scheduled to take the flight out the next morning to go back to the GPI. My mind was racing and trying to process all that had transpired. I thought about poor Parker. He was a nice kid, smart and strong, and he was on death row, time marching ever closer to his demise. It also occurred to me that in a small way, I had the life of the former Vice President of the United States in my hands. I wondered if I could stop the exchange if I wanted to. Could I tell CD I did not think Parker would be a good fit for Cheney? How would they receive that? What would I have to say to convince them he was a bad fit?

The bigger question I had, beyond him wanting to save his own life, was what Cheney planned to do with his new life. Did he someday plan to return to politics? I concluded, after his long career in government and obvious lust for power, that he most certainly would try. The American public would be blindsided; they would elect some guy named Parker. However, underneath would be the cunning, treacherous world of Dick Cheney. What did this man and CD have in store for the future? I surely did not feel comfortable having this knowledge. It was too much for one person. The information was too valuable. I was surprised CD allowed me to be privy to such a secret. And what was the deal about the Masons? What did that have to do with anything? I knew little about Dick Cheney except for what I knew of his career and what I had read in the newspapers, but I could tell that this man did not say or do anything without purpose. He wanted me to know the about the Masons. There was more to that than just joining a fraternity. And somewhere somebody was going to get a kickback or favor for giving Dick Cheney another life—you could bet on that.

The next morning I got on the flight back to San Francisco and then drove down to Big Sur. I had several hours to think about what had just taken place. What was happening at CD and GPI? What was going to happen to Parker and PJ? I felt like I was tied between two horses and being pulled apart—death was certain. I did not know what to do next. I wanted to help Parker, but I didn't know how to stop the exchange with Cheney. I would have to figure something out later. At this point I could not stop this train that Parker and Cheney were on. But, I swore to myself, someday, somehow the American people were going to find out about CD, the exchange, and Cheney. I still had a chance to try to save PJ. Her interviewer was not set to arrive for a few more days. I had to get her out of there. She needed to know what she was dealing with, or at least parts of it, to realize that her life was in danger. I felt sick to my stomach to have to expose her to more hardship. Some people believe there is heaven and hell, and some think that life here on earth is actually a test of person's spirit. Well, PJ had sure had more than her share of difficult tests.

When I arrived back at GPI, I went to Parker's cabin to talk with him. He was sitting alone in his cabin, reading a book.

'What are you reading?"

"The Templar Salvation by Raymond Khoury."

"Really? Interesting. Why that book?"

"I have always been fascinated by the Knights Templar," he said. We studied them in my world history class. The present-day Free Masons are supposed to be secret descendants of the Templars. Do you know who the Masons are?"

I must have had an astonished look. I replied, "You are the second person in two days to ask me that question." I thought it was a bizarre coincidence. "Parker, I met with your interviewer and he apologized for not being able to make it down here. He gave me the news that you have been accepted into a program which originates in Washington, DC. He instructed me to tell you that he will meet you there in a few days. He also told me that he would have his staff meet you when you get off the plane at Dulles International airport. Congratulations, Parker, good job. All your hard work here at GPI has paid off. So tomorrow you can pack, and the following day I will take you to the airport." After that, I gave him a hug.

Next I told Parker that we would be meeting a news reporter near the airport who wanted to interview him. She was doing a report on the American educational system.

Parker had a bewildered look on his face, and said, "That's weird, isn't it? Did any of the other kids get interviewed?"

"No, but I was asked by this reporter some time ago and I thought that since you were the class president you would be the most appropriate for the interview."

He thought about my answer for a bit. "What kind of questions is she going to ask me? What is it going to be about?"

"I don't know exactly, but probably about your life, as well as your experiences with the Institute. Don't worry about it. Just be yourself. It is for a research project as well. I'm sure you will never hear a thing about it when it is aired or published, if it ever is."

What I did not tell Parker was that I was lying. This reporter never contacted me. I contacted her. I called Channel 3 News and I told them the public's version of the program at GPI and asked them if they would like to do a piece on it. They replied that they would and that they would send a news team to do an interview. I had to be secretive about it because CD strictly forbade any interviews or exposure to the media of any kind. I knew that if I was ever going to expose this program I had to get some documentation somewhere as to what they were doing and who was involved. It was time to let the public know what their government was doing. People like Dick Cheney and others like him needed to discover that they were not above the law and could not take human life for their own self interest. The next day was going to be one of the most difficult days of my lives, and it would also put me at greatest risk—and I would never be able to turn back. Before I went to bed that night I stopped by PJ's cabin.

Penny Jo's Discovery

Iknocked on the cabin's door and PJ answered. She gave me a big hug and said, "I am glad you're back. I did not like you being gone. It made me nervous."

I looked her directly in the eyes and told her: "Meet me at Sand Dollar Beach at ten tomorrow morning. Don't tell anyone you are going to meet me. I have something important to talk with you about."

Her faced changed from happy to sad and nervous. She asked, "What's wrong? What's so important?"

I answered, "Don't worry. You trust me, don't you?" She nodded yes. "I will tell you everything tomorrow. Just try to get some rest tonight." I gave her a big, long hug and kissed her on the cheek, then went back to my cabin. I had to plan how I was going to get PJ out of here without her being exchanged and having her mind stolen. I wanted to be with her to take her to a place where they could not find her and no one could harm her. But I knew I could not go with her. CD could track my every move if they wanted to with the GPS attached to my brain. Somehow, PJ had to do it on her own, with little to no experience of the outside world. I could not let CD or the CIA know I intended to expose this entire program. I had to tell my boss that I needed time off to rest and recuperate after this assignment.

Sand Dollar Beach is the biggest sandy beach near Big Sur. I had a favorite secluded area at the northwest end, surrounded by very high cliffs and rock formations. I had discovered it on a previous visit to GPI. It was a secluded spot hidden from the wind and from curious prying eyes. It was great for sunsets. I brought my breakfast, coffee and a scone, and came out early to meet PJ. I wanted a bit of time alone to try to figure out how I was going to explain everything to her. I had been there for about an hour when I saw PJ walking down the beach, looking around trying to find me. I waved my arms so she could spot me. She ran toward me and as she got closer I could see a big smile on her face. When she got to me she jumped into my arms, like a smaller child would do when they leap off the ground into their father's arms. She put her arms around my neck and I held her off the ground, with my arms wrapped around her legs.

PJ said, "NOW! What is so important you want to tell me?" She had a silly playful grin on her face.

I took her over to my favorite spot, where no one could see us, and we sat down on the rocks. I said, "PJ, I have a lot to tell you. I am not sure how you will feel about me or what you will do after I tell you. But know that I have come to love you and that I care a great deal about you. I want to protect you. I see this wonderful sparkle in your eyes that reminds me of the twinkle of a distant star on a clear night. A twinkle that makes me wonder about our purpose in the universe. Maybe also a twinkle of hope, of hope that you can change this world and all the bad things that are in it."

PJ replied, "But how can I change the world? I am just one small person who does not even know where she is going."

"PJ, knowledge is power," I said. "I am going to share with you some knowledge that only few in the world possess. I am not who you think I am, and GPI is not what you think it is. Everything you have come to expect from GPI is a lie. Your life is in danger. No one at GPI, that I am aware of, here in Big Sur, knows of its true purpose except me. I work for a group of people who steal the bodies of young boys and girls and erase their minds. Then they replace their identities with those of another person. In other words, someone else's mind takes over each young person's body."

"That's not true. They can't do that. They do not know how to do that—that can't happen."

"Yes", I said. "PJ, they can do that and they have done that. Everyone at GPI is going to have a new identity exchanged into his or her body; it is the purpose of GPI. It is one of the reasons why GPI is so fanatical about the students taking such good care of their bodies. They have to make sure that someone wants your body when you are old enough to be exchanged so you have to be desirable and marketable."

"What happens to the person's mind who was in that body when that happens?"

I looked away. "It is erased completely, like they never existed, no trace is left. Essentially they die." We did not talk for a while, just stared out over the ocean.

PJ broke the sound of the waves crashing against the rocks. "What about me? What is going to happen to me?"

"Your interviewer is not really an interviewer, but rather someone who is interested in taking over your body. I am sorry, but it has already happened to the others except for you and Parker. I met with the person who wants Parker's body. It is ex-Vice President Richard Cheney. He is dying and needs a body right away; there is no way I can stop it. If I try to stop it now or go public, your life will be in jeopardy and they will probably go ahead with the woman who is coming and wants your body."

"Well, she can't have it," PJ shouted. "I don't want to die. I want to keep my body. I know my life has not been the best, but it is mine to do with whatever I want. I will just run away, somewhere they cannot find me." She was yelling angrily.

"You cannot just run away, since they will find you and force you to exchange. This is a very big, very powerful organization, involving the highest levels of many governments around the world. You have no idea what these people are capable of. They have unlimited resources of money, people, and technology. I have a plan to hide you until I can figure out a way to expose to the world everything that has been going on. I want to show the dark, hidden, illegal, and immoral things the government has been doing. PJ, to those in control of our government and of some big companies, it is all about money and power, greed and lust. It seems that those who are in the high levels of our government believe the people are there to serve their needs, rather than that they are there to serve the people's needs. This program has to be exposed, so that no one else has to lose their life or give up their body to someone who has enough money and is simply willing to pay a lot for it or give special favors in exchange for the process of becoming young again. This whole thing has simply gotten out of hand."

PJ then asked me the big question: "How do you know about all this?"

I looked deeply into PJ's eyes and held both of her arms. "I am sorry. I have known about this all along. It is happening all over the US. I know because I have taken over and exchanged with three other people. Three people who, like me, were lied to about the ultimate purpose of the whole thing."

She looked down, her expression was of total disbelief and shock. "I knew it. I knew it was too good to be true. Life sucks and it will never stop sucking. I hate it. Why me? Why is this happening to me? I never hurt anyone." She started to cry uncontrollably.

I held her tightly, pulling her head into my chest, stroking her hair, "I am sorry, but I will not let this happen to you. I am going to get you out of here."

"How? How are you going to do that?" she asked. "You told me they will find me and kill me. How are you going to protect me?"

I said, "We are going to fake your death. No one talks about it, but there have been several kids who have come here to GPI who have not been able to cope, and have committed suicide."

"How did they do it? How are we going to do that? What about my body? Aren't they going to find out?" PJ asked bewilderedly.

I told her, "Several of the kids who died killed themselves by jumping off the cliffs behind GPI into the surf and rocks and their bodies were never found; they washed out to sea or were eaten by sharks. We are going to make it look like you jumped off the cliff. No one will find your body. No one will keep looking or searching for you."

PJ looked at me and asked, "How are we going to do that? Won't they know?"

"We will write a suicide note," I said. "The other students and staff already know that you have been depressed about leaving and moving on, so they will not think it is that bizarre. But we have to move quickly. There is not much time, so we have to make plans. I have to take Parker to the airport tomorrow and I will stay near San Francisco tomorrow night. I do not want to be here when it supposedly happens, so no one will in any way suspect me or link us together. So it has to be tomorrow night. But we have a lot to do. We have to find a way for you to get out of here without being seen."

"But, where am I going to hide? How am I going to live?"

"Let me take care of that, one step at a time."

PJ stopped me, "Wait, you have taken over other kids' bodies? Is that what you said? So you are not really Adam? Who are you? How did you get this body? This is crazy weird, it is freaking me out. How long have you had this body? How long did you have the other's bodies? Who are you really?"

"I know you have a lot of questions, but you have to trust me at this point. We don't have a lot of time for me to explain. I can tell you that I am much older than I appear. I was a pilot, I worked for the CIA, and I have traveled the world, so I know a few things about hiding and keeping secrets. We will get through this, I promise. Trust me, PJ, please, you have to trust me. I do not want anything to happen to you. You will be the link that breaks the chain and keeps this from happening to other kids like you. This is wrong; it is murder. What I believed to be a good program in the beginning, and what was to be something to benefit all of humanity, has turned into a political and personal lust for vanity."

"I am not very strong and I do not know very much about the

world. I feel so lost and vulnerable. I don't know who to trust."

I again took PJ by the arms and, squeezing them tightly, looked directly into her eyes, "Penny Jo, you can trust me. I love you. I will die for you. I cannot live like this anymore. I will do anything to save you, protect you—please believe me. I want you to feel it right down to your bones and deep in your heart and soul, because it is true. I am here for you."

PJ looked back at me and softly said, "No one has ever told me they would die for me before. I trust you and will help you."

"Good," I said, "Be strong. We have a long, hard road ahead of us, but we can do this, one small step at a time. Do not worry about the distant future— think only of putting one foot in front of the other, small goals. Always remember to never, ever give up, and remember that even when things seem darkest, there can be a way out, there is always an answer. Right now, we have to plan your death. We have to kill you without being detected."

"Oh great, something I always wanted to do: plan my own death."

"The suicide note must written so they think you really did it and also so it points the way a bit."

"What should I write? What should it say?"

"Write the letter and put it on your bed. Make your bed very neatly. Then Sariah or a staff member will find it. The note should say:

I am sorry for causing so much trouble to everyone. I want to see my dad again, he will protect me. I do not want to live anymore. I do not want to leave here and I want to become part of the ocean for all eternity. Please forgive me.

And don't forget to sign it, PJ." I continued, "Just before you leave, make sure Sariah is asleep and put it on your bed. Tomorrow is high tide, so investigators should expect you to be washed out to sea, not left on the rocks, with few or no signs you were ever there. However, take a sock that you like to wear, one of your favorite gloves, and one of your shoes, and drop them in the rocks at the bottom of the cliffs below the compound as the only remnants of you left behind. Make sure you bring the other matching shoe and glove with you. We will throw them away where they cannot be found. Your personal items must look like they were washed up there after your fall. Your glove should look like it was torn from the rocks with some blood stains on it. You will have to go down there with your glove and pull it across some sharp rocks to make it look like it was torn in the fall. Also, run a knife through the middle part of your hand and put the blood on the glove, especially near the tears. Can you do all this, PJ?"

She looked at me a bit stunned and answered slowly, "I will do it."

"Next," I said, "you must not be seen leaving the area. I want you to hide in the forest until I can pick you up and we can leave here. So, to-day, put some food in a backpack and take it to the entrance of the trail we hiked the other day and hide it there. It is a full moon now, so you should not need to use a flashlight, but you might want to take one. Don't take yours. Steal one from one of the other students or take Sariah's. I don't want them thinking you took a flashlight with you to jump off a cliff: it does not make sense. Maybe in the early evening you could hang out a bit near the cliff's edge at the back of the compound, so someone will see you and can later correlate the two, and conclude that you must have jumped from near there. After you have picked up your personal items, hide up in the forest off the beaten path where you can see the parking lot for Sand Dollar Beach. When I return from taking Parker to the airport I will check in with GPI and let them tell me of your death. Then I will pack up and come to get you right after sunset. I will park in the parking lot, as if to think and to finally leave to go back to the east coast. I will tell CD that I want to drive back, not fly. It will buy us more time. Wait until after dark, then come and meet me down in the parking lot—hopefully no one else will be there—and then we can leave. Do you have any questions?"

"Yeah, I have lots of questions."

"PJ," I said forcefully. "Our lives and many other lives depend on us to carry this through. Be strong."

"Where are we going to go? How will we survive?"

"Remember, one step at a time. We will survive; I have a plan. I will tell you more when we are driving away from this place. Now I have to get back so I can get ready to leave and take Parker to the airport tomorrow. It might be good for you to say goodbye to Parker and be seen by others to be very distraught and sad over his leaving, which may not entirely be an act."

While getting ready to leave, PJ said, "Why are you doing this for me? Why me, why not one of the others?"

"Somehow I felt since I first met you that you were going to become an important part of my life. I felt close to you, even though I did not know you. I wanted to get to know you more; I wanted to see you happy someday. I still want that—to see you happy someday. Maybe someday, when this is all over, we can go live in Tahiti by the beach, secluded from the rest of the world, just you and me."

"That sounds wonderful," PJ replied with a half-hearted smile. She continued on, "Hug me, Adam, and never let me go. Promise you will come back for me, that you will never leave me alone."

With that said, I hugged her tightly and replied, "I will always come back for you and I will never leave you—or I will die trying, I promise."

PJ looked at me intently and said, "Kiss me. Seal your promise with a kiss." I kissed her long and softly on the cheek. She quickly pulled away. "No, not on the cheek, on the lips. Kiss me on the lips. I want to know what you feel for me, that I can trust you. You're not that much older than me, you know." I was torn. I knew I felt deeply for PJ. My body was drawn to her and got excited by a simple touch of her hand, my heart and soul ached for her, my mind was tortured over all she had been through and must go through now. I held PJ's face with both my hands on her cheeks and slowly placed my lips on hers. Her lips were soft and full; our lips melted together. I do not think I will ever forget that kiss. I could feel the heat from her face in my hands. PJ opened her mouth slightly as we kissed and our tongues gently met. I felt incredibly passionate and my heart was racing. I did not want to let go of her, so I stay connected and pretended for a moment that all of this was not happening. I imagined in that moment that we were just two young lovers on a beautiful beach, enchanted with each other, sharing a tenderness which would last forever. Our kiss seemed to last for minutes, then I slowly pulled away. Our eyes opened and remained locked on each other until I broke the silence.

"You had better go. I will see you soon," I said. PJ walked away. She was quickly out of sight, headed back to GPI.

I stayed behind for about an hour or so; just thinking of what lay ahead. For the first time in a long while I felt I had purpose. I felt like I had a reason for living that passion had returned to my soul. PJ needed me and I needed her. I also felt extremely sad for Parker and the others whom I had led to the gallows, without them even knowing.

Parker Departs

I watched from my cabin window as the students had a small going-away party for Parker outside. I saw PJ give Parker a big hug and begin to cry uncontrollably as the other students tried to console her. Later, I watched PJ walk away into the darkness and toward the cliffs, which would supposedly claim her life the next day. My mind froze for a moment, afraid, thinking maybe PJ would not be strong enough to handle all I had told her. Would she simply want to end it all today and commit suicide for real? Fear gripped me. I was worried and almost sickened about her and I could not sleep. Near midnight, I walked out to tell Parker he should go to bed soon, as we had a long day tomorrow. I asked him, "Where did PJ go?"

He answered, "She told us she was going over by the cliffs to think. She said she liked to hear the waves pounding against the rocks, that it was peaceful. I am really going to miss her and this place."

I said, "I know you will, but you will always have the memories. Now let's get some rest."

The next morning Parker and I met at the car and got ready to leave. He was a bit sad and said, "PJ told me she was going to come by and say goodbye before we left, but it looks like she changed her mind. I guess I understand that it's too hard. She was really upset last night."

"Did you see PJ after she went over by the cliffs?" I asked.

"No, I did not. I went right to bed after we talked. She is probably still sleeping; she likes to sleep late. Maybe it is best we do not see each other, since it will just get us all upset again."

"Yeah, I think you are right. Let's get on the road. It is about two hours to SFO," Once we got on the road we were both quiet until we passed some of Big Sur's incredibly majestic scenic coastline, winding road, ragged beaches, with the constant pounding waves splashing against the jagged rocks.

Parker spoke first. "I am really going to miss this place. It is the first place in my life where I did not have to worry much."

"Much," I said. "What was there to worry about?"

Parker looked out his window for a moment, "I always worry about something. Like, I wonder if I will be accepted by others, if they will like me. Or I worry about where I will be going after I leave here. I wonder if God is watching over me. Those kinds of things."

"I guess I am a bit surprised," I said. "You seem so confident, so precise in what you do. I think that is why everyone wanted you as class president."

"Yeah, I know, but it is a bit of a front, a shield I have to protect myself from getting hurt by showing others I am as good as they are," Parker responded.

I was taken aback. I thought Parker was this confident, strong, self-assured young man. But it appeared he was frightened and had low self-esteem. I asked him, "I did not know you were religious. Do you believe God watches all you do?"

"Well, I hope he does not watch ALL I do. I am ashamed of some of my life," Parker explained timidly.

"Why would you be ashamed? You having nothing to be ashamed of. You were a child when those things happened to you—they were not your fault. You are an amazing, talented, intelligent, and caring young man. You should not be worrying about anything, except maybe which girl you like the best, because you have so many admirers." I eagerly retorted.

"That's one of the problems," Parker explained, "I do not want a girlfriend, I don't like girls that way!"

I stopped myself for a moment, to be sure I had heard accurately what Parker had said. I softly responded, "Well, that is okay. You can like whoever you like, however you like. It is a free world and you live in America."

"Yes, but I am not going to be living in America. I am going to be overseas somewhere, somewhere where they might not accept that I am gay." Parker spoke very softly as he looked over at me, looking me directly in the eyes. "Just look at things here now," he went on. "The military has their weird policy and there is a big controversy over gay marriage. America is not as free as everyone likes to think. It is free as long as you are not gay. Then they want to either beat you up or take your rights away from you and treat you like you're not human. I don't understand why people care so much about what other people do with their lives. I have never hurt anyone or asked anyone else to be gay. Why do they want to judge me and treat me differently? I don't get angry at hillbillies, or rednecks, or heteros who just want to have sex missionary style. I don't get it, I just want to hide. I do not want people to know who I truly am, because they will just try to hurt me. I am really worried about what is going to happen to me when I get to where I am going."

I took my time to respond, trying to hold back tears that were making their way into my eyes. "Parker," I said, "I assure you, no one will ever hurt you again. I promise you that. You are a different person now. You are strong enough to fight back and to never let anyone take advantage of you. When you get where you are going, you will find peace." I had to look out my side window; the tears were starting to run down my cheek. I tried to wipe them away with my shoulder without Parker seeing me. I questioned myself whether or not it was such a good idea for me to take Parker to the airport, leading him toward his demise.

We arrived at the Hyatt Regency Hotel near San Francisco airport. We were to meet a reporter, Susan Welday, who would conduct an interview with Parker and it was all to be filmed. We went to Susan's suite and when she opened the door we saw the cameraman had already set up his equipment. Susan greeted us: "Hi, I am Susan Welday with Channel 3 News." She shook both of our hands and asked Parker to sit in a chair in front of the camera.

I asked her, "Do you mind if we get started right away? Parker has a flight to catch in a few hours."

"No, not at all," she responded, "Parker, are you okay with that? Are you ready?"

"Sure, let's do it."

"Parker, could you explain a bit about the Global Peace Institute, and how you were picked to attend the Institute?"

Parker began explaining very confidently as though he had done it many times before. "The Global Peace Institute, or GPI as we fondly call it, was like a heaven on earth to me. It is a program where abused or neglected children can live, attend school, do sports, and thrive in a warm, friendly, supportive environment which is designed to promote peace in the world. When the kids finish the program, they are sent away to some part of the world to further the cause of peace and help under-privileged children."

"How old are the students when they graduate?"

"The students are eighteen years old when they graduate. It's a great academic program at GPI."

"I understand there is a big emphasis on sports and health at GPI. What is that about?"

"Yes, that is true, GPI does require every student to participate in a sport, which they must learn well and excel at," Parker responded. "GPI believes that a healthy body is a healthy mind. And that focusing on a single sport intensely helps the student understand how to achieve a high level of ability and discipline. They also emphasize that it helps us, in particular, to focus on something and not dwell on the past. I trained in karate during almost all of my spare time. Most of the students at GPI had an extremely difficult childhood and many are trying to cope with what has happened to them. Through sports they can learn how to concentrate and remain focused. This contributes to making a better future for themselves."

"What about you, Parker? What was your childhood like?"

"Me?" Parker said while he looked over at me. "I am happy now, but I have not always felt that way. My mother was fifteen years old when she had me and since she grew up in a Catholic household they were embarrassed to keep me. I was put up for adoption. No one adopted me, so I was put in a Catholic orphanage, which was part of a church. I was raised by nuns and priests. They were very strict, but it was a nice place to live and they had good food. We had to go to church and wear uniforms every day, which all of us hated. Everyone there got a nickname from the other kids. They called me 'Pretty Boy Floyd,' because my name used to be Floyd Byrne."

"Your name *used* to be?"

"Yes, used to be. When students arrive at GPI they are all given new names, which for each new student is based on the year when they will graduate. The students' names of each graduating class all begin with the same letter. This year was the P class. Thus all the student's first names begin with the letter P. GPI believes this is another way for students to separate themselves from their pasts and move on. We all got to choose our new names. In some cases, like mine, I hated the name my parents had given me. Who wants to be named Floyd?"

"Your childhood seems like it was pretty nice," Susan went on to say."Why did you get chosen to attend GPI?"

Parker looked down into his lap. "Well, things have not always been rosy. When I was five I began to be an altar boy at the orphanage's church. There was one priest who would always say, 'You are the prettiest boy in the world.' He would often take me places with him, like to run errands. In the beginning it would make me feel special. It all started one day when we were running errands. I was six years old at the time. We stopped by a park to play at a jungle gym. The priest said to me, 'If you are a good boy and learn about becoming older, I will let you go play on the jungle gym for as long as you want.' He then unzipped his pants and pulled out his penis. He showed me how he wanted me to stroke it. Then he put my hand on his penis and had me stroke it by myself until he ejaculated. Then he let me go play. He said that I was such a good boy for learning how to become a man and I did not know any different. Afterwards, he told me, 'Fathers usually teach their sons how to be a man. But since you do not have one I will have to do it.' For a year or more he would take me to a park and I would jack him off. Then he would let me go play. About a year after that he started wanting me to put my lips around his penis and suck it until he ejaculated. He would always tell me after going somewhere together, 'Never tell anyone about what we do. It's our secret, like a secret between a father and a son.' I did not know any better. I thought all the boys were doing it like it was normal."

"I'm sorry Parker. Do you want to take a break?"

"No, that's okay." Parker replied. He paused for a few moments, in a quiet contemplation, then continued. "When I was ten years old, I got caught by one of the nuns playing naked in my bed with one of the other boys," Parker continued. "I was sucking his penis, just like I did the priest's. The nun spanked me hard and sent me to the same priest's office who took me out on errands. The priest was very angry, 'You have been very bad and have broken the trust between a father and a son! You have to be punished.' He sent me away and told me, 'Come back after dinner and clean my office.' I went back that night. The priest was very mad. 'You have to clean my office naked since you like to play naked with the other boys. Now clean off my desk.' He laid me across the desk on my stomach and tied my arms and legs down with neckties to the legs of the desk. He spanked me very hard until I was crying and was begging him to stop. He yelled at me, 'Promise never to play naked with any of the other boys again!' I promised. The priest then walked in front of me and made me suck him until he got an erection. Then he said, 'Now you are going to learn what it is really like to be a man.' He first put his finger in with some Vaseline on it, then he pushed until his penis went in my butt. It hurt so bad I cried, and he yelled, 'Stop crying.' I remembered that when I went back to my bed. I had blood and semen leaking out of my butt onto my underwear. I did not want anyone to see, so I threw them away in the trash. The priest stopped tying me up, but he still made me come to his office and lay across his desk to have sex."

"We can change to a different topic Parker if you like?"

"That's okay, I'll keep going, unless you want me to stop?"

"I want you to talk about whatever you are comfortable with."

"One day the priest forgot to lock the door to his office when he was in there having sex with me. A janitor accidently opened the door to do his nightly cleaning and saw us. He saw the priest with his penis in me and while I was straddled across the desk. The janitor was this big, old guy. He flipped out and started chasing the priest around with his mop trying to hit him. The janitor told the head nun, who took me away and cleaned me up. The nun asked me if that was why I was always running out of underwear. I nodded. The next day the nun took me the to county child care services and told them that the orphanage could not take care of me anymore, because I was incorrigible. I was then placed in a foster home with complete strangers. I was only there for a couple of months before I ran away. The police caught me hanging out with a bunch of homeless guys. The police put me in juvie, which is when GPI asked me if I would like to be in their program. What choice did I have? But, it turned out to be a good thing. They gave me a great education, and helped me to develop my mind and body. Now I am here, ready to go abroad in the name of peace to help other kids who are in bad situations."

"I am sorry, Parker, for what happened to you. What happened to the priest?"

"I don't know and I don't care. It is over. It was a long time ago, and I don't want to know."

It was so difficult for me to sit and listen to Parker tell his story.

I wanted to help this wonderful young man. I felt so sorry for him. What a terrible childhood. I wondered what he felt in the deep recesses of his mind about life and whether it was worth it. Maybe he just felt anger and wanted to point at men who try to hurt other young boys. I don't know. His exchange could relieve his pain and torment. I did not know how to stop it.

"How did GPI find you?"

"I am not really sure. I guess they have people looking on the police lists for runway kids or something. I heard that most of the kids who go to GPI are runways."

"Oh, is that right?"

I stopped Susan before her next question. "Susan we are running a little short on time. Are there any other quick questions, or maybe you would like to ask him more about what life was like at GPI?"

"Thanks, Adam, I will try to finish up. Parker, did you enjoy being at GPI, and would you recommend it to other kids?"

"Yes, I would definitely recommend it to other kids," Parker replied. "It is a great institution. We had great food, and great activities, all in a fantastic place with beaches, the ocean, mountains, and forests. It was really heaven on earth. The teachers really cared about the students as well. Mr. Pfafman used to help me so much with my studies, and he talked to me about life. Miss Anderson was a great English teacher and always had us read books that were meaningful to us. All of them told us that if we ever needed anything, day or night, they would be there for us and gave us their home phone numbers. I called my karate coach, Mr. Whitesell, one night about one in the morning. I couldn't sleep because I was thinking about a kata I was having trouble with. He laughed when I called and said he used to have the same problem, that he '...couldn't sleep until he got it right.' I know they are all proud of us for going out and challenging the world. You make great friends there—but, we are not allowed to contact anyone once we leave the Institute."

"What do you mean, you are not allowed to contact anyone once you leave?"

"That's right. The Institute felt it would be in our best interests to ultimately put our pasts behind us by not contacting anyone and by moving forward into our futures."

"Wow. That seems a little harsh, doesn't it?"

"Well, they have taught us a lot, given us a lot, and they seem to understand our needs," Parker replied. "So, we trust them. I trust GPI to do what is best for us, and if that is what they want us to do to help ourselves, I will do it. I would never do anything to jeopardize the Institute's program. It is worthwhile and it helps a lot of kids."

"Just a couple more questions—easier ones and more fun. You said you liked the food there. What was the food like and how were the living accommodations? And were the students a close-knit group?"

Parker smiled. "I loved the food there. My favorites were the German chocolate cake they would serve every Friday and the goulash they would have every Wednesday night for dinner. We lived in these great little cabins, two people to a cabin. The students were very close. We travelled around together as a pack. All the kids in a graduating class would stick pretty close to each other."

"I understand. Any love affairs with other students going on?"

"Not with me. I am gay. I guess all of us knew when we left there we could never look back. Consequently we stayed away from romantic relationships and from getting our feelings hurt by going down that path."

"You are gay? Did that cause any problems while you were at the GPI?"

"No, it did not. I do not think anyone knew. No one cared what your sexual preferences were. We all had our duties to take care of and did not worry about what others thought."

"Well, I think that is about it. Thanks a lot, Parker," Susan concluded. "I appreciate your time and that you've been so candid with me."

"You're welcome." Parker responded with a handshake.

I told Parker to wait outside. I wanted to talk to Susan for a minute, "Thank you for coming, Susan. Recall from our previous conversation that you're not to use any part of the interview until I get an okay from headquarters. They are very specific about these things since any breach could harm the program."

"I will archive the tape and wait until I hear from you," Susan assured me. "It was a great opportunity to talk with a graduate before he left to go overseas and was gone forever."

I looked at her and said, "Yes, gone forever. It was good you got to see him as he is, before life changes for him."

Parker and I silently went to the car for the ride to the airport, which was only a couple of minutes away. After we got in the car, I told Parker, "You did a great job back there. You should be proud. Never be afraid of who you are or to tell people who you are."

Parker replied, "Thanks, I will remember that."

I dropped Parker off at the curb for his flight, gave him a big hug, and watched him walk into the terminal. I cannot describe the awful feeling in my gut, tearing me apart, as I watched such a wonderful young man walk toward an oblivion I could not stop. I could not save him and it made the anger inside me swell up, like a raging fire, but a fire I had to control until the time was right. Right now, I had to get back to PJ. I had to try to save PJ. She was counting on me and I was counting on her.

Disney Dream

I needed time to think and did not want to be at GPI when PJ was to have committed suicide, so I got a hotel room in Santa Cruz, about half the drive back. I didn't want anyone, in any way, to link me with PJ. I had to think of what to do next, what to do with PJ. I could not take her with me and I could not be seen with her, since it would be too dangerous. I had to find her a place to live where she would be safe until I could sort through all this—and expose CD's secret program for stealing and exchanging bodies.

After I settled into my room I began to wonder how PJ was doing. It was just about dark outside. I felt bad that I had not had a chance to explain a lot to her. I hoped I had not frightened her to the point that she would lose it, or doubt me and try to tell someone of our intentions. I knew I was not going to sleep much that night. I thought and thought about where PJ could hide and be safe. PJ loved the water and I wanted her to be in a remote location where there were not a lot of people. I first needed to get PJ a fake ID, which would make it easier for her to get around without being questioned. I had an idea while I was sleeping and dreaming of taking a relaxing cruise ship around the world. It would be great if I could get PJ a job working on a cruise ship, maybe teaching swimming or surfing. A job like that would definitely keep her out of mainstream society, where she could possibly be identified. And on a cruise ship she should be safe since she would be at sea most of the time. In addition, there would be a lot of kids similar to her age from all over the world with whom she could share time and have fun. I wondered throughout the night if PJ had any trouble or if she did what we talked about. More importantly: was she able to do everything undetected?

I got up early, and after breakfast at a local Denny's restaurant, I drove the hour or so back to GPI. No sooner had I parked my car in the parking lot than Sariah came running over to meet me. She had tears in her eyes and looked liked she had been crying for a while. I said, "What's wrong?"

"PJ's gone, PJ's gone," she cried and threw her arms around me in a hug. Sariah cried uncontrollably for a few minutes before she could regain her composure.

"Sariah, what happened? What's wrong? Where is PJ?" I asked.

Sariah frantically replied, "PJ left a note on her bed last night. The teachers told me it was a suicide note."

"How do they know she committed suicide?" I asked.

Sariah looked down at the ground and then spoke slowly, "They found some of her things on the rocks below the cliffs this morning. After I showed them her note."

I told Sariah to go back to her room and try to relax while I talked with the staff to try to find out what had happened. I went to GPI's office and spoke with the superintendent.

He told me, "Sariah came to my cabin about 6am this morning with PJ's note. She told me that the previous evening some of the other students said they had seen PJ walking back and forth along the cliffs at the back of the compound, like she was nervous about something. Sariah was very upset this morning because she did not do something last night or say something to stop PJ. I went out to the cliffs and looked around and saw some clothing at the bottom of the cliffs. I called the police and they called out the Coast Guard to check around the area. I gave the police the suicide note. I feel really bad, but no one said anything about PJ being depressed or suicidal."

I told the superintendent, "I will contact CD headquarters and tell them. They need to stop PJ's interviewer from coming here and wasting her time. There will be no one to interview. I will also be leaving today as there is no reason for me to be here any longer."

I contacted headquarters and they told me to return to Washington, DC and await further instructions. I told them I needed some time off, a vacation, so they gave me three weeks before I had to report back to work. I thought that three weeks should be enough time to find PJ a place to stay and work and also enough time to make a plan for how to proceed from there. I spent the day packing up the rest of my belongings, and then I wanted to say goodbye to Sariah before I left. I felt badly for deceiving her in such a hurtful manner, but there was no other way.

I went back to Sariah and PJ's cabin and knocked on the door.

Sariah opened the door quickly, "Did you find her? Did they find her?"

"No, Sariah, they did not find her. She is gone; she died. It appears she was washed out to sea. They found her clothes on the rocks below the cliffs."

Sariah hung her head. "I knew I should have tried to find her last night and ask what was wrong. I knew it!"

I tried to console her. "It was not your fault, Sariah. Do not blame yourself. PJ's life was not your fault either. All of you kids here have had a hard time. Everyone deals with it differently. Everyone has a responsibility to himself or herself first. You need to take care of yourself, since you are a child, and let the adults do what they can and are supposed to do. It was the adults' responsibility to take care of PJ and also PJ's. PJ should have realized it was okay to tell someone if she was having problems, but she didn't. It is not your fault. We will all miss her."

"I will miss her so much," Sariah replied. "She was like a sister to me. I know she was leaving anyway in a few days, but this is different. Sometimes I hate this place, because I know all the kids here had terrible childhoods and just want to leave. But then I remember I have nowhere to go."

I hugged and tried to comfort her. "Don't worry. Someday everything will be all sorted out—you have a bright future ahead of you, so just concentrate on that. Try to get some rest for now and think of all the good times you shared with PJ. I will be leaving later on myself. I do not want to be here any longer."

Sariah looked at me and said, "I understand how you feel. I know you cared a lot for PJ. I wouldn't want to hang around either."

I left and returned to my cabin and waited for the sun to set. After it was dark I headed for the rendezvous location at Sand Dollar Beach to pickup PJ. I parked in the lot toward the south end, hidden from the bright moon, near a crop of tall pine trees, and waited. I had been sitting in the car for about thirty minutes when I heard noises in the trees behind where I was parked. Then I saw her. She looked tired and dirty from being out all night. I opened the door to the backseat from the inside and she got in. I immediately told her, "Lie down on the floor until I get down the road a bit. I do not want anyone to see you. How are you? I was worried. Are you okay?"

PJ replied in a muffled low voice from the backseat, "I'm okay. Let's just get away, as far away from this place as we can."

I drove south for about fifteen minutes and after that I was no longer worried about someone seeing us, as the Pacific Coast Highway is a narrow two-lane road and no one else was even on it. We left Big Sur and drove until almost midnight before we arrived in the small town of San Luis Obispo, where I decided to get a hotel room. PJ was worn out from staying awake the night before in the forest, after staging her suicide. She slept all the way down, until I woke her to go inside to the hotel room. After we carried our things in the room we both laid back on the beds, staring at the ceiling. We both must have been thinking similar thoughts, about what the future might have in store for each of us. I think we were both a bit scared and did not want to show it. After a while, I rolled over onto my side on one elbow and looked at PJ. "How are you doing? Are you hungry? You want a shower? Can I get you anything?"

She slowly turned just her head toward me. "Can you get me a new life? Not a new body, just a new life? Is that a big order? How hard is that for you, Mr. Government Agent?"

"You have all the reasons in the world not to trust me, or not to like me, or simply just to run away from me. But I hope we can work together and expose this whole operation. It is going to take some time and planning, and in the meantime I am worried for your safety. PJ, I care very dearly for you. I know that might seem a bit weird at this point, because you do not know anything about me except that I told you I have exchanged with three people. Why don't you take a long hot shower, clean up, and I will have a pizza delivered here to us. Then I can answer some of your questions. How is that?"

"Sure, I need a hot shower and I want to relax. Waiting out there in the woods I was so worried that you were not going to come back for me."

"I told you that I will always come back for you. You are my reason for living. We will do this together. Now, go relax and enjoy your shower. No more worrying, at least until I tell you to." I said sternly with a half-smile.

PJ got out of the shower, right after the guy delivered our pizza. She walked around wearing only a towel while drying her hair with another towel. She looked amazingly beautiful. Her body was slender and muscular, as her long wet hair fell across her back and dripped onto the floor. The towel covered only the top portion of her legs, which were long and very sexy. She was incredibly feminine for her age. I felt weird, admiring her, but I also realized my body was only a few years older than hers. My body was almost instinctively responding to hers, like any male in the presence of a young vulnerable female. It was difficult to control my hormone-enriched body. I wanted to hold her, caress her, kiss her and share our bodies like any two normal young people in love. But we were not two "normal" young people in love. I had to control myself, my urges, my needs and desires. I laid on one of the beds, on my stomach to hide my physical attraction from her.

PJ sat across from me on the other bed eating a piece of pizza and said, "I have never been out on a date. Do you know that? I feel like a weirdo. What other eighteen-year-old girl has never been on a date? There is so much I have never done. Will you take me on a date?"

"I would love to take you on a date. Where do you want to go?"

"I'm not sure. Where do most teenagers go on a first date—a movie, the beach, a hamburger joint? Where did you go on your first date—how many first dates have you had, since you have been in more than one body?" PJ asked. "Explain to me again what happened to you, how many people you have been. This is so unbelievable."

"Adam is my fourth body. My mind is that of Frank Freiberg, and he had his first date at a county fair with his high school sweetheart. It was common for that time and place to take your dates to the fair, to go on carnival rides, to eat cotton candy, and to win prizes for your girlfriend."

"What happened to Frank?"

"Frank's body died after his fighter jet was shot down over Afghanistan. After that, without my prior knowledge or permission, I was then put into the body of a 19-year-old serviceman. Don't get me wrong: I was happy because I did not want to die, but I was sad he had given up his life for me. I found out later he had not been told the truth either about what was going to happen to him. What happened to him was that the military asked for volunteers to be part of a secret program, which they were only told was in the interest of national security, and so a lot of young men and women volunteered for it. The program was for them to give up their bodies, so that others like me could exchange into them. At first it was a test program simply to see if it could be done. After that the military realized they could save money by exchanging people like me in whom they had invested a great deal of time and money. It was not long after that that other government agencies started using the exchange program for their own private programs, like the CIA and the FBI."

"After Frank died, I became a CIA operative. I was educated at Berkeley, learned Arabic and was sent to Yemen as bait to a capture a high profile terrorist, except that I was killed in the process. I was then exchanged again, sort of as a test, since I was exchanged into a twenty-two-year-old girl's body, which apparently had not been done before. I was chosen by the FBI to become a female undercover officer to infiltrate a global human sex trafficking ring. I liked that body and I liked learning all about being a woman. But, ultimately before I could enjoy being a woman, I was kidnapped, raped, tortured, and killed. After that, I was exchanged into Adam's body. I never had a choice. No one ever asked me what assignment I wanted, what kind of body I wanted, if I wanted to stop, or if I thought it was right or wrong. I feel like I was just a piece of equipment the military and government used as they would a combat vehicle. If I got damaged they would simply put me in a new vehicle or, in my case, a different body. And then I met you and your classmates."

"I'm sorry, Adam. I had no idea. I thought you were just another guy who was out to take advantage of us. I had no idea you had been through more shit than we had."

"Well, I am not sure I have been through more than you guys. It was different. But what is for sure is that it has all gotten way out of control and that it has to be stopped. Who knows what some pathological people in places of high power are doing with this technology. I am willing to bet their ideas are not all to serve the people of this country—more likely to serve the interests of a few rich and powerful people, from what I have seen. This technology could be used to benefit mankind, but not this way, not just for some elitist's vanity. One of our most controversial vice presidents, Dick Cheney, is going to exchange into Parker's body, and it sickens me to death. You can bet Cheney has some ulterior motives, besides saving his own sorry skin. Cheney was a less than moral government official and the worst part of it was, he did not care to conceal it and professed it was for the greater good of the world. He was one of the key officials who believed in the torture of prisoners, in the rendition of people all over the world, in holding people in secret prisons without charges for unspecified periods of time, in war without basis—and ultimately was involved in the illegal exposing of a CIA operative. Cheney was not what we need in our government and surely we do not need a Cheney Number Two, especially without disclosure of his true identity."

"Is he why you went to Wyoming?"

"Yes, Cheney wanted to meet with me. He could not come to GPI to see his new body himself. Too much was at risk for him. He wanted to keep it secret. Also, all the interviewers who came to GPI were not interviewers at all, as you now know; they were the people who took over your classmates' bodies. There never was a peace program abroad. It was all a lie to manipulate and deceive."

"Wow! How big is this program? How many people have been exchanged, or died, or lost their identities?"

"I do not know how big it is, or how high in our government it goes, or if we have infiltrated other governments or corporations with our exchanged operatives. I am sure it has spread quickly and pervasively, like a cancer. I want to make sure you are in a safe place, first and foremost. You are the most important thing to me."

She looked intently at me. Her gaze hung with me and seemed warm, open, and sympathetic. "Adam, I am sorry for all you have been through, and I thank you for all you are doing for me. You are the only one I can trust. I will do whatever you want. You are like my guardian angel."

PJ came over to my bed, laid down next to me, and kissed me on my cheek. She let her towel fall off and I could see her naked body next to me. Her small breasts were so perfect, so untouched and innocent; her waist and hips with the curves of a young woman were still growing into her adult form. I wanted her so badly, all parts of me, the young and the old. I had felt so alone for so long. I desired the touch of a woman, a companion, someone who understood me. I also felt the desires of being a young man wanting someone to love and feel special with. I wanted to hold her and make her feel how special I really felt she was. But it also felt wrong—all the pieces did not fit, at least not yet. Maybe someday they would, but not here, not now, not this way.

"PJ, I can't do this. I can't do this here, right now."

"Adam, make love to me," She said softly and yearningly, almost as if it would hurt not to.

"PJ, you are a beautiful woman and I love you. I want to make love to you and forget the entire world, except for you. But in the morning, we will have to wake up and see the world for what it truly is. When we get together, I want it to be a special time and place, where we can be at peace and see things clearly. Not like this, not stressed about what the future will bring." I pulled PJ's towel back over her and held her tightly. We laid together for almost an hour without saying a word, then PJ said, "I'm still hungry!"

I laughed, "The pizza is cold now."

PJ replied with a laugh, as she danced in a couple of circles across the room. "I don't care, I am happy I am here with you!"

"Me, too," I said. "We also need to get some sleep and head on down to LA tomorrow." We finished our pizza and fell asleep in each other's arms, as if the outside world could never find us, and we were at peace, even though it was only for a short period of time.

The next morning we checked out and continued down the Pacific Coast Highway toward Los Angeles. I asked PJ, "How would you like to go on a cruise ship, a big cruise ship?"

"I would love to! You and me on a cruise, that would be wonderful—like a first date!"

"Well, I would not be able to go with you. I need to get back to the east coast and plan how this is all going to go down."

"You're going to leave me alone on a cruise ship?" she said dumbfounded. "Isn't that a bit weird. Won't people be suspicious?"

"Well, my idea is to get you a job on the ship. Disney has a cruise ship that departs out of Long Beach, and we can try to get you a job on the ship. That way, you would be out of the area and hard to find, even if someone was looking for you. You would be around other people your age, or almost, and I would not have to worry about you. All of your needs would be taken care of by the ship. You would have a place to live, food to eat, people to meet, and you would be safe. I think you would like it, and it would be a huge change from the Institute. And we could communicate by the internet. Maybe we could set up bogus Facebook profiles and post things to each other on that if we need to. I made you a fake ID card under the name Susan Meyer."

PJ looked out her side window with a sad expression on her face. "I don't want you to leave me. Can't you take at least one cruise with me?"

I said lovingly and with consternation, "PJ, I would love to, but time is of the essence and also I do not want to be seen in public with you. Remember, CD can track my every move with GPS. I do not want them to be able to track you or me on a cruise ship. All they know is that I am taking the long way home right now and they have no reason to be suspicious, or if they ever do find out anything there is no way they would be able to know where you are from tracking my route."

"I understand," PJ responded softly and dejectedly. "I think it might be fun to work on a cruise ship. What would they have me do, I wonder?"

"I am not sure. We can check their website when we get in tonight and see what is available."

It was a beautiful day in Los Angeles as we drove down the winding coast highway. PJ had never been to LA, so we stopped at Venice Beach to play in the waves and look at all the attractions. PJ saw the carnival rides and said, "Hey, there is a Ferris wheel. Please take me—it will be like your first date! Please?"

"Yeah, that would be fun. Let's do it!" We got on the Ferris wheel and PJ sat close to me. She put her head on my shoulder and I put my arm around her. It felt so good. Like I was a teenager again. I actually felt my heart beat faster as PJ sat close to me. It was wonderful to be young and in love experiencing it all over again. The moment seemed perfect.

We got a hotel room near LAX. I discovered Disney had open walk-in interviews for cruise ship workers every day from 8am to 5pm. I told PJ we should go there the next day to and see what we could find out. Back at GPI I had already made a copy of PJ's birth certificate when I was reviewing her file. The next day I took PJ to the interview and they were very happy with her. Disney was looking for lifeguards to work at the ship's pools during the cruise, which was perfect for PJ as she was an exceptional swimmer. At night, PJ would also work as a server for the dinners. PJ told me, "I also want to try out for the many shows they put on for the passengers. I have always loved Disney! Maybe I could dress up like a Disney character and be in a show." PJ genuinely seemed excited about starting a new life and a new adventure. And I was happy to know she was not going to be killed off and that she would be in a safe happy place where I did not have to worry about her. The unfortunate part was that Disney wanted her to start in a few days for her first cruise. I had hoped we would have more time together before I would have to leave her.

PJ and I decided to spend a couple of days exploring Los Angeles, which really is a unique and beautiful city. We spent a day at Disneyland and a day at Universal Studios, and a day at Sea World down in San Diego. It felt exciting and rejuvenating, exploring like a kid again, taking my girlfriend to all these places she had never been before. I also, in a way, felt like a father taking his daughter for the first time to all these special places. I really enjoyed the looks on her face as she saw so many things for the first time—it was an incredibly gratifying feeling and made me so happy. But, it also made me sad, because it made me miss my family, Frank's family, and my own children. I wondered what they were doing, what their lives were like.

On what was to be our last night together, until a time neither of us could guess we decided to stay in the room and again order a pizza. PJ loved cheese pizza, I think mainly because they never served it at the GPI since it wasn't healthy enough. We laid on one of the beds together, watched TV, and ate pizza. PJ said to me, "Adam, I am worried about you. What will I do if something happens to you? How will I even know?"

"If you have not heard from me in three months, assume I am dead and go on with your life, however you want to lead it. You will live like people are supposed to, without the interference of the government, a free person, independent and able to make your own decisions. Disney has a lot of resources, so whenever you decide to leave they can help you find another job within the company, or give you a good reference."

"But what if I want to contact you? How do I do that?"

"Let's try not to use email, since it's too easily tracked. Why don't we post ads on Craigslist—ads like, 'men looking for women' or 'women looking for men.' I will always put in my headline, 'Exotic bald man seeks strong swimmer type.' I began to laugh uncontrollably.

PJ, also laughing, "Yeah, and I will always make my headline, 'Hot Character seeks Disney Companion.'"

"I think that is a good starting place, anyway." We both got quiet and PJ started to cry. I pulled her to me and wrapped my arms around her; she put her head on my chest.

"I am not sure if I can do this. I am going to miss you so much," PJ uttered. "I wonder if I am ever going to see you again. Please don't forget about me. Please come back for me."

"PJ, I will never forget you and I will come back for you. Try to enjoy every day, every moment——it is what life is about, happiness and joy. When the time is right I will let you know what to do next, just like we planned."

PJ looked at me and I at her, and with fear in her eyes she said, "I am so scared."

"I am, too, but we will get through this. We have to do this. We will be helping a lot of people——always remember that. I will miss you every day, every minute I am away from you."

"I will miss you so much, my heart already aches for you." We didn't let go of each other throughout the entire night as we slept. We got ready quietly the next morning and I took her to the dock at Long Beach where the Disney Cruise Ship "Dream" was moored. PJ got out of the car and we hugged tightly for a long time. She said in an upbeat way, "Life is like a dream, just like this ship's name. Who knows where the dream will lead us." She turned and walked away, up the gangplank, and disappeared into the ship. I stood and watched from across the parking lot as tears ran down my cheeks. I felt so alone again. I wondered when I would see her again, and my heart was aching. I did not know how this nightmare was going to end, but I hoped it would be soon so I could come back for her.

Reunited with Miriam

I was glad I had a long drive ahead of me. I enjoyed driving; it allowed me time to contemplate, especially if there was something bothering me. I figured it would take me three days or so, with stops, to drive back to Washington, DC. I planned on driving straight east from Los Angeles, across Arizona, through Flagstaff, then on to New Mexico where I would find a place for the night in Albuquerque. I thought that Parker would be gone and that Cheney would have taken over his body if all had gone well. I wondered what Cheney planned to do, if and where he planned to go to college, or whose skin he was going to get under next. I really felt like this guy had to be exposed somehow, so he could not be allowed to go into politics again.

I was baffled by Cheney's talk of the Free Masons and what that had to do with anything. I knew Cheney was not making idle chit-chat, so he had a purpose—but what was it? Did he want me to join so I could do something for him, or was it somehow to keep me from talking about his exchange? I already understood that once you join the Masons and learn of some of their internal secrets, no one quits and lives to tell about it. I would rather simply not join and not learn of their dirty little deeds, especially if I had to die with those secrets. I thought I had better try to find the guy Cheney wanted me to contact, just so it would not raise any suspicion.

I thought that what I needed to do was to keep building a coalition of people who knew about what the government and CD were doing. When things go public, there would be several others who would know of the program, just in case I met with an untimely death. I had to find people who would unquestionably believe my story and be able to convince others of its veracity. The first person who came to mind was Miriam, my wife. Miriam would know very quickly when I talked with her that it was truly her husband Frank in another man's body. But how would I get her to talk with me or, if was she remarried, what would I do? I wondered how the kids were doing. I missed them so much. Funny enough, there were only about ten years of difference between them and me now, so I could be a long-lost cousin or son of their dad's buddy. It was settled in my mind. I would go to Indiana after New Mexico to see my family. I did not even know if they lived in the same place or if they had moved.

It took me about one and a half days to get to Fort Wayne, Indiana. When I arrived I got a room at the Hilton hotel in the middle of the downtown area. I did not want to just go up to the house and say, "Hi, I am your dead husband in a kid's body." Miriam was a science teacher at Carroll High School, in a rural area of Fort Wayne. I would call her and tell her that my father, an old military friend of her husband, had told me to ask her for help about where to live since I just got relocated here for a job. I waited until evening and then thought I would try the old phone number from six years ago to see if it still worked.

At about 7pm, I called the number and it rang three times before a young female voice answered. "Hello," I said. "Is your mother home? May I talk with her?"

The voice said, "Sure, hold on," and I heard her yell in the background. "Mom, someone wants to talk with you on the phone."

The mother responded, "Who is it?" The girl said, "I don't know, some guy."

Then I heard the mother pick up, "Hello, can I help you?"

"Is this Miriam Freiberg?"

"Who is this calling, please?"

"This is Adam River. My father was a military friend of your husband and he told me to call you. I just got relocated to Fort Wayne for a job and thought you might be able to answer some questions about the area and where to live, things like that. I don't want to be a bother, though."

She seemed startled and did not respond for a brief period of time, then said, "Yes, this is Miriam Freiberg. How did your father know my husband?"

"My dad's name is Captain James River and he flew with your husband in Afghanistan." There really was no such person. I knew she did not know all the guys I had flown with over there. "My father knew your husband was from here, so when I got my new job he thought I should stop by and check in on you to see if there was anything I could do for you—and that maybe you could tell me where to live as well."

"Wow, I haven't talked about my husband in a while. It brings back a lot of memories. I do not know how much I will be able to help you, but if you tell me what you need, maybe I can help."

"Well, maybe I could come by tomorrow to say hello and ask you some questions?"

Miriam paused for a moment. "Sure, why don't you come by for dinner at 6pm. How old did you say you were?"

"I'm sorry, I did not say. I just graduated from college. I am 23 years old,"

"Oh okay, that's fine. Great, so I will see you tomorrow at 6pm."

"Thank you very much, I will look forward to meeting you tomorrow. Goodbye."

I was happy, yet amazed and stunned at the same time. I had just talked to my wife for the first time in six years, and the young voice must have been my daughter, Emma. This was so crazy. I was supposed to be dead; they think I am dead. I will have to be careful about telling them, or maybe I should just tell Miriam. I decided I would wait until after I met them all before I thought any more about how I would tell them what had happened to me. I was getting more excited about seeing my family after six years of being away. I wondered what had happened to them in that time. I imagined the kids would be much bigger. I couldn't wait to see what they looked like. Tomorrow would probably seem like it was going by slowly. I couldn't wait to see them.

At 6pm I was standing in front of my own house, the house I had bought and used to live in. I had finally come home, almost like nothing had changed and everything I had experienced had been just a dream. I imagined I would walk through this door and see Emma and Justin, still eight and seven years old. Miriam would be the same as I remembered her six years ago. But things were different, very different. I had to control my emotions: no tears, no show of joy, no excitement, no hugs. I rang the doorbell and a few moments later the door slowly swung open. I saw a five-foot-four inch, dark-haired, beautiful young teenage girl with her hair tied back in a ponytail and braces on her teeth. She was wearing black shorts and a purple 'Juicy Couture' sweatshirt. I said, "Hi, I am Adam," and put out my hand for a handshake.

The young girl put her hand out to shake mine and said, "Hi, I am Emma." I could not take my eyes off of her, since she had grown so much. I realized everything I had missed since I had been gone. I had not thought I would ever see my family again and then there I was, in front of my daughter, but she did not recognize me. I was totally different, a stranger. If only she knew I was her dad inside and how much I wanted to hug her and not let her go.

"Hi Adam, I am Miriam." A bit startled out of my fixation on Emma I saw Miriam walking toward me in the hallway. Miriam looked more beautiful than I had even remembered her.

I started to walk toward her and began to raise my arms instinctively to hug her and kiss her, but caught myself before it was noticed. "Hi, Mrs. Freiberg. Thanks for having me over. It was very nice of you,"

"Not at all, no problem. Come in and make yourself comfortable. This is Justin." She pointed to the living room, where I saw a teenage boy, with dark chocolate-colored hair styled like Justin Beiber's, wearing a black tee-shirt with a red swirl design and blue jeans sitting on the floor in front of the television playing a video game.

"Hi Justin, I am Adam. What are you playing?"

"COD," Justin replied.

"COD. What is COD?"

"COD is a video game, Call of Duty. This is Black Ops. It's a war game."

"Oh, is that your favorite?"

"One of my favorites. The other is Assassin's Creed. It is a game about a group trying to kill Knights Templar in Rome a long time ago."

"That is the purpose of the game—to kill Knights Templar?"

Justin paused the game and looked up at me. "No, you try to find the secret artifacts the Templars took from Jerusalem during the First Crusade. When you find something you either get points or special powers."

"Oh. Very interesting game. I guess you learn a bit about history as well."

Justin turned back to his game and muttered, "Yeahhhhhh." He was a handsome teenage boy, tall, it appeared, skinny, with his mom's olive skin—and he seemed to possess a lot of confidence by the way he looked directly at me and answered my questions. There I was, home again with my family. I could not believe it. I felt so happy to be there, and I never wanted to leave again. Miriam spoke as if to break me out of a trance, as I must have been staring into space. "I fixed spaghetti. I hope you like it. It's simple and easy, and the kids love it."

"I have always liked spaghetti, especially with meat sauce and artichoke hearts. It is my favorite sauce," I said.

"Really," Miriam quickly responded. "My husband used to like the same sauce, and the kids like it, too. So you're in luck."

"Great. Maybe we have similar tastes."

"Maybe." She went off into the kitchen area. I noticed Miriam was not wearing a wedding ring and I did not see any signs of a man living there. She must not have remarried, but I did not want to ask. Miriam called from the kitchen, "What kind of a job did you get here? They are hard to find these days."

"General Motors hired me for their light truck factory here. I'll order parts and make sure they arrive on time for the assembly line." I walked into the kitchen and saw Miriam stirring the pot of spaghetti cooking on the stove.

"Oh, GM is a big company, you should do well with them. Do you want to live in the south part of the city? That is where the plant is."

"I'm not sure. I want to look around a bit and not rush into anything. Where do you recommend?"

"Well, you are young, good-looking, and single. I would think you would want to be over by the college, in the east part. There are more young people over there."

"That's what I wanted to talk with you about, to get your opinion. Do you like it out north here, in this area?"

"Yes, but I work at a high school just down the street, where Emma goes. Justin's school is close by, too, so it's easy for me. Maybe I could show you around a bit on Sunday? There are a lot of open houses we could look at. I like going through open houses."

"That would be great, if you don't mind.

"The kids would be bored, I am sure. The kids always keep themselves entertained. I'll show you around. It will be fun."

"Great. Thank you very much."

The few hours I was able to spend with my family went by in the blink of an eye. I was again sitting alone in my car in front of the house. I thought about them and was happy they were okay, seemed happy, and were well taken care of. The kids were so adult-like, polite, and entertaining. I had tried to study them without appearing too much like a stalker. Miriam was nice and she looked amazing. On my drive back to the hotel I wondered if maybe I was doing the wrong thing by being here and if I should disrupt the wonderful life they have made for themselves, without me, their father and husband. But I thought their lives could still be good with me in it, since even though I was not in the same body, I was the same person. The kids could still have a father and Miriam could still know her husband. Maybe I was being too overly optimistic or simple. This whole situation could put their lives in danger, or at least be very disruptive. I thought that maybe I could just tell Miriam and not tell the kids until they got older. I had a lot to think about.

The next morning I got a call from my handler, Samuel Jackson at CD. I guess his real name was something else but that is what he called himself. Samuel had been assigned to me when I exchanged with Adam. He wanted to know, "When are you planning on coming back to Washington, because they have another assignment for you? I see you are in Fort Wayne. Are you checking up on your family? It was probably a good idea to see them and help them if you can."

I was a bit stunned by his statements. First, that indeed CD was checking on their operative's whereabouts. Second, that they had another assignment for me. I thought I was going to be doing this recruiter job for a while. Sam had this weird sense of humor that made it difficult at times to know if he was kidding around or serious. I could tell he was serious this time.

"Expect me back sometime next week."

"That's fine. Enjoy your time with your family."

For the first time in a long time, I felt scared after that phone call. I knew they had no idea what I was up to. But they knew where I was located, and they knew I had been with my family. I again wondered if I was putting them in danger and I knew I could not have that. I knew that Miriam would understand my situation and would want to help me in any way she could. She was a strong person, with strong convictions about the government and how democracy was supposed to work. I knew she would want to help if she knew what was going on.

On Sunday I drove out to pick up Miriam. I arrived about noon. She was pulling weeds in the front yard and came out to the car. I greeted her. "Hi, how are you?"

"Great, how are you?"

"Fine. Where are the kids?"

"They are over playing with friends for the afternoon."

"Is it okay if I drive? I've been studying the maps of the area and want to become familiar with the roads." Of course I remembered the roads very well, as I grew up there. I wanted to drive and not worry about Miriam being distracted if I said something shocking. We went to a couple of open houses nearby and then I drove to a place known as Devil's Hollow. It was a place where Miriam and I used to park and make out. Devil's Hollow was on a road that winded down to a small canyon, where trees hung over the road and blocked the sun from coming through even on bright sunny days. Kids used to like to come here because it had an eerie feeling to it, since it was dark and secluded all the time. When we got near the area, Miriam commented, "Wow, I haven't been here for a long time."

I said, "Really? You mean, Devil's Hollow?"

Miriam looked over at me, "How did you know it was called that?"

"I learned lots of things about the area before I came here."

"Oh. A little weird you would learn about a random place where kids hang out."

I found a place to park the car on the side of the road. Miriam quickly said, "Why are you stopping?"

"Miriam, I don't have a lot of time. I need to tell you some things about your husband and about what happened after he died. I am not who I said I am. I work for the government."

"What do you want with me? What do you do for the government?"

"Miriam, I'm part of a secret project, a very secret project. If anyone knew I told you there would be big trouble for you and maybe your family.

"Then don't tell me. I don't want to know what you are doing. Take me back home. You are scaring me."

"Miriam, remember the night you and your husband parked here before you were married?" I asked. "He was just your boyfriend at the time and cop pulled up behind you and turned on his red lights. Remember how scared both of you were? The cop came up and shined his flashlight in the car and asked you what you were doing out here. Remember how Frank said, 'Oh nothing, Officer, we were just talking.' The Officer then asked you, 'Miss, are you okay? Are you here of your own free will? He is not hurting you?' And you started laughing, 'Oh, I'm fine, Officer. This is my boyfriend, he would not hurt me.' Do you remember? The Officer walked away laughing, and said, 'Okay, you two have fun.' You were so scared when the cop first pulled up."

Miriam had a blank look on her face as she looked at me. She said in a voice I could barely hear, "How do you know that? No one could know that except my husband, myself, and the cop."

"I know because I am your husband. I'm Frank. I was put in this body after Frank's body was killed when his plane was shot down."

"That can't be. I saw Frank's body when they brought it back from Afghanistan. Frank's dead. You are not Frank, that is not possible. Who are you, why are you doing this?"

"I am part of a secret government program in which they can store a human being's memory and entire identity in a computer. They can transfer that stored memory, that identity, into another body. That is what they did with me. Before I deployed to Afghanistan they attached a device to the back of my brain, inside my skull, to accomplish a download. They stored all of my memory on computer. When I was killed—when Frank's body died—they took my stored information and uploaded my identity into another body. It was like waking up from a night's sleep in a new body: the same person, with the same thoughts and memories, but in a different body."

"If you are Frank, why didn't you come back sooner? Why didn't you come back to your family? I don't believe you. Frank would have come back for us."

"Miriam, remember on our wedding day, after we finished saying our vows and turned to walk down the aisle and out of the church? You whispered in my ear, 'I'm afraid I am going to stumble and fall, I am shaking so much.' And I whispered back in your ear, 'Never worry, I will always be here to catch you if you stumble or fall. I am your safety net.' Or when Emma was born and you were holding her in the delivery room and I said, 'Now there are two angels in my world.' Or the first gift I bought Justin after he was born, a fighter pilot jacket for a five year old, and told you he will grow into it. Do you remember?"

Miriam began to cry. "Oh my God, Oh my God. Is it possible, Frank, is it you? Oh my Lord, how can it be?" Miriam cried uncontrollably and I held her tightly.

"I'm sorry for not coming back sooner. They had me doing all kinds of things and it was not possible to come back. I was afraid you had forgotten me or got remarried. I love you so much, I have missed you."

We sat and talked for most of the afternoon, reminiscing about the many events that had happened to us since we had met. Miriam now was completely convinced it was me. She just could not believe the government had the ability to exchange one person's mind into another person's body.

"How could the government keep this from us? What about the families of those who died? Why couldn't they tell us?"

"Because they are taking other people's bodies and using them for their own benefit. Those people were not told what was going to happen to them. It is all a big lie. There are people making decisions as to who is going to live and who is going to die. It has gotten completely out of control."

"I need your help. I have to expose this operation. There is a girl who was about to be killed and her body used for an exchange. Her life is in danger, so I have hidden her. There could be many others like her all over the US—who knows how many are involved. I also do not know what else they are using the program for. It has to stop! They are taking young servicemen and women's lives without their knowledge and telling their families they died in combat. I was just notified yesterday that I have to get back to Washington as they have another assignment for me. I have no idea what it is or what will happen to me. I want you to help me to document the situation so that if anything happens to me, you can take it to Congress and let them know what is going on. You cannot trust anyone. You cannot imagine how high up in our government this goes, and it also involves many other countries and people. It even involves the ex-vice president, Dick Cheney. He just exchanged into a young man's body a couple of weeks ago because he was about to die."

"What are you going to do? How are you going to expose it?"

"I don't know yet. I want to have a few people in place when I do go public, so that others can support me and back me up."

"I will always be here to catch you when you stumble or fall."

We hugged and I said, "We should probably get back. The kids might be wondering where you are."

I drove back to the house and we fixed dinner together, just like we used to. I barbecued chicken on the grill. We spent the evening together, as a family. I felt so happy, yet so scared of what the future might hold. I left after the kids went to bed.

The next day, Miriam called in sick for work and we met after the kids went to school. Miriam came to my hotel room. Before she arrived I set up a video camera to record my personal interview. I wanted to have Miriam with me in the video to show we had contact with each other. I wanted to document the different lives I had had, the people whose bodies I had taken over, whom I worked for, and what I had witnessed. When Miriam arrived we immediately got started, as I did not know how long it would take to record all the information. It took about four hours to get down most of the information I wanted to disclose. I then told Miriam, "I will upload this video onto my computer and I will send you an email. But first I want you to create an email account from a public computer, like at the FedEx Office, and that way the account will not be traceable to your home computer. I will then send this video to that email account and it will be stored there. I will include with it various email addresses of important government officials and news media personnel who can help you distribute the video in the event I am killed or go missing. I will also send you the email address of the young girl, named PJ, short for Penny Jo. In addition, I will give her the email address we create. In addition, I will send her and give you a hard copy of this video to hide somewhere, not in your house. Finally, I will email you the contact information of a news reporter named Susan Welday in San Francisco who can help you break the story. Please check the email address once a week for any updated information I might have, but never check it from work or home. Hopefully, after the story breaks we can uncover others like me who are willing to come forward and tell their stories. Now, I must leave and go back to Washington to find out what they want me to do next. There is no reason for them to be suspicious, so just carry on with your life just like you were before I came a few days ago."

I saw a soft warm smile on Miriam's face and her face lit up a bit. "What are you thinking?" I asked.

"I was thinking that my life is not the same as it was a few days ago. Everything has changed. I have my husband back! I do not hurt anymore. It is like some weight has been lifted off of my heart and I can breathe easier now. I look forward to the day when this is all behind us and we can be a family again. It doesn't matter whose body you occupy—you are Frank, the sweet, caring, loving man I have known for most of my life."

I smiled back at her and hugged her tightly. I felt like I had years before, in love with this woman, and I did not want to let her go. I forgot for a moment I was in Adam's body and lowered my lips to meet hers. I held her tightly and we kissed and kissed, our passion welling up and releasing to each other. We fell backward on the bed and began slowly to undress one another. Miriam pulled my shirt off and saw the tattoo they gave me after my first exchange. "What is this tattoo? It's kind of in a weird place if you want others to see it."

"It is not for everyone to see. I was given the tattoo after I received the brain implant. It is a way for those who know about the program to recognize exchangers."

"What is the tattoo of? What does it mean?"

"It is the logo of Crystal Discovery."

"It is kind of a weird logo. It looks like it should mean something. It looks like a device of some sort."

"Maybe, I don't know and don't care." I wanted to be with her and not think of my past. I gently nudged Miriam's upper body down on the bed, running my hands slowly over her breasts. It was easy for me to go slowly since there was no tension. I remembered each part of her body, which I had not touched for many years. I watched Miriam lay back and close her eyes as I kissed and caressed each part of her body. We made love and stayed in bed for most of the afternoon. I felt so alive, so invigorated, like I had been given several shots of adrenaline. I had not felt like this in so long. I was happy. We both dressed slowly, in part, because I think we both understood we were not sure when we would see each other again.

Miriam broke the tension. "I feel like quite the cougar today."

I laughed and teased her, "Yes, you are such an aggressive woman, making love with a man half your age."

"Well, now I know why cougars are prowling around for younger men! But they do not get what I have, a younger man's body, with an older man's heart and brain. I am the lucky one."

"No, I am the lucky one. You're a great woman."

Miriam went to the door and turned around, looking at me, then hugging me. She said, "You never stop amazing me. I somehow always knew you would come back for me. Although, I thought it would be after we both died and we were in heaven. You came back from the dead. We will get through this. I do not want to lose you again. The children and I both need you and want you in our lives."

"I have thought about you every day, through it all, and I can't wait to be back with you," I replied. "I want to move away and go someplace where we can live in peace, all together, as a family. And grow truly old together, naturally." Miriam pulled on my hand as she walked out the door and the door swung closed behind her.

I stood and faced the now closed door. Tears began to run down my face and I hung my head down. I felt like I had to climb a large mountain before I could reach my family again on the other side. I knew there would be many dangerous twisted roads ahead and any wrong turn could send me to my death. I had to remind myself to take one small step at a time and that all of us would get through this. I packed my bags and started off on my trip back to Washington DC. I arrived back at my home, a small studio apartment in Georgetown, after about twelve hours.

Meeting a Mason

The next day I called Samuel Jackson at CD and told him I was home. He said that there had been a meeting set up with Assistant Chief John Dexter for the next day at 8am. Dexter was the point man between secret government funding and CD. I asked what the meeting was about and he informed me he did not know of its purpose. I was a bit nervous, as it was not normal to meet with the Assistant Chief. Normal protocol was for operation handlers to inform field operatives of their new assignments. It crossed my mind that somehow they had discovered my relationship with PJ. Maybe they even knew of her whereabouts. I had to remain calm when I met with him and not reveal any nervousness, which might trigger suspicion.

I decided to head down to Martin's Tavern, just down the street from my house, to get a beer and a bite to eat. I had sat down at the bar and was ordering when a man came up and sat down next to me. He was in his early 40s, white, clean-cut, and looked to be of Irish descent, but did not look like the political types who frequented this area. He also did not look like CIA or FBI. He ordered a beer and said, "Hello, Adam, how was your trip?"

I looked at him and replied, "What trip would that be?"

He said, "My name is Jonathan Rex. I am your Mason sponsor."

"Really," I said, "I was not aware I needed a sponsor."

"Yup, you do and I be him," he said. He raised his beer up as if to toast mine and said, "Cheers, mate."

"Do I have a choice in this matter?"

"Of course you do, Adam, I was told you were new to the area and wanted to find a lodge you could join. You came very highly recommended. Have I offended you in some way?"

"If you call being followed and tracked like a wounded animal offensive, yes, I would say you have offended me. I would imagine the normal manner someone joins an organization is that THEY find someone to sponsor them and contact them about joining. Not the other way around, as has occurred here."

"Adam, don't shoot the messenger. I was told to find you. I was given your address, where you might hang out, and what you looked like, and told to approach you. That is about it."

"Well, I'm sorry you were given this assignment. I would have thought a simple phone call would have been sufficient. Your showing up like this makes a person wonder what else you have been watching me do and for how long. Is that the trust and loyalty I can expect if I join the Masons?"

"You do not act like other guys your age, I will give you that. Most guys who are asked to join the Masons are usually excited about joining; not everyone is asked. Where did you go to school?"

"Listen, Jonathan, when is your next meeting for new recruits? I will go and listen to what they have to say. We both will fall in line and win medals for doing what is expected of us. How is that? Do you have a time and place for that? Where do we go from here?"

"We have a new members meeting coming up at the end of the week. The lodge is located just down the street here on Wisconsin; the address is 4441. Do you know it? The meeting room is in the rear. Come on Friday night at 7pm. We will have a meet-and-greet for new members."

"Great, I will do my best to be there," I replied sarcastically. "Do I need to wear a funny hat or anything when I come?"

"No, you get one of those later after we make you pee on the cross and take an oath to the devil," Jonathan replied, laughing. He finished his beer and got up to leave.

"Are you going to be following me around anymore? Is that standard Mason operating procedure?"

Jonathan walked away and said, "Nope, you are on your own for now."

I found the entire Mason thing so strange. There has to be something meaningful involved or Cheney would not have taken the time to set this up or want me to become a member. I thought I would play along and see where it took me. I did not think it was wise at that point to turn down the offer. I didn't want to piss someone off, raise suspicion. I was paranoid walking around, thinking someone would always be watching. I had to be careful what I did and who I saw. I finished my food and went home. I needed a good night's rest for my meeting with the Assistant Chief in the morning.

I arrived early and waited patiently outside the office. After a few moments AC Dexter came out to greet me and take me in his office. He sat down and proceeded to talk. "Adam, I hear good things about your work. I read your file and understand you have been through a lot these past couple of years. I brought you in for two reasons. First, there is a project I want you to finish that has to do with your recent visit to GPI."

My heart began to race. I thought for sure it was going to have to do with PJ. They must have been watching me the whole time and knew what I did with her. Shit, they had probably already killed her. Goddamn it. This fucking machine has got to be stopped, I thought to myself. They are probably going to set me up to be killed if they found out about PJ. God, what do they want with me? How much do they know? Why am I here?

AC Dexter continued. "Parker, the student you introduced for the former Vice President, is no longer needed. We need you to contact his previous interviewer and get that exchange completed."

I spoke up. "What happened to the former Vice President? Didn't the exchange work?"

"It worked fine for a few weeks, and then a different opportunity came up, so Parker was no longer needed, but he is available now. That is why we need you to get a hold of the interviewer as soon as possible and make that exchange happen. Parker is at the George Washington hospital intensive care unit; we did not want to reinsert his former self back into his body, just to be exchanged again. We are keeping him there until it is time for new the exchange to take place."

"Second, You are being promoted. The former Vice President was impressed with your work and thought you would be an asset as an aide to the Senate Intelligence Committee. He thought that with your background, you could help guide those dumb-fuck Senators on matters dealing with terrorism and national security issues. Apparently, there are too many Democrats working over there right now and nothing seems to be getting done. How does that sound to you? I know your handler Sara told me you are getting tired of traveling all over the country and have been looking for a new place to work."

"Thank you. It would be great not to have to travel so much and to put down some roots here in Washington."

"Super, I will make it happen. You can plan on starting over there next week. Try to take care of the Parker exchange as soon as possible."

"Yes, Sir."

The A.C. stood to shake my hand and said, "Congratulations, Adam. We need more men like you in this country."

I shook his hand and replied, "Thank you, Sir, I appreciate your confidence." I left his office and my head was in a spin. As I walked down the hall away from his office I thought, what the hell just happened? What did I just sign up for? I knew right away that I could not exactly have turned the position down. What would he have thought of me then? What was I supposed to have done?

What seemed apparent, though, was that my plans and my people had not been detected or compromised. PJ must still be okay and my wife and children must be safe. I would just have to move forward. I kept thinking, though, that if Cheney was not with Parker anymore, where the hell was he? He did not just die, that was obvious or he would not have recommended me for a promotion or to join the Dixie Cup Hat wearers club. Cheney was up to no good, that was for sure. He really hated leaving politics and it is my bet he is doing all he can to get back in the game. But where was he? Or, more precisely, who had he become? That was what I needed to find out.

I immediately got on the phone and contacted Parker's original interviewer, an ex-MIT professor who was dying of cancer. The professor was one of the forerunning scientists involved in the development of the human genome project. I was happy to process this exchange because at least it represented someone of value to society who was going to get a second chance at life. With his knowledge and experience, maybe some greater good could come from his future discoveries. The professor had worked with human genomes, but had also done major studies with non-human species' DNA structures. The other species were dolphins and killer whales, two of my favorite animals. The professor, according to his dossier, was going to return to MIT to continue his research on the relationship of these two animals to humans. I contacted him and asked him to come to Crystal Discovery as soon as possible. He told me he could be on a flight within a few hours. The professor had no relatives and lived alone, so there were no loose ends to have to tie up in this case to protect confidentiality. It was a pretty clear and easy transition. I called Samuel Jackson and told him to tell the Assistant Chief that the Parker matter should be completed within the next two days.

Now I had nothing to do for a couple of days before my Masons meeting on Friday and my new job starting on Monday. I needed to do some research about the Senate Intelligence Committee as to what they were involved in at this point and who was on the committee. There must be a special reason Cheney wanted me to try to influence or provide information to someone on the committee, but what? I thought there must be Democratic senators who were blocking a bill, order, or revenue request which either Cheney or CD wanted passed.

I would have to wait until I got over there to find out what was going on, as all the meetings are restricted.

Friday night arrived and I found myself at the Masonic Lodge with several other new guys, waiting to be brought into a "recruit" meeting room. It seemed that even the Masonic Lodge itself had a veil of secrecy. Outsiders were not allowed to enter some of the higher echelon meeting rooms, where the long-standing members discuss their activities. We had several speakers come and talk before us and give their reasons why we should join. They told us we were a select group of men and that we should be proud to be a part of such a globally prestigious organization. The only thing they asked us, the only requirement to be a Mason, was that you had to believe in God. You could be of any religious faith, but you had to believe in God. The last thing they had us do was swear an oath never to reveal the secrets of the order. I already knew about this requirement and that if you violate this oath, it is understood it is the last thing you ever do. We were told to start attending meetings as often as possible, as we would be taught and should learn as much as we could. There would be nothing to take home, since nothing was written down and everything was passed on verbally and must be memorized. I didn't see Jonathan the entire evening. However, the other men had their sponsors with them standing up for them as they were given the oath.

After all that had happened the last couple of weeks I simply wanted to get away for a quiet, relaxing weekend. I thought about renting a boat and taking it out on Chesapeake Bay. I decided I would wait until morning to decide. I walked home and went to bed.

Finding a Mole

The next morning I turned on the news only to discover that the breaking story of the day was that ex-Vice President Dick Cheney had died from a heart attack in his home in Wyoming. I thought to myself that it wasn't breaking news, at least not to me, since I knew that it was going to happen several weeks ago. But I also tried to think of where Cheney might have gone and whose body he was now occupying. Why did he not like Parker's body? Parker's body was ideal for anyone, so why was there a problem? I thought that in order for me to expose this program and Cheney, I needed to find him first. I also considered the difficulty of the task, because he was no ordinary guy. Remember, Dick Cheney is the guy who started and ran a "Black Ops" program within the CIA for eight years without any member of Congress, the President, the CIA Director, the Defense Secretary, or the Joint Chiefs of Staff having any knowledge of its existence. Finding a mole like Dick Cheney, if he did not want to be found, was going to be nearly impossible.

I decided to pack it in for the weekend and just stay home. I wanted to do some research on my new job and my new colleagues. I looked up the members of the 111th Congress, Senate Intelligence Committee. There were fifteen members, eight Democrats and seven Republicans. I knew right away the fact that the Democrats held a majority and that Dianne Feinstein, the Chairman, was a thorn in the ex-VP's side. It was my bet that he wanted me as part of the committee, with my background in the military and counter-terrorism, in an attempt to sway votes to the Republican way of thinking—or more precisely, Cheney's way of thinking. Dick Cheney never did anything without a reason. The Senate Intelligence Committee controlled the purse strings for billions if not trillions of dollars worth of military contracts and secret operations. I thought there was a possibility that Cheney was again involved with Halliburton, the company he was CEO of from 1995 until he started to help with Bush's presidential campaign in 2000. I needed to start working with these fifteen committee members to find out if there was a link between any of them and Cheney. I spent the remainder of the weekend researching each and every committee member to learn about them before we met.

The Senate Intelligence Committee, it turned out, had a meeting on Monday and I was the last item on the agenda before lunch. I was to be introduced in front of the entire group as a research assistant and analyst, at the disposal of all committee members and their staff. Apparently the committee was working on a high-priority project, which needed to be completed as soon as possible. I was assigned an office next to the committee's vice chairman, Christopher Bond, and told that if I had any questions to contact him or his staff. The day was overwhelming. Only a few short weeks ago I was on a pristine beach on the west coast with no one around. Now, I was in the middle of Washington, DC on a committee involved in some secret operation, which in some way I was going to be a part of. I contacted Bond's lead staffer and asked what the primary order of business was for the committee. He told me, "The committee needs to make a decision within the next month on role of the US military in Afghanistan."

"How that can that be? We have thousands of troops dedicated to the mission in Afghanistan."

"Yes, but the President and China are working on a deal to determine who controls the lithium mining operations in Afghanistan."

"Lithium mining operations—what are you talking about? What happened to destroying Al Qaeda and their terrorist networks to combat terrorism and implement democracy in Afghanistan?"

"Afghanistan is not about Al Qaeda and terrorism anymore. Afghanistan sits on the largest lithium reserves in the world—lithium, which is what is found in computer and electric car batteries. If the United States is to gain more energy independence it needs lithium, and Afghanistan is the Saudi Arabia of lithium. The United States does not want to be without such a valuable commodity. Why do you think we are over there? It is like what Dick Cheney once said, 'The good Lord didn't see fit to put oil and gas only where there are democratic regimes friendly to the United States.' Well, the same is true for lithium. The US needs that lithium and China wants it, too. The Senate Intelligence Committee is trying gain the rights to the lithium, since we are the ones over there fighting for a more democratically friendly Afghanistan. The Chinese want to come in and mine it, but they do not want to be involved in the security to get it out. They want the Afghans to be in control of the government so they can manipulate them for the lithium."

I concluded our conversation by saying, "Thanks a lot for the information. I will get started on learning more about the situation."

"Senator Bond's staff will help you with anything you need." He replied, "Welcome aboard."

I was a little bit in shock over what I had just heard, although the continued war in Afghanistan beyond that of destroying Al Qaeda and their training camps was beginning to all make sense. It also made sense why the USSR wanted Afghanistan. The US wanted control of the valuable minerals; I should have guessed that before.

The next morning when I arrived at work I wanted to contact as many of the Senators on the committee as I could to get an understanding of their position regarding Afghanistan. It was a hunch that all the Republicans were in favor of the US retaining control of Afghanistan, so I wanted to start with the Democrat Senators. After contacting the Democrat Senators on the committee, I discovered that all of them, except one who was out of the country, were against the SIC bill that allowed the United States to maintain sole control of Afghanistan's mineral rights after a democratic government was installed. Most of the Democratic Senators voiced concern that Senator Whitehouse (Rhode Island) had been out of the country, meeting with Afghan and Chinese leaders, for longer than expected and his return was overdue. The Senators stated that no vote could take place until that his return and that he was staunchly against the United States maintaining a presence in Afghanistan. Moreover, when he returned to vote on the bill it would be defeated, giving China access to Afghanistan's mineral wealth.

After work that night I needed time to think about all I had learned. It seemed to me that Afghanistan was Iraq all over again. Iraq was about oil and Afghanistan was about lithium. The bill in the SIC committee seemed to be deadlocked unless someone could be persuaded to change his or her vote. I felt like I was assigned this job for a purpose, but I did not really know what that was yet. Maybe what Cheney had in mind for me to get one of the other Democratic Senators to change his or her mind and vote for the bill. I thought about how amazing it was that so much went on behind the scenes in Washington, DC. I laughed at the thought that it was likely that none of these Senators had any idea CD existed and that this was their committee which was supposed to maintain oversight over all intelligence projects and expenditures. I wanted to meet with Senator Whitehouse when he returned from his trip.

I was sitting at my table, drinking my Pilsner and eating my French dip sandwich back at my favorite bar, Martin's Tavern, when someone approached my table. I noticed the pants first, as I had my head down to take a bite out of my sandwich.

"Hi again, Adam. How was your first meeting the other night?"

I looked up and saw Jonathan, my Mason sponsor. I responded, "Oh, I see you are still following me around."

"No, no, I thought I might find you here. You are kind of predictable. I wanted to apologize for not making it the other night and to see how things went."

"Fine, I guess. I am not sure what I was supposed to think."

"Well, you could have got up and left before you took the oath of the order."

"Yes, I suppose I could have. But it seems the Mason creed is about helping others and promoting a healthy society, and I can't find much fault with that. Besides, it can't hurt to be part of such a renowned organization, especially in this town," I said, while I finished chewing my sandwich. "What else can I do for you tonight?"

"I was told to tell you, from the highest degrees within our order, that there they are watching your progress and that they want you to know that people are rewarded when they do things for the common good of the order."

I paused for a second, trying to understand what he was talking about, then said, "Okay, what does that mean? Obviously, I am being watched. What do they want me to do?"

"Adam, we are here to help all new pledges and members, not just you. It is our responsibility to help and guide, just like parents guide their children to be productive members of society. I am sure you will recognize your purpose when it is revealed, that's all. And we are here if you have a question or need guidance."

"I will remember that, thanks. I have had a long day today, I need to get home and get some rest. I am sure tomorrow with be another long day."

"Yes, I am sure it will be and I hope you take on the challenges tomorrow brings."

I quickly responded, while I turned away from him and started to eat more of my sandwich, "God, do all of you talk like Shakespeare with riddles and codes? Never mind. Don't answer that, goodnight."

Jonathan walked away and said, "Goodnight, Adam," as he disappeared behind a crowd of people in the bar.

The next morning as I was getting ready to go to work, I got a call from AC Dexter's secretary at CD. She told me that the AC wanted to see me at 9am and that it was important. After I hung up, I wondered what the hell was going on. I felt like I had on a choke collar and every time someone wanted something, all they had to do was yank it and I would do whatever they wanted. I got the impression that that was the way things worked in Washington, that everyone had a collar on, and that there are different people holding on to the leashes. I was happy I never had to work in this town.

I arrived a few minutes before nine at the AC's office. The secretary knocked on his door and escorted me in. I saw Dexter sitting behind his desk and another guy sitting in front of his desk whom I recognized from pictures to be Senator Sheldon Whitehouse. Neither got out of his chair. Dexter spoke first. "Adam, this is...."

"Yes, I know. Senator Whitehouse from Rhode Island—nice to meet you." I extended my hand to shake his.

"Very good," Senator Whitehouse said. "I knew I would be impressed with you, Adam." He acted like he already knew me. The Senator turned back to Dexter and smiled.

Dexter spoke again. "Adam, we want to offer you a very special assignment, one which will change your stature in this community and among your brethren forever. Do you want to hear about it?"

"Sir, if you are offering an assignment then I am sure you have the utmost confidence I can fulfill the mission, otherwise you would not be asking."

"Quite true, Adam, but this is a bit different because it is one which will require you be brought deeper into CD's organization. You were there from the beginning and have a lot of experience, so we wanted to offer it to you first," Dexter said.

Senator Whitehouse spoke. "Adam, I had a good feeling about you when I first met you. I know from reading about you that you can handle this with perfection."

"First met me—Sir, have we met before?"

"Yes, we met at my home in Wyoming a few short weeks ago,"

the Senator replied. I felt like I had just been hit by a blast of arctic air which froze me in place; I could not talk for a moment. Then he spoke again. "Adam, I appreciate all the work you did getting me Parker, but a situation came up which needs our immediate attention." I was stunned and couldn't believe it. I looked directly at him and saw Dick Cheney behind the Senator from Rhode Island's eyes. Cheney had Senator Whitehouse killed, and I had a good idea why and continued to listen. Cheney in Whitehouse spoke, "Adam, the bill in the SIC is monumental to the national security of the United States. It will ensure the prosperity of this country for years to come; otherwise we will be at the mercy of those who hate us and control all the energy resources in the world. I cannot let that happen. We need you to exchange with the Senator from Indiana, Evan Bayh. I understand that you have been doing your homework by learning about all the Senators on the committee. With you and me on the committee we will have the necessary votes to pass the bill. Once the bill is passed and recognized by the global community, we'll be able move on with our next lives."

I sat down at this point, next to Senator Whitehouse's body. I then asked, "After that, what happens?"

Dexter spoke, "That is up to you Adam. Whatever you want. If you want to be returned to Adam's body, we can put it on ice for you until you return, or we can find you someone else. Your choice."

"What are we going to say about Senator Bayh?"

Cheney looked at me. "Adam, that is being handled. You do not need to concern yourself with that aspect."

I sat back in my chair for a moment and then flashed back to last night when Jonathan came to my table at the bar. Son-of-a-bitch, Jonathan already knew about this. It's what he was referring to when he said something about taking on the challenges tomorrow brings. This whole thing is so big, so powerful—what was I supposed to do? I had no choice. They really were not asking me to do this. I did it or

I was dead, period. I looked over to Dexter and Cheney. "Of course I will take the assignment. It is the right thing to do for our country."

Both men looked back at me and at the same time said, "Adam, you are good man."

AC Dexter then spoke, "Adam, here is a dossier on Senator Bayh. Go home and prepare as much as possible and come back tonight at midnight and we will make the exchange." As I stood up and began to leave, the AC spoke again. "Do you want us to keep Adam or would you prefer to change?"

"I would prefer to keep Adam, I was just getting used to him," I replied with a grin to both men, as if I was part of their little brotherhood now. They both laughed and I said, "Thank you for this assignment. I won't let you down."

"I am sure you won't," they both said at the same time.

I walked out of AC Dexter's office, and when I was in the hallway out of everyone's view I shook my head in total disbelief. I wondered how I was going to pull it off. How was I going to stay alive to expose this massive conspiracy? It was too big, I thought. My heart was racing so fast I thought it was going to jump out of my chest. I had to stop for a second and recall my pilot training, that when things really got hairy in combat you had to calm yourself and act with precision, with purpose, slowly and methodically. This was one of those times that separates a mediocre type from an expert. I had to be the expert. I could do this.

Becoming a Senator

I came back at midnight, and for the first time in my exchange process I voluntarily laid down. I do not know how they got him here and maybe did not want to know, but Senator Bayh was lying on a gurney near mine. The exchange took nearly twenty-four hours. I woke up in much the same way I always had: I thought or felt like I was still Frank. But this time, I had aches in my joints and did not feel as energetic as I had in past exchanges. I thought for a second. Of course—Senator Bayh was not nineteen, but rather fifty-five years old. I spent much of the next day getting used to my new body. There was a bit of an acclimation period; I could not move as fast and my thinking was clouded. It was almost like waking up from a hangover. I also spent time reviewing Bayh's case file. It was much more of a challenge to learn about someone as complex as fifty-five-year-old United States Senator, as opposed to a nineteen or twenty-year-old who had little life history and all ties to the past severed. I had to attempt to fool not only a wife, but the Senator's staff and his children!

CD had set up a plan to have Bayh taken from his office. They called his wife and told her the Senator would be working away from home for a few nights on a special project. She was used to such calls. The Senator's staff was told the same thing and further that the project was secret and that they could not disclose the location or any other information about the project. It is amazing how easy it was to cover the kidnapping of a US Senator. CD was familiar with covert operations and understood the difficulties I was up against. Dexter and Cheney decided that when I returned to work, I would pretend to have laryngitis. In this way, I would not be expected to respond to questions I did not know the answers to. I had only about a week before the vote on the bill took place. Hopefully, I would not have to put up with this charade for long.

I was very concerned and upset about what they had done or intended to do with Senator Bayh's body when I finished with this operation. I wanted to ask the AC Dexter, so I called him to have a few questions answered. I was thinking I might be able to use my time as Senator Bayh as a lynchpin on stopping the CD exchange program. The AC answered the phone when I called his private office number. "Hello?" he said.

"Chief, this is Evan Bayh." There was a pause.

"Yes, Senator," he said with a chuckle. "I did not recognize your voice at first, but now I do. What can I do for you?"

"Are we on a secure line?"

"Yes, of course, it is always secure," he replied. "What do you prefer I call you? It must be confusing. I want to call you Frank, since that is what I have always known you as."

I said, "No, I prefer to be called by my name. Who I am, Senator Bayh. It keeps things less complicated and straight in my head."

"Of course, I understand. What can I do for you?"

"I would like to know what is going to happen with the Senator after the mission is complete. It will help me develop my covert scenario with his wife, children, and staff. I do not want to say or do something that could in some way jeopardize the exit strategy of mission."

Dexter paused for a moment, then said, "Very good, I understand. The Senator is going to be involved in a car accident on his way back to Washington, and he is going to sustain a head injury with a resultant concussion and amnesia. Don't worry: we are not going to terminate him. We are going to put him back in his body, but simply erase the past few weeks so he won't remember a thing."

"We can do that now?" I interjected.

"Yes, we have been making a lot of new discoveries. But as far as the Senator is concerned, he is on his way out of Washington. He did not seek re-election, so no one really gives a shit about him after this vote. We are going to remove his utility hardware after we are done with him."

"I see. Good, that gives me a clear picture now on how to handle the situation with his family and staff. Thank you." I replied hesitantly, as I was thinking about what he had told me. "I appreciate your time, Chief," I said and ended the conversation.

AC Dexter replied, "No problem. Call any time. I am always available to help a Senator."

After that he hung up the phone. I thought for a moment and again realized just how much power a few men had. They could make a Senator vanish, erase his memory, put him back in his life—and he would not even realize what had happened to him. Well, maybe I could change all that. Maybe I could help him remember and fill in the blanks.

The vote on the SIC bill was scheduled to take place in four days, which should give me enough time to think about how to use the Senator's position to help shut down CD and the Exchange program. I was very nervous about going to the office for the first time. I normally have handlers run interference for me with details to help make things work smoothly. But on this mission I had limited resources, because only a select few were allowed to know about the exchange. I had the AC call ahead and contact the Senator's top aide to inform him about my laryngitis so I wouldn't be doing any talking. I told my aide to leave me alone in my office and hold all calls. I also had Senator Whitehouse to help me find my way around and possibly help me out of any predicament I could get into. I texted ahead and had my aide meet me in the parking lot and escort me to my office. I did not want to have to try to answer any questions. I would let my aide do all the talking.

There was not a lot to do around the office, as most of the staff was in the process of moving to a temporary office in the basement. This was to be Senator Bayh's last few days in office, as he decided at the last minute, right before the primary election, not to seek re-election. He bewildered a lot of people by making a monumental decision without consulting others or his party.

At one point my top aide, Phillip, came in to my office. He said, "Don't forget to clean out your office safe, Senator Bayh, and leave it empty for the incoming freshman Senator."

I replied, "Phillip, could you empty it for me and bring me the contents, then leave it open? I also would like to leave a gift in there for incoming Senator." I wondered before I asked him if he had the combination because I surely did not. He did not bat an eye. He immediately went to the safe, opened it, and brought me the contents. They appeared to all be documents from the completed Senate bills the Senator had helped to pass and was holding onto copies as keepsakes, nothing secret. Then I noticed an envelope wrapped with a red, white, and blue ribbon tied in a bow. I saw it had already been opened and appeared old, as it was a bit yellowed. I unwrapped the bow and pulled out a single sheet of 8 ½ by 11 paper, tri-folded. I read the letter, which was written by Senator Nelson W. Aldrich of New York in 1911. In it he congratulated the incoming Senators on their Congressional victory and spoke of the ritual of writing a letter to the incoming person to occupy the office. The letter read:

DEAR SENATOR,

TO WHOMEVER IS ENTRUSTED WITH THIS OFFICE AND THIS LETTER, I CONGRATULATE YOU. YOU ARE A BUILDING BLOCK IN THE HISTORY OF THIS GREAT NATION. YOUR DUTY IS TO RISE ABOVE THE CORRUPTION AND VANITY OF YOUR SINGULAR BEING AND REPRESENT THE PEOPLE OF THIS NATION, AS YOU WOULD WANT TO BE REPRESENTED. NEVER FORGET WHO PLACED YOU HERE. THEY ARE THE VOICES THAT CRY OUT FOR YOU TO SPEAK ON THEIR BEHALF. YOU ARE NOT HERE FOR YOU, BUT FOR THEM. THE ANSWERS YOU SEEK ARE IN THE TRUTH. GOOD LUCK.

Amazingly, the letter was signed in succession by all the Senators from the past one hundred years to occupy this office. I also noticed a symbol at the bottom left-hand corner of the letter. It was similar to the tattoo I had received after my first exchange, but without the letters CD. I thought it was strange, as Crystal Discovery obviously has not been around for one hundred years. I wondered about the origin of the symbol. I thought that this letter was only supposed to be in the hands of a Senator. What if I kept it until after Senator Bayh was returned to his own body and I exposed CD? Senator Bayh would have to realize I had been in his body and in his office going through the things from his safe. There are only a few people with access to the letter, but none would have recognized the value it had to me. I placed it in my jacket pocket.

I was reminded by my staff that there was a meeting at 2pm with the SIC to discuss final aspects of the bill before the vote in two days. I advised Phillip, by writing on a piece of paper, that I wanted him to escort me to the meeting and that I did not want to talk with anyone along the way.

He replied, "Of course, Senator. We can take the secured route to the meeting room."

I was anxious about being detected once I was in the meeting, since all these men knew Bayh quite well. I was afraid they would ask something that would throw up red flags. Philip came and got me at 1:30pm. I thought it would be a bit strange to get there a half-hour early. We left my office and went to an elevator, which needed a bio-identification of my right-hand to operate. Fortunately, the elevator's computer told me when to put my hand on the device. Otherwise, I would have stood there and looked stupid, like I had never done it before. I assumed we would take the elevator up to some floor inside Congress to a meeting room. Instead, we took the elevator down for seemed like a long time. Once we stopped, we exited into a parking garage and got into an awaiting limousine which took us down a two-lane tunnel. We traveled in the tunnel for a couple of miles, before it opened up into another large parking garage. We again entered an elevator, which took us up to the third floor. I looked around when we got out of the elevator and noticed there were a lot of military personnel around. Phillip escorted me to the meeting room and we went inside. I immediately saw Senator Dick Cheney Whitehouse sitting at the large table.

Senator Whitehouse got up when he saw me and came over to shake my hand. He said, "Hi Evan, I understand you have laryngitis. Sorry about that. Let me help you to your seat. I will act as your voice during the meeting, if that is okay with you?"

I let out a low groan as if to indicate a yes. I looked out the window and noticed we were on the other side of the Potomac River from Congress. It seemed we were in Arlington, Virginia.

Cheney saw me looking out the window and said, "How was your ride over to the Pentagon, Evan? Okay, I hope?"

I looked back at him and nodded, with a smile. I was amazed for a time, thinking about how much the people of this country did not know about the internal workings and capabilities of their own government. I thought I knew a lot, but I did not know there was a secret underground road from the Senate to the Pentagon. It looked as if there was an entire city under Washington, DC, the Potomac, and Arlington. The other members of the SIC arrived and the door closed. The Chairman, Dianne Feinstein, brought the meeting to order and said there were only two orders of business. The first was the bill regarding Chinese access to Afghanistan. The second was a covert operation spooling up in Egypt, about which the CIA was not being cooperative. The SIC had oversight authority on all intelligence community covert operations. Thus, they had a Congressional duty and authority to know what was going on. The chairman asked for volunteers for a group to investigate the Egyptian action, for which I did not volunteer; I watched Cheney remain quiet. In addition, Feinstein asked for discussion on the Chinese connection to Afghanistan and whether there was anything that needed to be done prior to the vote. Cheney-Whitehouse made a motion for the vote to be closed instead of an open ballot. He argued it would be in the best interest of future political compromise, within this group and in open Congress, not to know how each Senator voted on this bill. The other Senators quickly agreed and the motion passed. Cheney-Whitehouse was smart to ask for this. In that way, no one could be sure how each of us voted and who had changed their votes. The meeting was then adjourned.

I stood up and Senator Cheney-Whitehouse came over and shook my hand. "Good to see you again, Evan. I am sure you want to head home to see your beautiful wife now!"

I smiled and nodded a yes while I looked directly at him. He seemed to take this all in stride, like it was something he did every day and was very calm and cool with it.

He said, "Evan, why don't you let me give you a ride home? It is right on the way for me."

Again, I nodded. I also gave him a thumbs-up. I was glad I did not have to play charades anymore with Bayh's aide or with anyone else I might bump into.

When we got into the limo for the ride to my house, Cheney-Whitehouse said, "Good job back there, Adam. This will all be over soon and you will be back in a more comfortable environment—your old clothes, if you will." Then he made a couple of telephone calls on the ride back, which I was happy about. I was not in the mood to chit-chat. We arrived at Senator Bayh's home and I got out.

Cheney-Whitehouse said, "Why don't you take the day off tomorrow and I will pick you up at 8am, on the day after tomorrow. We will go vote and be done with this."

I replied, "That sounds great. The less contact with everyone, the better. But it will be a hard sell for a day or so with Evan's wife, Susan."

Cheney said, "Good luck with that. I'm sure you will do fine. Susan is a beautiful woman." Then he drove off.

I used my key to open the front door and let myself in, to my house, which I had never been in before. I hung my coat up in a hall closet and began to give myself a tour. I said out loud, "I'm home."

Susan called out from somewhere in the house, "I'm in the kitchen."

Now all I had to do was find the kitchen. I kept putting myself in these awkward situations, in which I was at a complete loss of awareness of my surroundings. When I finally found the kitchen Susan was busy cooking, so she did not seem to notice me. I walked in and said with a raspy voice, "Hi, how are you doing?"

"Great. I feel a bit like a stranger, we haven't seen each other in a while."

"I definitely know what you mean. My mind has been elsewhere lately."

Susan continued talking as she came over and puckered her lips in front of me, waiting for me to kiss her. "I thought I would fix us some dinner, since I have to leave for Indiana tomorrow for a board meeting. I will be gone several days." Susan was an attractive, blond-haired woman in her forties, about five-feet-six, very well-educated and with a busy career as a board member of a large company back in Indianapolis. I returned her kiss with a quick peck on the lips.

"I'm working from home tomorrow. I have a bit of laryngitis and don't want to make it worse by talking a lot at the office."

"I know. I talked with your staff today, and they said you couldn't talk. I was concerned about you."

"No worries, I'm fine. I just didn't want to strain my voice anymore. Thanks for cooking dinner."

"Do you want to pour the wine? White or red tonight?"

"Red is my mood."

"Great, I bought a nice Syrah recently."

"Tonight I want something with a little strength to it, some complexity, some variation in flavor. You like complexity, don't you?"

"Of course I do. You know reds are my favorite."

I poured us both a glass of wine and held my glass up to hers, after I had handed it to her, and said, "Cheers. To our next adventure."

"Cheers. Do you have some big adventure for us? Something you are not sharing? A vacation in the Caribbean perhaps?"

"Not exactly, but I do need to talk with you about something," I said as I turned away to take a seat at the dining room table.

"Okay. I hope it's nothing too dramatic. Life has been too complicated lately, although I talked with the boys today and they are doing fine."

"Good, glad to hear that," I said with a deadpan tone.

Susan stopped working on dinner and turned to me, "Okay, now you are beginning to worry me. You seem like something is bothering you. Are you okay?"

I took a sip of wine and put the glass down while I examined the wine's dark purple color. I then replied, "I like tasting wine, because no matter what variety you choose, you may think you know what it is going to taste like, but every winery and every year is different. It's almost like the bottle is wearing a mask, until you really taste it and let it reveal itself in your mouth for awhile."

"What is up with you? Are you taking medication? Since when are you a wine connoisseur?"

"I am just being a bit contemplative. I never stop being amazed at the complexity of life at times. Let me help you put the food on the table." We carried out a great baked salmon, with roast potatoes and broccoli.

"It's nice to be together," Susan said warmly as she looked directly into my eyes.

"Let's enjoy the dinner and talk after. Dig in." After we finished, I sat back and drank another sip of wine. Then I began, "Would you agree life that is not always as it appears?"

She nodded.

I continued, "You know there are many secrets from work which I cannot share with you?"

She again nodded and quietly responded, "Yes."

"Well, I am about to share something with you which could put your life, and my life, in danger," I said. "Susan, what I am about to tell you is something you can share with no one, and you'll have to pretend I never told you until the time is appropriate. For the last several years, the government has been working cooperatively on a secret project dealing with the transfer of one person's mind into another person's body. They have developed the technology to completely download and store an individual's identity on a computer hard drive. They can also take that identity and upload it into any other person they desire, after completely erasing that person's mind, which is similar to erasing a computer's hard drive and reinstalling a different version on it."

"Why are you telling me this if it is secret?" Susan responded. "You have never done that before. What are you talking about—erasing people's memories and putting someone else's memories in their place?"

"Yes, that is exactly what I am talking about: the mind of one person exchanged into the body of another person."

"What happens to the person whose mind was erased?" Susan asked more intently.

"Well, that depends. It could be saved and reinstalled at a later time, or it could be deleted and that person would never exist again, essentially being killed."

Susan paused for a moment, looked directly at me, and said, "Okay, and what is our government doing with this technology? Who is exploiting this technology for personal or political gain?"

"It's interesting that you should make that quantum leap, which I guess in today's world is not such a leap," I said. "There is going to be a vote the day after tomorrow in the Senate Intelligence Committee, and it was not going in the direction some would have liked so some people decided to use this technology to alter the outcome."

Susan replied with her voice cracking, "Are you saying that some-one has been exchanged into the committee, to vote in favor of one side or the other?"

"Yes, that is exactly what I am saying," I stated emphatically.

Susan stared at me for a moment, "Who did they exchange?"

I looked directly at her and said, "Me." I watched and waited to see how she was going to react. I saw her hands begin to visibly shake. She tried to drink a sip of wine, but only lifted the glass about half way to her mouth and stopped, then put it back on the table.

"Who are you?"

"That is a very complicated story, Mrs. Bayh. What I can tell you is that I am not your husband. I may look like your husband, but I am not. It may seem impossible, but technology has come a long way in our lifetime and corruption's evil shadow is right there with it. Your husband is not the first person I have exchanged with; there have been others. But this exchange with your husband is an attempt to tear apart the fibers of our government as we know it. You thought I was Evan. What scares me is the thought that there could be many others like me out there. I do not have the answer to that, because I am not privy to that information. Your husband's seat on the Senate Intelligence Committee is the reason I am here. He was going to vote against a key bill, which could be worth billions and billions of dollars to the United States and to companies in the US. There are those in private enterprise and in this government who do not want to see this bill fail and who will go to any lengths to ensure its passage, including murder."

"C'mon Evan what is this all about? Is this a joke?"

"No, Susan. This is not a joke. It is real, it is happening. And I need your help."

"How do I know you are telling the truth."

"I know you are aware the government runs many secret operations that your husband is privy to, but he could never share with you. Well, I'm sure you can think for a moment and realize there is truth to what I am saying. If you give me a chance I can explain more and we can go from there."

"Okay, go ahead," Susan said slowly.

"My name originally was Frank Freiberg. I was an Air Force Captain and my body was killed in Afghanistan. A secret program within the government called 'Operation Crystal Discovery' was able to save my identity by storing all of my brain's memory before I died. Afterward, they were able to restore my identity in another person's body, that of a military volunteer, someone who was misled about what was going to happen to him. What I thought was a good thing, by being saved from death, has evolved into a confusing web of deception, corruption, and murder. I do not want to be a part of this corruption any longer, but I feel like I am trapped in a cage with an enormous beast and I really do not know how big this beast is. I cannot see all of it or to what level of this administration it reaches. For now, to get Evan back in his own body I have to play along and finish this mission—otherwise he dies. I need your help. I do not want you to do anything, except live your life. Unfortunately, you must live it with this knowledge. When I have all the chess pieces in place, then and only then can I try to bring down this beast and have it exposed. The public needs to know what has been happening."

"You must think I am out of my mind. But you know your husband and he would not be talking like this or saying crazy things. I am also a husband, and I have a family of my own, a wife and two children, who live outside of Fort Wayne, Indiana. In two days, you're going to be told your husband was involved in a car accident and suffered amnesia as a result," I explained.

"Where is Evan right now?"

"Let me explain as best I can, Susan. The husband you know, who has lived fifty-five years with all his experiences, knowledge, memories, and identity, is stored in a computer behind the veil of a secret program. And behind that veil, there are only a few people who know of the computer's existence. The other part of what you know as your husband, his body, is right here in front of you. But that is not the part you want, the part you fell in love with and have been married to for so many years. I want to help you get both parts back together. When your husband returns I want you to tell him what I have told you. The police will tell you he hit his head in the accident and received a cut and some bruises to the brain."

I went over to Susan, turned my head and bent my left ear forward to expose a fresh cut near the hairline with stitches. "This is the cut they will tell you he received in the accident. However, this is where they attached the device to be able to download your husband's memory. Also, tell him I took something from his office safe which is about one hundred years old. Evan is a smart man; he will realize he did not really change his vote on the latest SIC bill or get amnesia and that something is very wrong. He was right about the government when he decided to not seek re-election: it has gotten out of control, it is ineffective, and it has become a repository for so many with only their self-interests in mind. But America needs more people like Evan to fight for the true rights and freedoms of its people."

She sat back in her chair, now able to raise her glass of wine to her mouth and sip. She said, "Not your typical quiet dinner conversation. This is impossible to believe on the one hand, and in an insane way plausible on another. I do not know what you want me to do. It sounds like you do not want me to do anything, except tell Evan he had an out-of-body experience to some extent. I do not know if he will believe me."

"Susan, trust me. Evan has been in the government and has been involved in secret programs for a long time. He knows of the capabilities of some people and to what lengths they will go. I will contact you in the future and we will, together, stop this cancer in our society from growing anymore."

"How will I know it is you—really you? What will you look like?"

"Good question, because I am not really sure who I will be. Where is the most exotic place you have ever traveled?"

Susan thought for a moment, then replied, "Madagascar. Evan and I went there on vacation once; it was beautiful, tropical, and exotic. Why?"

"Because we need to have a code word so you know it is indeed me you are talking to. Did you do anything extraordinary while in Madagascar?"

Susan stared off for a second and said, "I did fall in love with this endangered Lemur called an Indri. The Indri sings almost like a humpback whale."

"Okay, then when I contact you again I will use the word Indri in a sentence and you will know it is me. So tomorrow you will go see your children and stay in Indiana for a few days like nothing is unusual. The police will contact you to tell you that Evan has been in a car accident. At that point, Evan will be safely returned to his body and you can come see him. We'd better get some sleep now."

I got up the next morning after Susan had already left for the airport. All I wanted to do that day was simply stay in and not venture out to cause any problems. I wondered how PJ and my family were doing. I missed them all very much.

I used Bayh's home computer to post an ad on Craigslist in the Los Angeles personals. The headline read, "Exotic bald man seeks strong swimmer type." I put a short note with it, which read, "Would like to meet someone for long-term relationship. I know you are out there somewhere and I hope you are doing well. I cannot wait until our paths cross and we never have to leave the warmth of each other's embrace. I will be thinking of you until that time."

I wondered when her ship would be in port or when she would have access to a computer. I would have to wait to hear from her. I also wanted to write an email to Miriam, but did not want to risk too much in case it was intercepted. I did not want them to know I revealed everything that has happened to me. If the wrong people found out, her life could be in danger. I just wanted to relax for the day. I would not know what was going to happen to me until after the vote. I had to think over all the details, as I felt it was about time to go public and tell the world what had been going on.

The next day, precisely at 8am, a limo pulled up out front and I went to meet it. I opened the door and saw Cheney-Whitehouse sitting inside and he said, "Good morning, Senator Bayh, how are you today?"

"I am great, but I wish I were young again. I have too many aches and pains in the morning at this age."

Senator Cheney-Whitehouse laughed. "I completely agree with you, Adam, it is much nicer being young and full of energy with no pains to wake up to. How was your visit with Mrs. Bayh?"

"It was nice. She prepared a pleasant dinner for my homecoming, then she headed back to Indiana yesterday. So I did not have to answer a lot of questions and feel awkward about answering them."

"Good, good," Senator Whitehouse replied. "We should be finished by noon, and then I will escort you directly back to CD, where you can immediately start your exchange back to Adam. We need to get Senator Bayh back in his body to not draw any attention to him."

"That would be great. I will be happy to get back to normal."

Again, Senator Whitehouse chuckled and said, "Normal, what is normal for you? I bet you must feel strange as to what normal is anymore."

"True, but that is why I want to go back to Adam and try to live a normal life."

Senator Whitehouse looked away and replied, "I can understand that. It will be over soon."

We arrived at the Senate and were escorted by our staff from the front door right to the same meeting room we had been in a few days earlier. When we arrived, everyone else was already seated and waiting for us. We took our seats and Chairman Feinstein brought the meeting to order, "Gentlemen, we have had a lot of time to think about this. Let's get right to the vote so we can continue with other business." A staff member handed out vote cards to all of us. We wrote our vote down and passed them back to the chairman. The staff member opened the vote cards and read each one out loud. The SIC bill passed, by one vote. The Democratic members looked at each other in disbelief. The meeting was adjourned and we all left. Senator Whitehouse stood up, shook my hand and said, "Well done. Now this country can get on with the real order of business. Senator, let's get you back to where you belong."

Senator Whitehouse and I rode in the limo out to CD. He spent most of the time on the phone talking to people about the bill's passage. I quietly looked out the window and admired Virginia's beautiful rolling hills. When we arrived I was immediately taken into the exchange facility to begin my return to Adam.

Egyptian Mission

I woke up with the distinct hangover-type feeling which typically accompanied each exchange. A headache, weakness, slight dizziness—things were hazy and I could not think very quickly and everything was slow to make sense. As soon as I was oriented enough, I was anxious to go to the bathroom and see myself; it was a weird notion since I understood who I was supposed to be, but given what had happened to me I wanted to confirm who I was. I wanted to be back with Adam, because I had gained a certain comfort level with him. Indeed, when I looked, it was Adam I saw in the mirror. I smiled at myself and said, "Welcome back, I missed you." I stayed at CD for most of the day to make sure I did not have any medical issues and that it was safe to drive. AC Dexter came by to see me before I left.

"Adam, I was very pleased with the way you handled this mission. Great work. Take next week off to relax and rejuvenate. Do you have any preferences for your next assignment?"

"If you don't mind, let me think about it for a couple of days and I will get back with you. But I am thinking about an intelligence analyst position in some warm country."

Dexter chuckled and smiled. "I understand. I will see what I can do. Enjoy your time off."

I went back to my place in Georgetown and enjoyed a good night's rest. The next morning I walked to the Starbucks just down the street for a mocha and a bagel, and to read the newspaper. The front page of the *Washington Post* had a picture of a car mangled into a tree, with the headline, "Indiana Senator Recovers from Head Injury." I felt like my life was playing out like some sort of espionage novel. I thought of when I used to be a pilot. It was all I had ever wanted to be—a pilot and a father. It seemed I couldn't be either. I felt lost in a world I did not create, which was out of control, much like *Alice in Wonderland*, and I couldn't find my way back. I did not know whom I could trust to help me expose this labyrinth of corruption, deception, murder, and treason. Who would believe me? I could not believe it myself. Looking at the newspaper, I wondered if the *Washington Post* could be my platform for the news bomb I wanted to drop to take down the organization.

I looked at the article on Bayh and found the reporter's name, Elizabeth Broadwater. I knew I could not directly contact the reporter. There was too much information and it was too sensitive. I would have to do it covertly. At first, I could slowly feed her information she could investigate. I decided to FedEx her a very simple letter including contact procedure.

I thought the letter should say: "Bayh's accident was staged and his last vote was not his own. If you are interested, post a Craigslist ad under the category, 'furniture for sale'. Have the title of the ad read, 'Antique Oak Chest with Cedar Lining." I would then begin to give her all she needed to know to break the news story. I was about to get up and walk back home when I felt a hand on my shoulder.

"Hi Adam, nice to see you again. " I looked up and saw Jonathan. "You mind if I sit down?"

"I am not sure why you find it necessary to approach me this way. There are a lot ways for you to contact me to let me know you would like to meet."

Jonathan smiled for only a moment, then raised his coffee cup to take a sip. "Adam, the lodge would like to begin your training. There are some things you need to learn before we can move forward. Tonight we have arranged a special meeting for you, at 7:30—are you available?" He looked around at the other people sitting around drinking their morning coffee, as though someone could be watching us.

I thought to myself that it wasn't like I had a choice. I was afraid to turn these guys down. I felt like they wanted me for something, like I was being groomed. I replied, "Sure, I am off this week, so tonight would be fine. Will you be there?"

"No, I am not needed for what you will be learning. I will tell them to expect you. Oh, by the way, how is your Arabic? You haven't forgotten it, have you?"

"My Arabic? No, I haven't forgotten, although I have not spoken it in a while. Why do you ask?"

"The brotherhood thought it would be a useful tool to have within our lodge, in view of current world affairs. Also, of course, it would help if we had a pledge who wanted to join who does not speak English. The Masons don't discriminate based on race, you know."

"I know. Only women or those who do not believe in God are excluded, right?"

Jonathan got up, pushed his chair in and said, "See you soon, Adam. I enjoy our little meetings. Have fun with your training."

I felt I was always being watched. It was too easy for this guy to find me—not that I was trying to hide. But it was a bit unnerving, especially at this point, when I had not done anything yet. I would have to be particularly careful once this thing started to unwind to not be discovered. I was thinking about Miriam again and missing her. It had been weird; for a period of time I used to think I would never see her again. I would recall fond memories, but it felt almost as if she had died. It was not until I saw her that my feelings came back to the surface and I started missing her again. But I also thought about PJ. I wondered how she was doing and what she was feeling. I needed to check Craigslist to see if she had posted a reply to my ad. I knew I had strong feelings for her. I liked those feelings and felt almost a need to be near her.

I went to a FedEx Office to send the note off to the *Washington Post* reporter, Elizabeth Broadwater. I wrote down the sender's information as Randy Edwards, my second exchange body, and his family's address in Collierville, TN. I used one of the public computers there to check the Craigslist personals. I did not want the computers to be traced back to me. I was excited and happy to find a posting, "Seeking bald man for LTR."

The posting read, "Need LTR with you. Would like to meet you ASAP. Miss you in my life. I am well and will be available this weekend, in Cabo San Lucas. Will call. What number? Can't wait to see you. Always yours aboard DD."

I replied to the ad, "Glad you are well. Miss you. Things continue to be complicated here. Will meet you Saturday. Can't wait to see you! Mystery Man."

I wanted to visit Miriam and the kids this week as well. I used the computer to call Miriam on Skype. She did not answer her phone. I left a message that I would be there in a few days. I then wrote her a short note to her new email address, cougarinafort@gmail.com. "Hi, all is well. Wish I could be there with all of you. Know that I am thinking of you. More to follow." I signed it, "Love, The chameleon."

At the Mason meeting I was the only student along with the five Masons who were going to be my teachers. I got the impression they were various ranks or degrees as they call them, but they would not say. At one point they told me that there are three degrees of Masons and that the top degree is called a Master Mason. Further, Master Masons have levels from 4 to 33, with each level signifying increased responsibility, knowledge, dedication, and secrecy.

Simon, the leader, introduced the other members who were to be my instructors. Simon was physically the largest of the group, which I found to be interesting. He was probably six foot six, easily two hundred and sixty pounds. He looked like he was a television evangelist, very proper and straight-laced; he was stone-faced. I got the impression he did not trust me. Or possibly he did not like the reason I was there; I wasn't sure which. Maybe he just had a terrible personality or perhaps a bad home life. He introduced the others: Peter, Matthew,

Thomas, and Andrew. I could have sworn I was either at a KKK meeting or one of the first gatherings of our forefathers. There was something subliminal about these guys that just made me uncomfortable. They always watched me, and watched my reaction to their teachings.

My training on the initial night was to focus on the history of Jerusalem and the First Crusade—a strange place to begin, I thought. Andrew began my instruction. I think he was the lowest rank out of the group, which is why he taught the rudimentary lesson. Andrew looked to be of Irish descent, with red hair, blue eyes, small in stature, something like five foot eight or so, one hundred and sixty pounds. He gave me information about King Solomon's Temple, which is believed to be the first temple of Jerusalem. It was built around 960 BC as a temple of worship, but primarily as the sanctuary for the Ark of the Covenant. The Ark of the Covenant, from historical accounts, was the container built for the tablets inscribed with the Ten Commandments, which were given to Moses by God on top of Mount Sinai. To date, no one acknowledges the whereabouts of the Ark of the Covenant. He went on to tell me that King Solomon's temple was destroyed around the middle of the 4th century BC. It was believed that the Ark of the Covenant had been removed by Babylonian invaders before the temple was destroyed.

Matthew got up to teach next. He wore a long black robe that hid a lot of his physical features. I would have guessed him to be five foot ten or so. He had a slight beard. All of these guys, except Simon, appeared to be in their late thirties. Simon, he looked like he was in his late fifties. Matthew must have been Italian, since his arms never stopped moving as he spoke.

Matthew continued the instruction and talked about a second temple, built in the same place as the first, which was subsequently destroyed by the Romans. He said that the Muslims took Jerusalem from the Romans around 637 AD and that the area was holy for Jews, Muslims, and Christians, because of the significance of the temple mount, where the Al Aqsa Mosque, a.k.a. the Dome of the Rock, was built in 691 AD. It is believed by Jews to have been built around the exact rock where Abraham was about to kill his son Isaac before God stopped him. It also is believed by Muslims to be the site where Muhammad ascended into heaven with the angel Gabriel.

Thomas stood up next to begin his lecture. He said that although it was not known for sure, it was believed that the Ark of the Covenant was returned at some point to Jerusalem and placed beneath the Dome of the Rock Mosque, which was the sacred rock. The actual sacred rock is apparently many levels below the top of the structure. Few are permitted admittance to the area. Furthermore, the Ark remained in Jerusalem for centuries, until the time of the First Crusade and the capturing of Jerusalem by the Knight Templars on July 15, 1099. However, there was no evidence that the Knights discovered the Ark after the city's fall. Some believe that the Muslims fled the city with the Ark of the Covenant through a secret tunnel, discovered only recently, beneath the sacred rock. But Muslim faith prevents any further excavation at any location on the temple mount, so there is no way to confirm this theory.

Thomas spoke of a group of Muslims, not unlike what the Knight Templars were for the Christians, called the Brotherhood of Muhammad. He went on to say that they were a group of highly skilled warriors whose duty was to protect the city of Jerusalem and its most valuable antiquities. It was further believed that the Ark of the Covenant was carried out of Jerusalem by the Brotherhood of Muhammad before the final Templar assault, which resulted in the city's takeover.

Peter taught the final lesson for the night. He wore an ornamental cloak, similar to what I have seen priests wear at Sunday masses. It was bright green with gold trimming and had the distinct red cross of the Knights Templar on the back. Peter was a strange character. Maybe he was a priest among the Masons, although I am not sure if they had them. I would characterize him as a cross between the devil's brother and a vampire. He had very pale skin with dark hair. He was a very hairy guy, with long thick locks on his head, long sideburns, and a lot more hair on his forearms and the back of his palms, as well as his fingers. He put me on edge. I was just waiting for him to start flying around the room.

Peter concluded the evening by talking about a place called the Hall of Records. The Hall of Records was believed to have been built at the time of the Great Pyramid, 5000 BC, to house all of the documents of human history up to that time, much like a library. He spoke of evidence, in recent history, of the discovery of the location of the Hall of Records under the right paw of the Sphinx in Giza, Egypt, at the same complex as the pyramids. Most importantly, he said, Masons believed that the Ark of the Covenant had been there at some point and could even still be there. Finally, he said there are supposed to be documents from throughout human history there, even when people lived on the Continent of Atlantis.

"Atlantis?" I asked.

"Yes, Atlantis. There is enough evidence from throughout history to prove the existence of Atlantis. By discovering the location of either one of these great artifacts, we could understand our actual origins."

Simon thanked me for my attention and told me to come back the following night when they would provide me with more instruction. He also emphasized that anything discussed within the walls of this lodge should never be shared with anyone outside the lodge, even with other Masons. The last thing he said was that the Masons and the Templars have survived for hundreds of years based on one premise—loyalty.

I nodded and said, "I completely understand and hold sacred all that you have shared with me. Thank you. Goodnight."

As I was leaving the lodge I noticed a plaque above the door of the room I was in. It had a symbol on it, the same symbol as the tattoo

I had received from CD after my initial exchange, except it did not have the letters CD on it. I asked Peter, who was walking next to me, "What does that symbol mean?"

He said, "It is the square and the compass, the universal sign of Free Masons. It derives from our early days as Stone Masons and the tools they used to construct sacred structures and monuments. It is also a reminder of what we need as individuals to build humanity for the future."

"Interesting," I replied with a smile, and left.

I walked to a local pub to get a bite to eat. After I sat down and was about to drink a beer and eat my food, I saw a news flash on television that Senator Whitehouse had just died of a massive stroke. I felt like I was somehow responsible for his death. I felt more urgency to expose this entire conspiracy before more people died. I thought back on my training as an intelligence operative and realized that I had to be patient. I could not make the final moves until all the pieces were in place. I was sad for Senator Whitehouse's family and what they must be going through. I tried to imagine what my family went through when they were told of my death. I knew I had to do everything possible to protect my family; I did not want them to have to go through anything like that again. I couldn't wait to see them.

The next morning I received a call from AC Dexter at Crystal Discovery. He told me, "Senator Bayh is out here and wants a tour of the facility. Do you know anything about this? Why would he want that?"

"I have no idea, Sir. That is very strange. What does he want?"

"He wants to see all the documents for the projects we are working on."

"That is bizarre. Why would he all of a sudden want to do that? Do you think he remembers anything from the exchange? Could he have seen anything while he was being taken out of there?"

"Bayh said he received information that his traffic accident had been staged, that he never hit his head, and that his mind had been altered. I told him I did not believe such a thing was possible, that the police had investigated his accident, and that he had taken a severe hit on the head. I also explained to him that the doctors reported he had amnesia from his head trauma and that it would probably be temporary and that his memory of the past couple of days would probably come back to him very soon. But I don't think he was buying it. I'm not sure why he would correlate anything to CD, do you? I don't think it is possible he could have remembered the exchange. He was unconscious when he was taken out of here. You know what it is like after an exchange—it takes time to regain all your thought processes, right? I can't imagine how he would remember anything or why he would come here. He was asking if we have any black ops programs that deal with mind control. I told him that all of our projects are registered with the SIC and that he was already aware of all our programs."

"What do you want me to do?"

"I'm not sure; I will be in touch. We do not want any link between Bayh and CD. Thanks for your help," the AC answered and then hung up.

I was a bit stunned Bayh would do something so blatant. I called Phillip, an intern at Bayh's office, to find out why Bayh would go to CD. Apparently, earlier in the day Senator Bayh had made several phone calls to fellow Democratic SIC members, advising them of his belief that there was a conspiracy to sway his vote and that he may have been drugged or had his mind altered.

Phillip said, "I could tell he was upset with himself. I thought he might still be suffering from the bump on his head from his traffic accident. Or he was trying to cover up a deal he had made with someone for his vote on the SIC bill. He was very upset."

I didn't know what to think. I thought I had made it clear to Susan that his life would be in danger if he tried to expose anything before I told her the time was right. Why would he go out there? What did he expect to find? This was not good.

To distract myself, I began to pack my clothes for the trip to Indiana and Cabo San Lucas. My mind drifted to what it would be like to lie on the warm beach in the sun with PJ. I began to get more excited about seeing her and getting out of this snake pit. I thought it would be nice to take all of my family—Miriam, and the kids—and get PJ from Cabo, and then travel somewhere remote and never come back. We could be one big happy family. I also thought about the Masons meeting scheduled for later that night. I did not want to go, I would rather just get on the road to Indiana. I was thinking that maybe I should stop by Indianapolis and talk with Susan Bayh—maybe she could explain some of her husband's actions. I also needed to check on Craigslist to see if the *Post* reporter had responded to my note.

I took a break to drink a soda and to relax. I thought about the Mason meeting of the night before. It seemed really strange that they would begin my training the way they did. I wondered if they taught all new Masons the same things in the beginning. I got on my computer and checked Craigslist under the "Furniture for Sale" category.

I found an ad titled, "Antique oak chest with cedar lining for sale." It said, "If you want to discuss terms, meet tomorrow at the Lincoln Memorial around noon and wear a baseball cap."

Good, I thought, this reporter wants to learn more, but I have to think about how much I want to tell her. I finished packing and got some dinner before my next training session with the Masons.

Jonathan was standing at the front entrance, when I arrived a few minutes early. "Hi, Adam. How did you like the training last night?"

"What training?"

"Nice, good job. He laughed. "That was a little test to see if you would talk about the training, not really though, but I appreciate your response. Adam, I am sure you have lots of questions about all of this and I'm sure you realize there is more to this than the obvious. There are people in this organization who want you to be part of a very important mission—maybe one of the most important missions in human history. The information you are being taught is very important. Please pay close attention. I know you are a specialist and that details are natural for you, but your life might someday depend on your retaining this information. I will tell you more when the time is appropriate. Enjoy your evening." He turned and walked away.

I thought to myself that I had known these guys had something in mind when I was brought in. Cheney must have recommended me for some reason; it all started with him. I wondered where ole Cheney was. Probably having a good time.

"Welcome back, Adam," a voice said from behind me. I turned and saw Simon and the others.

"Hi, how are you?" I said.

"I'm great," Simon said. "The others are ready to continue your training. Do you have any questions from last night? Let's go inside and get started. We have a lot to cover."

"No, no questions. It is all very fascinating."

"Are you religious, Adam? Or did you have a religious upbringing?"

"No, I am not religious. My mom grew up Catholic and wanted us to be raised Catholic. My dad was a Lutheran."

"What do you think is the single most important event to have happened to mankind, as the foundation of Western and Middle Eastern religion?"

"I don't know—maybe the building of Jerusalem?"

Matthew interjected, "How about when God gave Moses the Ten Commandments?"

I slowly responded, "Yes, I would say that was an important milestone. The premise of the Ten Commandments has been handed down through generations upon generations. People readily accept them as coming from God himself."

"Indeed," Peter said. "What if we could disprove the existence of or authenticate the tablets known as the Ten Commandments? How many people have actually seen the tablets? Or do people simply believe by faith on their existence, because it has been passed down by word of mouth for the last 3300 years? How about if we could find Atlantis?"

"Well," I said, "It would be a pretty big discovery to find either."

"Exactly. It might change the way people view the world, history, and religion," Peter said. "They might be found together."

My next question seemed obvious. "Do you know where the tablets or the Ark of the Covenant are?" I asked. "Do you think the Ark is on Atlantis? Isn't Atlantis, if it was a real place, destroyed and underwater?"

"We believe," Simon responded, "as we have for centuries, since the First Crusade, that the Brotherhood of Muhammad has them and has been keeping their location secret from the world. We believe that there may be no tablets with the inscription of the Ten Commandments and that the Ark of the Covenant may actually house something else. There is documentation that anyone who goes near the Ark dies a painful death from their skin falling off. We believe this is consistent with radiation poisoning."

"Radiation poisoning—where would that come from?"

All the Masons looked intently at me. "We are not sure; that is what we want to find out."

I stopped for a moment, turned, and walked away from where we were standing. All kinds of thoughts rushed through my mind, as I tried to review my history, information and beliefs. I could not put anything together; it was like my brain was on information overload. But I realized that these guys wanted me for something special, and so now they had my interest. I could sense that this was extremely important to them and thought that I might be able to use it to my advantage somehow.

Peter asked, "Would you like to start where we left off last night?"

"That would be great."

THE EXCHANGE

Andrew started first. "There is a man named Zahi Hawass. He was the Chief of Egyptian Antiquities. It has been reported from our sources that one of Hawass's teams discovered the location of the Hall of Records. In 1993, Hawass was fired from his position because a very valuable artifact was stolen from the Giza Plateau. It was never revealed to the public what the artifact was. Our sources tell us the artifact was the Ark of the Covenant. We have had emissaries in Egypt for centuries trying to find out the location of the Ark and steal it. We want you to exchange with Hawass, who is believed to be either a member of the Brotherhood or an associate, and who knows where the Ark is located. Hawass is coming to the United States in two weeks for a conference in Chicago. We want you to be ready to make the exchange at that time."

I thought it was elementary of me to question how they knew about the exchange process or that I was capable of doing it. I had to assume that they knew at least as much as I did about CD and probably a lot more.

"Well, this is not exactly the same as you asking me to hold office in your local chapter. I will need a little time to process this."

Simon spoke: "Adam, you are uniquely qualified man, in a unique place at a key time. Think of the revelations for humanity of such a discovery. I am sure you will make the decision that is best for all. Why don't you take a few days to think it over."

"I will." I left the men in the room where we had had our conversation and walked home. I had so many things on my mind.

Bayh Goes for a Walk

The next morning I was supposed to meet Elizabeth Broadwater from the *Washington Post* at the Lincoln Memorial, but I did not want to reveal myself to her yet. It was too risky. I wrote her another note: "Follow lead from sender of the first note. More later." I then posted another ad on Craigslist to her: "Check behind the information sign at the front of the exhibit." I would stop by there before visiting my family. I finished packing my things for Indiana and Cabo.

I drove down to the Lincoln Memorial, but since there were an inordinate amount of police in the area the streets to the Jefferson Memorial were blocked off. I parked the car and had to walk a couple of blocks to get to there and then placed the note. I figured it would take me about twelve hours to get to Indiana. I wanted to stop by Indianapolis and talk with Susan Bayh first, to see if she knew anything about why her husband would have gone to CD. My idea was I wanted to make sure I did not drive out of my way and go through Indy, so that it appeared that I was simply on my way to Fort Wayne. I could never know when someone was monitoring the path I was taking.

I arrived into Indianapolis about 10pm. I had planned it that way, as I did not want anyone to see me driving to the Bayh's private home. Susan had given me her address when I had met her in Washington and she had told me to stop by anytime to say hello. I wanted to talk with her to find out if she had told Evan anything which would have prompted him to go to CD. The Bayh house was gated. I rang the intercom from the front gate. Susan answered the phone for the intercom. "Yes, who is it?"

"Susan, this is a friend," I said. "I met you a short time ago in

Washington. A friend of mine told me to stop by and said you were on a committee to save the 'Indri.' There was a pause on the other end. I could hear her breathing, but nothing was being said. The buzzer opened the front gate and I walked up to the door. As I approached, it I saw Susan standing next to the door. I said, "Hi, Susan. I hope I didn't frighten you."

"I actually did not think I would ever hear the word 'Indri' again."

"Really? What is going on?"

Susan closed the door and we walked over to an adjacent room with two couches. "Here, sit down. Can I get you anything?"

"No, thanks. I can only stay a short time."

We sat down facing each other. "Wow, you look a lot different than the last time we were together," Susan said with a surprised look on her face.

"Yes, I know. I have been with this body for a while and plan to keep it that way," I said.

Susan lowered her head and looked at her hands, then spoke. "I talked with Evan a couple of days ago about what you told me to tell him. He did not believe it. He told me he was supposed to know of all secret ops programs going on, but had never heard of such a thing. He was confused, though, because he never would have voted for the SIC to continue funding in Afghanistan. All he wanted to do was get out of Washington and come home. He knew Washington is full of corruption, self-serving people, and gridlock from very opposing views."

"Evan went to the place where the exchanges are done and caused quite a stir. My boss called me to try to find out why he would go there. Why do you think he went there?"

"Well, I don't know for sure. He told me he would try to get some answers, but I don't know what his plan is."

"I understand. You have to get a hold of him and tell him to not do anything out of the ordinary until I am able to expose this program. Now is not the time and I am not ready yet—do you understand?"

"Yes, yes. I'll call him tomorrow and talk with him. Should I tell him anything about you—your name, or who you are, that you stopped by?"

"Yes, tell him I stopped by and talked with you. Tell him not to ask any more questions, especially about Crystal Discovery."

Susan nodded her head. "Okay, I will do that. I'm worried about him. He sounded so confused and upset with himself about the vote. He could not figure out how he could have voted that way, as well as how some new technology or black ops program got by him."

"Great. Tell him that after this news story breaks, I will get in contact with both of you to explain more. He can then bring the entire situation before the Senate and the American people. I have to go. Susan, it was great to see you again. Be careful. Do not put anything past these people: there are major stakes at risk here."

"Oh, I can only imagine—or should say I *can't* imagine how far some people will go to get what they want."

"Goodnight, Susan," I said as I walked out the front door and into the darkness.

"Goodnight, Mr. Lemur." I chuckled to myself as I walked back to my car to drive to Fort Wayne.

I drove into Fort Wayne at about 1am and called Miriam. "Miriam, I am sorry for calling so late, but I did not want you to worry. Do you mind if I come by?"

Miriam, groggy from being asleep, "What's going on? Are you okay? Why do you want to come by so late? Sure, come over. Do you want me to make some coffee?"

I laughed into the phone, "No, no coffee thank you. I have a lot going on, but I have a couple of days and wanted to see you and the kids. Do you mind?"

"No, I don't mind. I would love to see you and I'm sure the kids would enjoy seeing you, too. We'll have to come up with something to tell them in the morning,"

"Okay, I'll see you in a couple of minutes." With that I hung up the phone.

When Miriam answered the front door, her hair was messed up, she was wearing a robe and she looked tired, but to me she looked beautiful. It was as if I had come home from a long time away. I gave her a big hug and kissed her on the cheek.

"Why are you here so late?"

"I only have a few days, then I am off again."

"Well, come in and put your bag in my bedroom. We can tell the kids you came in unexpectedly overnight. I'll get up before them so they won't know you slept in my room. Now, come to bed and we can talk about it tomorrow."

Miriam led the way to her bedroom and I followed. I put my bag down and watched her take off her robe, which exposed her beautiful, naked body. She looked gorgeous. I felt like I was coming home from a long tour abroad and we were reuniting as we had many times before. I took off my clothes and slid between the sheets next to her. In the darkness of the room, there was nothing to tell us that this wasn't just like the old days, nothing to tell us we weren't the same people from years ago, doing what we would always do when I returned home. My hands were soon exploring and touching Miriam's soft, warm body all over. I listened to her sounds of pleasure as I caressed and touched her in places she had not been touched in a long time. We kissed and kissed like teenagers in the back seat of car parked on lover's lane. We were soon making love, sweating and feeling so in the moment. When we finally relaxed, we laughed and she said, "Wow, you feel so young. I didn't want to stop, you felt so good."

"Yes, well, the years have been kind to me." I laughed. "I am so happy to be home, here with you and the kids. I don't ever want to leave you guys again."

"But you said you can only spend a few days. Do you have to leave?"

"Yes, I was only dreaming, or trying to wake up from the bad dream my life has taken. But for now, I am here with you and only you. I want to hold you all night." We fell asleep. I remember Miriam getting up in the morning to get the kids off to school, while I stayed in bed to get a few more hours of sleep.

After Miriam got Emma and Justin off to school she came back into the bedroom. "The kids asked me why your car was parked in the driveway when they got up this morning," Miriam told me with a grin on her face.

"What did you tell them?" I asked with a smile, as I rolled over to pull her down on top of me. She reached down to kiss me with her soft, full lips.

"I told them you just came in to ravage my body and have sex with me."

We both laughed. "You feel so great to hold. I'm glad to be here."

"I'm glad you're here, too. I don't want you to leave. I told the kids you came in late on business and were asleep in my room, and that they were not to disturb you. I was up before them, so they were none the wiser. How are things with you?"

"There are a lot of things going on. For one, I joined the Masons in Washington."

"The Masons! You mean those guys who drive around in little cars at parades with funny little hats with tassels on them?"

"Well, not exactly. These guys have very old ties to a group of Christian soldiers during the Crusades. You know, like in the movie, *National Treasure.*

"Uh oh."

"Yes, well, they are tied to the exchange organization. They want me to go undercover in Egypt and exchange into a famous Egyptian archeologist."

"Why on earth would they want you to do that?"

"They want me to find the Ark of the Covenant, Atlantis, or something. They are not being exactly clear."

"Really, I thought that was all myth and legend. Do they really exist?"

"Yes. These guys believe and have obviously convinced Crystal Discovery to exchange me into this Egyptian guy so I can go find them. This is extremely serious to them. I don't want to do it, though, so I am going to refuse. I don't want to exchange again, or go to Egypt on any treasure hunt where I could get killed. I want to stay with you guys and live out a boring life. And, I wanted to expose this tragedy of our political system. Let's take the kids to the Family Fun Center, drive the go karts and play video games tonight. Then we can get a pizza or something, and just have some fun with them."

"Well, that sounds like fun. I am sure the kids would love it."

"Great, it can be a carefree, fun evening for all of us—like old times." Miriam and I were able to relish each other's company until the kids came home from school. Then we had to act a bit more serious and reserved.

When Emma and Justin came through the front door, they politely said, "Hello Adam."

"Hi guys. How was school today?"

"Oh, school was the same as always," Justin responded and Emma nodded in agreement.

"How would you like to go out and have fun to tonight, and maybe get a pizza!"

"Great—no homework!" Justin exclaimed.

"No, after your homework is done we can go."

We had a great evening out racing go karts, playing video games, and eating pizza. We were a family again—well, almost. They did not know I was their supposedly dead father. But maybe someday I would be able to tell them. Miriam, the kids, and I all came home tired. The kids went to bed. Miriam turned on the television to watch the news and relax. I sat down on the couch next to her.

I was astonished to see a news alert about Senator Evan Bayh. The news reported that Bayh's body had been found yesterday morning near the pond at the Jefferson Memorial in Washington, DC. He apparently had committed suicide after a short walk. The cause of death was a gunshot wound to the head: he left a suicide note. They said that according to coworkers, he had been distraught over his recent vote on a key SIC bill and his resignation from public office. I could not believe it. He did not kill himself or leave a suicide note. He was murdered. It took them such a short time to set up his death, after he visited CD just the morning before. Those who are in control will go to any length, including killing a standing Senator, to protect their interests. I felt like my life was worth very little if they were willing do that. I had to protect myself by making myself valuable, or at least by making it painful for them if they tried to kill me.

I said to Miriam, "I just met with that Senator's wife in Indianapolis before coming to Fort Wayne. She apparently did not know he had died yet. God, I feel terrible. I thought that those sons-of-a-bitches might do something like this. Damn it, I should have gotten him out of Washington and had him hide. Now he is dead. Did you ever create that email address I asked you to?"

"Yes, I have it written down in my address book and I already sent you an email."

"Okay, good. I haven't emailed the video to anyone yet. But I need to do that to protect us. I will get my laptop and do that right away, so others have a copy. I'll send it to Susan Welday, the reporter in San Francisco, and to Susan Bayh. I'll give you a hard copy of the video to hide, and I'm also going to make a copy of it for Elizabeth Broadwater, the *Washington Post* reporter. I don't want to reveal to her my identity right now, but I will later when the time is right. PJ also needs a copy. I will mail her one. I'll create a website and a separate email account, which will release all of the information on a date in the future, in case something happens to me. I feel this whole thing is going to implode very soon," I said in a worried tone. "I need to leave the day after tomorrow. I don't want to spend a lot of time here in case I raise suspicion about my intentions here or bring anyone snooping around."

Miriam looked at me with a sad look on her face, "Oh, you just got here. I don't want you to ever go."

"I know. This will all be over soon." We went to bed and wrapped ourselves around each other and stayed that way most of the night. I got up before the kids woke up and moved to the couch so they would think I had slept in there all night.

The next morning after the kids left for school, Miriam and I decided to spend the day together—something we hadn't done in years. Miriam called in sick for work and we got in the car and headed to northern Indiana, to the Chain-O-Lakes State Park. It's a group of lakes in a heavily wooded area, with lots of secluded spots and a few mom and pop restaurants. The drive took about an hour. We enjoyed the bright, sunny day and the relaxing green scenery of Indiana farmland. We found a lookout point over one of the lakes to sit and talk.

Miriam spoke softly and directly, she seemed troubled. "I need to talk with you about something that has been bothering me."

"Yes, what is it?"

"Since you were here last my mind has been very busy, running through many scenarios and situations. I am worried about how things will be between us."

"What do you mean?"

"Well, you are half my age—or at least your body and appearance are. How are we going to deal with that? What do we tell people? That you are a distant visiting cousin or something? What do we tell the kids? And what is going to happen in the future when we get older? I am 23 years older than you. I do not think you will want to be with an old woman when you are in your prime."

I looked directly into Miriam's eyes. "Babe, we have to take this one step at a time. I love you no differently than I did when I was in a different body. I am the man you married, you are the woman I married, and our children need us."

"But things have gotten so complicated and confusing," she replied.

"The world is indeed complicated. I am sure many generations of couples have said that to each other. We simply have to keep breathing, keep learning, and keep trying to do the right thing. I know I want to be with you. You are a wonderful beautiful woman."

"Yes, and when I close my eyes, I forget for a second that this whole awful thing has happened and I feel I am just with you: my Frank."

"Exactly, I am the same person, just in a different body."

"And, a gorgeous young body, I might add. I bet all the young girls find you quite sexy and appealing. I am a middle-aged woman and quickly getting older. You are more like the kids' older brother than my husband. I don't know what to feel. I have had dreams in which I've been exchanged to a younger body, too, and we've been given a second chance to go through life. Part of me wants to exchange like you did and be a younger, prettier woman."

"Miriam, who knows what the future holds? Maybe that will be possible with technology when all this gets sorted out. Maybe we can have younger clones we can exchange with—who knows? Or maybe they will figure out how to stop aging. I have done some reading and I've heard of a new concept called 'singularity,' which is a time in our future when death could be cured liked a disease. We simply have to keep trying every day to do our best and live for what we can do now."

She put her head down and became sad. "Yes, but I will be dead long before you die. Then what? Where will your life be then? You will want someone your own age or younger then. You should be with someone your own age."

"I am with someone my own age: you. You are my own age. You are who I want to be with. And maybe before this is over, I'll exchange into someone who is more my emotional age, the same as you."

"Are you crazy? Why would you want to be in an old man's body closer to death? I would do anything to be younger again, to be like you, and to have it all to do over again. Everyone wants that. I just don't think our future is going to be easy. We won't be able to be a normal family or to have a normal marriage. It is all too weird, like something out of a sci-fi movie. I think you really need to consider what you want to get back into."

"I know exactly what I am getting myself back into: my family, you and the children. I have never been dead. I am here, now, the same man I have always been. Well, I know more and have seen too much in my lives, but I am indeed the same person you married and the same person who is a father to our children."

"Frank, it is a fantasy. You are living a fantasy. What are we going to tell the children? And if you tell them, what are they going to tell their friends? What are they going to think? I think it is too much for them to handle. It's bizarre, freakish," Miriam said cold and bluntly.

"Well, soon the whole world will know what has been going on. The whole world will know what has been going on in my life. Don't you think our children should hear it from me or from the two of us first? Or maybe, before they find out, we should take them away from here, someplace where the world is less prying."

"Frank, I do not know what is going to happen. I am just not convinced that it is truly you inside this other person's body. How could it be? You are not Frank anymore. You are someone else. You are different. Too much has happened."

"What are you trying to say? What do you want me to do, to feel?"

She looked at me with a sad, worried look on her face. "I can't tell you what to feel. I don't know how I feel about all that has happened and who you are now. The children are going to be freaked out; it is not healthy for them. I want to protect them and let them be normal kids. I just want you to think about all this and consider what is best."

"Miriam, I understand that all this must be a nightmare for you. I have thought about it for the last several years, before I ever came back here. I thought it was important for you to know the truth, about what happened to me and where I was. I thought that maybe there could be a chance for us. I realized there were going to be difficulties—there always are. We will overcome them together as we always have," I said emphatically.

"I don't know. I just don't know," Miriam said with her head hung down.

We drove to a nearby restaurant and had a quiet lunch overlooking the lake. After lunch we drove back to Fort Wayne to pick up the kids after school. We did not talk a lot during the drive back to Miriam's house. As we got close to her house, Miriam said, "Frank, maybe it would be a good idea if you were not here when the kids get home from school. Let's just take some time and try to figure this all out so we're sure we are doing the right thing. I feel so confused and hurt, like I am losing you all over again."

"Miriam, I'm sorry," I said softly. "I didn't want to hurt you by telling you all this. I want what's best for you and for the kids. I will leave and keep in touch. I am sure you will hear more in the news when all this breaks. I will try to keep you out of it."

"I am sure time will help us understand all this." After we arrived home, I picked up my things and put them in the car.

I stood by the front door and said, "Well, I guess this is goodbye for awhile. I can't tell you when I will be back again. I promise I will let you know as soon as I can. I will keep in touch." I extended my arms out for Miriam to come to me so I could hold her. She came to me and we kissed and hugged.

She began to cry. "Frank, this is so difficult. My heart and soul are being ripped out of my body. I don't know what to do. I feel great when you are here, but when you are gone I feel lost and vulnerable. I wish I knew what I was supposed to do," Miriam said through the tears falling down her face.

"We'll sort it out. I still want to be your knight in shining armor. Say hi, to the kids for me, and tell them I had a great time with them last night." With that, I left and drove off to the airport. I bought a ticket there and headed to Cabo San Lucas, Mexico, to meet PJ. I was so torn to leave Miriam—it was so confusing. PJ was then waiting for me and I wanted to be excited for her when she arrived.

PJ in Mexico

After traveling all night, I arrived in Cabo the next morning around noon. I did not even have a hotel room reserved. I wanted to stay close to downtown, because that was where the cruise ships come in. I decided to on a Mexican hotel, rather than American, to try to remain a little more off the radar. I found the Pueblo Bonito Sunset Beach Resort and Spa. It was not exactly downtown, but only short walk away. It was beautiful here and so warm and nice, exactly what I needed after everything that had happened. It would be great to live out my years here, escape and hide from everyone, except all CD had to do was search for my GPS and they would know exactly where I was. AC Dexter did tell me to take some time off, so there should be no suspicion for me being here in a resort town. It was Friday and PJ's ship should arrive the next morning at eight. I was excited to see her and find out how she had been doing. All I wanted to do was relax by the pool and catch up on my sleep.

On Saturday, I got up early and went down to the cruise ship dock for coffee and a bagel. I wanted to be there when everyone got off the ship, so I wouldn't miss her. We hadn't made any formal plans to meet. I sat on a bench close to the pier disembarking area with a Starbucks triple-shot mocha. I was there until almost nine. It seemed a majority of people were already off and only a trickle were still leaving the ship. Then I saw her pop out of the ship, like a Disney character from behind a curtain on stage, with a big smile on her face. She wore dark shorts and a light blue tank top, and had a great tan. I wanted to run down the pier and hug her. It was funny, those feelings I was having. It was as if at times, my body took over and washed me with excitement and carefree feelings, I loved it! I sat there and did not move. I wanted her to see me before I got up. It was nice just to sit there and watch her search for me. She was looking and looking all around. When she reached the top of the pier, near the boardwalk, she saw me. I had a huge smile on my face. She ran over and as I stood up threw her arms around me. We hugged for minutes, slowly pulled our faces back from each other and quietly looked into each other's eyes. I was so happy to have her in my arms again. I was so relieved to see the joy and life in her eyes, as if I was looking all the way down into her heart. She was such a sincere, open, emotional person. I felt such intense care and love for her. It was magical. We slowly moved our lips closer and closer together, without saying a word. Our lips touched ever so gently and softly. We still had our eyes open and locked on each other. After a few seconds, we closed our eyes and kissed long and intensely. The feeling of her body next to mine, the warmth and softness of her full beautiful lips were almost indescribable. The sun was shining and I could feel its heat, there was so much energy between us, you could almost see the sparks. I pulled a few inches away from her face and said, "I am so happy to see you."

PJ smiled, "I missed you so much you have no idea. I would lay awake in my bunk and wonder where you were and what you were doing. I'm glad you are here now!"

"Are you hungry, what would you like to do?"

"Where are you staying? What do you want to do?"

"I'm at a nice resort hotel a few minutes away, I have no plans. I thought we could just relax by the beach, go snorkeling, whale watching, para-sailing, or whatever. I just want to be with you. I want to hear all about your travels on the cruise ship." We turned and began to walk down the boardwalk of shops and restaurants. We held hands like young lovers who could not get close enough to each other. The ones many people are disgusted to see, because they cannot keep their hands off each other, kissing, touching, and holding hands!

PJ seemed to contemplate for a few minutes, then said, "Let's just walk around for awhile. I feel like a hamster being let out of his cage, I want to stretch my legs."

I laughed. "Yeah, I bet. It's a long time to be cooped up on a ship. How do you like it, working on the ship?"

"It's great. Disney is awesome, the people are awesome, the food is awesome, my friends are awesome!"

"Wow! Sounds pretty AWESOME."

PJ looked at me and burst into laughter, "Well, what do you expect, being locked up on that big thing, with a bunch of bratty kids running all around trying to drown each other in the pool. Oh, my bed sucks, I can tell you that, but I am on the top bunk of three fortunately! The people in the lower bunks always have to deal with people in the upper ones using their bunks to step up to get into theirs. Actually, Adam, I really like it. Thank you for helping me get the job and keeping me safe. How are things with you? Are you getting any closer to exposing what these people have been doing?"

"I really am not sure. I think so. This is so big, so complex. It scares the shit out of me. And I am still afraid for you. We have to be very careful. I still need you to stay with Disney until I can expose this monster. I sent you an email with an attached video of me explaining everything in case something happens to me. You can send it to news media if you don't hear from me in three months. Like we have talked about before." I continued, "Just before I came here I was basically forced to exchange again."

PJ interrupted, "Really?"

"Yes, with a senator who was voting on a key piece of legislation. Then after I exchanged back to Adam, they killed him. They also killed another senator who exchanged with ex-vice president, Dick Cheney. There are a lot of people dying at the hands of very self-centered, egotistical, power-hungry maniacs. I have been asked by the Masons, who are somehow tied to Crystal Discovery, to exchange into some Egyptologist. They want me to find a lost or stolen ancient artifact."

"What do we do now? What is the plan?"

"I'm trying to set up a journalist with the *Washington Post* to blow the lid off this. I want to try to make it so the leak is not tied back to me. Otherwise, they will kill me. I also don't want them to realize you're alive. I'm in the process of feeding information to the reporter at the *Post* for her to investigate. She'll have to learn to trust me and the information I am giving her. When she trusts me, I will give her all she needs for her to print the story."

I began to jump and skip along the boardwalk. "But, hey. What does that have to do with us having a good time down here in Mexico? You know what they say, what happens in Mexico stays in Mexico!"

PJ looked at me weirdly, like I was high on drugs. "I have never heard that expression."

"Okay, let's go on a whale watching trip. You go out in these small rubber boats and go really fast to try to find the whales, then you stop and the whales come right up to your boat! It sounds really fun."

"Sure, sounds wonderful."

We went down to the pier area and found the whale watching tours. They left every hour and were about ready to leave when we signed up. There were two other couples on our tour. The operators gave us life vests and snorkel gear. Apparently we were allowed next to the whales once we found them. The boat ride out to where the whales would normally hang out was quite exciting, with waves breaking over the front of the small rubber craft. We probably went about thirty miles per hour. Our guide, Anton, a dark-skinned Mexican guy who spoke broken English, pointed ahead and we could periodically see humpback whales breaching in the distance. Anton told us to get ready and slowed the boat as we got closer, then stopped so we just floated with the current and waves. It took about a half an hour for three or four large whales to come within a few feet of our boat. Anton said if we wanted to, we could swim with our masks and snorkel. PJ and I jumped in. The other women said they were afraid, but still got in the water as well. I was amazed at seeing the huge creatures right next to us. It was like swimming next to a moving submarine. The whales would sometimes swim directly at us, like they were excited to see us. I took my life vest off and just kept my mask and snorkel on. I then dove down as far as I could on one breath to get as close to the whales as possible. I had never experienced anything like it. I felt so happy. I looked down and saw the whales and looked up and saw PJ. After a couple of minutes, PJ took off her life vest and also dove down with me to play with the whales. Life seemed so simple, so peaceful, far from the ugliness of Washington, DC and the people there. As I was diving, it occurred to me that while I was underwater my GPS could not be tracked. I had never really thought about it before. There were places the GPS signal could not get in or out of, like underwater, in large buildings, deep inside a ship or submarine. It got me thinking. How could I use this notion to keep them from knowing where I was on a more permanent basis? I was lost in thought for a moment, until the next thing I knew, PJ pulled my mask off my face as a joke and swam off. I chased her back to the surface, where she was laughing uncontrollably.

"What were you thinking down there? How to be a whale?"

"No. I was just lost in thought for a moment, don't you ever do that?"

"Of course. I do it all the time, until someone smacks me and says, hey snap out of it. Then, I realize I was being goofy weird, like staring off into space or something."

The guide called us back to the boat, as our tour time had ended. It had been so much fun to be out on the water, with PJ, the sun, the whales, a perfect day. After we got back to the dock we walked to my hotel room to clean up.

"God, I can't wait to take a real shower, not one in a tiny little cubicle, where everyone else is yelling at you to hurry up. I am going to take a long hot shower."

"Sounds great, maybe I will join you?"

"Join me. Where in the shower?" PJ asked, looking a bit astonished.

"Yes, in the shower. What do you think of that?"

"Well, every girl needs a little shower boy to wash her back." We both laughed and then quietly walked on a beautiful red brick street the rest of the way to the hotel.

When we got in the hotel room, PJ looked at me in a seductive, playful manner and said, "I will be in the shower, if you need me." Then she winked at me. She had this amazing playful part of her personality, which was so alluring, even in a difficult if not dangerous situation. I guess she has had most of her life to practice, trying to make the best of bad situations. I imagine we all have coping mechanisms within us to deal with situations that befall us, pain, torment, abuse, poor living situations, hopelessness, despair. For me, I have always had hope to get me through, hope I can and will survive. I have always had someone or something that gave me a purpose to live. I couldn't imagine not having that, not having someone in the world I wanted to see again, be with again: it must feel so lonely. I laid back on one of the beds and continued to think about my life and how to keep PJ away from any more danger or torment. I really admired her for her courage and patience. I was not sure I had that much when I was her age.

My mind wandered back to Miriam. She seemed so distant when I had left, almost angry at me, pushing me away. I could understand why she would; this was confusing. I was sure she did not see me as the man she was once married to, and I was sure she was afraid for the children. What were they supposed to think? How could they comprehend all this? It was probably better they never know and just let them hold fond memories of their father. Maybe it was best I never go back there, maybe it was wrong of me to go back there in the first place. It really was too much for anyone to handle; it was even difficult for me to think about. It all seemed like a dream, not reality. But, I was here. PJ was here.

I had always tried to live in the present, take stock and realize I am still breathing; still alive. Interesting, being alive. I have had to really think about what it meant to be alive. It's a basic human instinct to fear death and want to be alive. People throughout history have done terrible horrific things to one another in an attempt to stay alive, prolong life, and avoid death. But, inevitably we all must die, at least up until now. I wondered what humanity would gain, or individuals would truly capitalize on by living multiple lives? I see most people wasting away their lives, the only lives they have been given. What would people do it they had to live multiple lives to live? Would things get worse? Would they get more complacent and lazy because they would figure, well, I will put it off until another life? Or get fat and not care, because they would know they could simply exchange into someone else later? How many people would actually take advantage of having a second, or third, or fourth life? What good have I done? I was just a government puppet. I don't even have control over my own life. I truly do not have freedom. Maybe we all are a slave to one thing or another and it doesn't matter how many lives we have, we will not overcome that barrier. I just want to find peace, a smile, contentment, and the comfort of knowing those I love are safe and not going to be hurt.

PJ came out of the bathroom after an hour or so, and awakened me from my daydreaming thoughts. She said, "Hey, what happened to my shower boy, he never showed up?"

"Oh, sorry my mistress, I forgot," I replied indignantly with a hint of playfulness.

She came over and slowly sat down beside me on the bed, wearing only a towel around her body and another one around her hair. "How was your shower?"

"Awesome, really warm and long and relaxing. I loved it. Now, where are you taking me for dinner?"

I responded as if I were offended, "Wow, you are high maintenance." I changed my tone to soft and loving, "Well, not really. I would love to take you to dinner and look at you from across the table all night." I loved the banter between us. It was so fun and endearing. She made me feel like we were alone in the world and all our cares were gone. I really felt twenty-three again when I was near her. That's what life was about, happiness and joy, laughter and fun, being with some-one you enjoyed being around.

"I want to have some good ole Mexican food, tacos and beans. I am tired of all the seafood they have on the ship and it's all so formal at all the meals. Let's do casual."

"Casual is good: shorts, t-shirts, and sandals, how is that?" I said.

"Cool, it will only take me a second to get ready." I watched her disappear once again into the bathroom. I retreated again to my thoughts. Wow, this girl and I really seemed to be on the same wavelength. Was that possible? How could that be? I was so much older. Maybe she did not realize it and forgotten my real age, and just saw a young guy in front of her. Or maybe it was just me, maybe I saw this young girl in front of me and forgot I was much older than her? Whatever it was, it felt wonderful and I didn't want it to stop.

She again snapped me out of my thoughts, "You ready? Let's go." She looked great, so simple, so innocent, so happy, just wearing a light grey t-shirt, short black shorts, and flip-flops. I grabbed her hand and pulled her toward me so we could walk holding hands, like a young couple in love, swinging our hands back and forth.

We found this great little hole in the wall Cuban restaurant that served chips and tacos. It had a nice courtyard in the back, where we were all alone sitting on black wire mesh chairs. After we finished our simple meal, I looked over and gazed at PJ as she was finishing her last bite of refried beans.

She noticed my stare and asked, "What are you thinking about?"

"Ah, I was thinking how happy I am here with you. This is so peace-ful. I don't want to go back."

"Then don't. Stay with me or we can go somewhere together."

"PJ, you know that is not possible. I have this leash called a GPS attached to my fucking brain, they track me like I'm a damn dog."

"Ah, I forget about that thing," she said with resignation.

"Yeah well, I never forget. You know, it's funny. On one hand I'm so grateful to have been saved from death and to be alive, and on the other I feel the life I have been given is not my own. Without Crystal Discovery I would never have met you," I said looking down at my hands on the table, but with a warm affectionate tone.

PJ leaned over and put her hands on top of mine. "Adam, we will get through this. I know it sounds cliche, but I feel it."

I looked up at her and smiled, "Hey, who is supposed to be the older, more mature person here, me or you?"

"Me, of course"

We both laughed. I looked over at her with a more serious expression and her eyes met mine. "You know, I went back to see my family. I told my wife all about what happened to me and about you."

"Really? What did she say? How did she react?"

"Well, she didn't believe it at first, then she thought it was wonderful. We didn't tell the kids. It was so great to see them. They are getting so big. Then, I went back a second time to check on them, right before I came here. The second time she changed her tone. I think she questioned my intentions. She asked me to leave. I don't think she wanted me to come back again. I guess it was all too confusing for her."

"What did you think when you saw her? What did you feel?"

I looked intensely into PJ's beautiful grey/blue eyes, "At first it felt like I had hardly ever been gone, like I had returned home from a long mission. But looking in the mirror reminded me that was not quite true. It would have been one thing had I been returning home forever, never leaving again, and was not being manipulated. But she knew what my life had always been about, and it was not about being at home, as a family. She saw a twenty-three-year-old boy in front of her and couldn't connect the dots that it was her husband from yester-year."

PJ asked, almost in a fearful voice, "Do you still want to be her husband?"

Squeezing her hands, "I thought I did when I went back and saw her and the kids. But, I think I realized her husband was killed in that plane crash in Afghanistan. Life is an evolution. I am not the same person I was the last time she saw me, the man she married a long time ago. We are light years apart. I am here with you and you are part of my life now. My family will always be a part of me and I need to do whatever I can to help them and protect them. I am not sure they want me to be around, to be a part of their everyday life. It would be too confusing."

"Do you think you will ever get married again?"

I laughed "Hmmm, I wonder what the marriage laws are on that? I guess we vow to stay together until death do us part. So, if the body that vowed dies, I guess that duty is fulfilled. Interesting thought, maybe you get one marriage per body? What do you think?"

PJ responded with a frown on her face, "Well, I am never getting married, it all seems such a mystery; commitment."

"I see. A free spirit, right?"

"Yup, that's right!" She got out of her chair, "Now, let's get out of here; too much serious talk. Let's walk down by the pier, then let's go to sleep. I am looking forward to sleeping on a soft, big normal bed, not a hard small bunk bed."

"Now, that sounds like a great plan."

We walked quietly hand in hand, taking moments to look over at one another from time to time without saying a word, sometimes with a squeeze of each other's hand.

Back in the hotel room, PJ walked over to me sitting on the edge of the bed, still dressed in shorts and t-shirt. She stood in front of me and slowly pulled her t-shirt off, exposing her smooth teenage tanned skin, and bra. She then reached back and undid her bra, letting it fall to the floor. She looked at me with an incredible fragile intensity. Part of her appeared so frail, so innocent, needing to be held and protected and another part of her seemed strong, in control, precise in her thinking, and confident. She reached down and pulled her shorts off and stepped out of her flip-flops, standing there in only her small black lace thong. Last, she untied her hair from a ponytail and let her beautiful long hair flow around her shoulders. She looked incredibly beautiful, such a woman, so feminine. I felt like she wanted to grow up too fast. I think she wanted me to feel like she was the only woman for me. I wanted her so much I ached from head to toe, to hold her, touch her everywhere, to feel her warmth, her skin, to let go of my inhibitions of my many lives and just be a normal twenty-three-year-old boy. But, in my heart I knew I was not a boy, I was a man. I was not sure how I felt, it just did not feel right. Maybe someday it would, maybe when she was older and all this was behind us. I loved her so much. I looked deep into PJ's eyes, in as much of a loving and caring way as I could and said, "Come here," as I pulled her down onto the bed next to me. "PJ, we have a lot of life ahead of us. I want you, need you, and love you."

PJ put her hand over my mouth, "Make love to me, Adam."

I reached up and pulled her hand away from my mouth just enough, so I could speak. "PJ, I can't do this. I don't feel completely right with us together in this way yet. Someday, someday I am sure we will, but not now, not tonight. Lie here with me, be as close to me as you can. "

"Then take me, I am yours," she said with such an intensity I could feel her heart pounding next to me.

I put my hands on both sides of her face and pulled her lips to mine. We kissed so passionately, I was lost in the moment, like time was frozen. It was amazing how much energy our minds and bodies could create, our feelings felt endless. We separated for a moment and I said, "PJ, I am yours. We are together, right here and right now. Let's be happy, we have so much. We have each other." I held her tightly and close to me. We fell asleep in each other's arms.

The next morning I woke up to the sun shining brightly in the window. I rolled over and saw PJ was just waking up. She looked at me and said, "I love you, Adam."

I stroked her hair, looked deep into her eyes, and said, "I love you too, Penny Jo." We gazed at each other for a few moments without moving. Then I said, "Let's get some breakfast I'm starving!"

"Me, too."

We got dressed and went down to the dock area. We found the Cafe Canela, not too far from the Disney Dream, and sat down for coffee and a scone. It was a beautiful day. "I don't want to get on the ship tomorrow. I would rather stay here with you."

"Believe me, there is nothing I would rather do than stay here with you!" We both smiled at each other and drank our coffee.

"What are we going to do today?"

From close behind me, a man's voice, slightly familiar, spoke in a clear, distinct, strong tone. "Are you enjoying your time in Cabo, Adam?" I turned to see where the voice was coming from, my heart sank and began beating very rapidly when I saw who it was.

"Jonathan, what are you doing here? Following me around again, or maybe, hopefully, you are coincidentally here on vacation as well?" I felt instant fear. What was he doing here? Did he know who PJ was? What did he want? Was he here to kill us?

He started to pull a chair out and looked at me. "Mind if I join you?" he asked, as if we had a choice. PJ looked at me. Jonathan turned his attention and looked at PJ. "Hi, I'm Jonathan."

PJ responded without losing a beat. "Hi, I'm Susan. How do you know Adam?"

"Oh, Adam and I are in the same business back in Washington, colleagues you might say," Jonathan replied with a smirk on his face, while taking a few grapes in a bowl off of our table. "How do you two know each other?"

I quickly jumped in, "Susan works on one of the cruise ships. I met her yesterday when she first arrived. We have been hanging out."

Jonathan looked again at PJ. "Nice, I need to meet a playmate while I am down here. Do you have any friends you can set me up with?"

PJ began drinking her coffee again. "My friends are all out doing their own thing today. We have to leave at five tonight."

"Ah, too bad, it could have been fun, the four of us," Jonathan said in an almost evil tone.

"Susan, would you excuse us for a second? I would like a moment to talk with Jonathan alone."

"Sure, I need to go to the ladies room anyway."

"Great." I looked at Jonathan, who wore a sarcastic-looking smile. I moved my face closer to him and said, "Look, I'm not sure what you are doing here, but I'm tired of your little games. I owe you nothing and you have worn out your welcome. You and your strange friends, with your strange ideas and your treasure hunting, are going to have to find someone else to be your pawn because I am not playing along. I have better things to do."

Jonathan was not even slightly moved by what I said. He grabbed another few grapes and began to eat them, then looked intensely at me. "Adam, this body of yours is on temporary loan. It is not really yours, so you will do as you are told. I noticed you went back to visit your family back in Indiana. How are they? I am sure you want to keep them nice and safe and sound, don't you? Did you go back to take a look at them like some sort of peeping Tom or did you tell them all about what has happened to you? No, matter, I don't really care. What is important is you are going to do what we want, or something will happen to them. Maybe you do not realize how important this is to us, to this country, and to humanity. The timeline has changed. We need you back sooner. Hawass is changing his schedule and cutting the conference short. He's leaving to go back to Egypt in three days, so we need to get you in position for the exchange."

"So, if I am hearing you correctly, I have no choice in this?"

"Adam, you have always known this. This is our business. I have tickets for us to leave on the American Airlines two o'clock flight through Dallas to Washington. Enjoy the rest of your morning with you cute new friend and I will see you at the airport." He got up and walked away.

I could not believe this. It was happening again so quickly I didn't have time to make adjustments like I needed to in order to blow up the operation. I only had two days, once I got back to Washington, before I had to exchange with Hawass. I looked up and saw PJ walking toward me from across the cafe. I raised my arm up, to indicate to her it was safe to return. She looked a bit shaken, and said as she walked up to me, "Is everything okay? Who was that guy?"

"He is somehow tied to CD through an organization called the Free Masons. They are group of men that evolved out of the crusades. It was him and his buddies who want me to exchange with the Egyptian guy. Now they are threatening my family if I don't do it. The good thing is that apparently they have no idea who you are." I moved forward and kissed PJ on the lips, then said, "And by the way, that was very quick thinking to give him your fake name. You did not stumble a bit. I knew I loved you for a reason." PJ smiled at me, like a young girl who just got an "A" on her math test. "I need to get you back on that ship. I do not want this guy to see you again. I do not want him to put two and two together, ever." I said sternly. We walked back to the hotel room and started to pack up.

PJ came over and hugged me tightly, "When am I going to see you again?"

"You know I don't know the answer to that. Let's setup a Facebook account like we talked about. I will make a fake account name. Hmmm, let's see, maybe, Johnny Desperado, after the restaurant we ate in last night, and you could be?"

"I will be Angelique Aqua. Part of the name is from 'Beauty and the Beast,' the show that is playing on the ship."

"Great, then we can stay in touch that way."

PJ hugged me again. "I'll miss you. I can't wait until we don't have to leave each other and this is all over."

"Me, too. Me, too. We need to get you back on the ship. I will also email you the video I told you about. Remember, three months. Then go to the news media with it, okay?"

"Yes, yes, I will do it. Just make sure you get back before three months and don't let anything happen to you." PJ picked up her things, stopped before opening the door, and hung her head down. When she turned and looked back I could see tears in her eyes and one tear from each eye rolled down her beautiful face. She blew me a kiss, grinned half-heartedly and walked out the door. I slowly gathered the rest of my things and left for the airport. I could not get the last seconds of PJ's face, with tears in her eyes, out of my head. She had a presence, an energy, which was intoxicating to me. It gave me strength to win the battle against these vicious people.

Treasure Hunt

At the airport, I picked up my ticket and went through customs to the gate. I was sitting in the waiting area when I spotted Jonathan walking toward me. This guy was like a stalker with a GPS tracking device linked to his brain. I do not like his mechanical, emotionless, almost robotic personality. He is not unlike some I have met when they are on a mission, who have no time for patience or emotion, unless of course it is required to elicit something they need.

"Hi, Adam. Glad you could make it," Jonathan said with a sarcastic grin, as he sat down next to me. "You know, it doesn't have to be this way between us. We are both doing what we are told. It is the way the world works, eh?"

I replied matter-of-factly, "Well, even if I have to do what I am told, I don't like being treated like some circus animal who has to act on command by some callous trainer. And you don't seem like you are exactly enthusiastic about what you are doing, coming down here to retrieve someone who is actually needed for a mission."

"Adam, we all have our different roles, and for now, this is mine: making sure you do what is expected of you. I think if you actually knew how significant this mission was, you might act differently. But, you know, as agents we are not privy to the big picture. We are pawns who simply act as cogs in the wheel," Jonathan replied.

We waited quietly, until the flight boarded. Fortunately, we did not have seats next to each other. The flight connected in Dallas and then it was a red-eye onto Washington. I slept most of the way.

Once in Washington, I went home and cleaned up before I had a meeting with AC Dexter. At home, I wondered if I would ever be back here again. The Middle East has always had their age-old rivalries and battles. It is not exactly the safest place in the world. To be a spy, well, that just makes life worth a little less. I hadn't spoken Arabic in a while; any slip of accent could prove fatal or, at minimum, delay my getting back. It could jeopardize my family's safety. How did I get into this mess? And more importantly, how was I going to get out? I did not have time before I see Dexter to contact the *Washington Post* reporter or anyone else to help me uncover this story. It was too dangerous. The pieces were not all in place to blow this whole thing. I needed to find out what this was worth to them, and how my family was doing.

I walked into AC Dexter's office and saw Simon, from my Mason training. He was already seated in front of the desk. He looked over at me. "Good Morning, Adam. I trust you had a good flight."

I did not respond, but simply pulled out the second chair in front of the desk and sat down.

Dexter looked at me and said, "Adam, I am going to get right to this. We really want you to be involved in this project."

I interrupted him. "Is my family safe?"

"Of course they are safe, Adam. We would never do anything to harm them."

"Well, Jonathan implied if I did not cooperate, they would be in jeopardy."

"No, that is not true. You have my word on that Adam, that is not what we are about. You have been a loyal agent for a long time and have amazing technical experience and are a valuable asset to this organization. We feel you have a very special skill set to handle this mission. You have military, tactical and strategic intelligence, and you have experience in the Middle East theater, Arabic, and exchanging that make you very unique. I personally would not have asked you to do this mission if we had someone else with such expertise. I know you are ready to take a less stressful job and maybe retire from field service. What do you think? Are you in?"

I knew he was asking politely because I had no choice. They were not asking. "Of course. It sounds like one of the more interesting missions I have been on. And I get to speak Arabic, which I enjoy. Let's get to it." I wanted them to think on some

level, I really was into this and I did not have to be trailed everywhere I went. Simon spoke up, "Great. Hawass changed his plans for some reason and is supposed to leave tomorrow night for Cairo. We are going to pick him up tonight, when he returns to his hotel room, and bring him here for the exchange. All you have to do is get on that flight tomorrow night. It should give you time to adjust and we will have an operative meet you when you arrive."

Dexter spoke next. "Adam, why don't you spend the day here and relax? Maybe get some sleep. I am sure you are tired. When we have Hawass, I will come and get you."

What Dexter was really saying we wanted to keep an eye on me and they did not want me getting any ideas about jeopardizing the exchange. I understood the subtlety; it was not my first such meeting. I went to sleep in a hotel-like room they had at the facility. At about one the next morning they came to get me. My next exchange began.

After the usual grogginess of an exchange, I prepared to leave. This time, I delayed my trip to the mirror. I really did not want to look at myself. I had already noticed that my shape was much different than Adam's thin, fit, young body. I already had a backache and I had not done anything. My stomach was sticking out over my waist, my legs were thick and heavy, and I had wide feet. I felt old. I finally went to the mirror and saw a dark-skinned man with short-cropped, all white hair. His eyes were set widely apart, thick eyebrows, narrow-set big ears, and a short neck. But he did have nice white teeth. He was a far distance from Adam. Adam was like a close friend; it was weird how I felt about him. I knew he was now me and I him, but yet there still felt a distinction. Would I ever truly be one with him? I did not know; I still felt like I was Frank at the deepest level. I soon found myself on a long, fifteen-hour flight to Cairo. The good news I was on an Emirates

Airlines new Airbus A380, a double-decker airplane, and I had my own first-class suite. One has to try to enjoy the moments in life.

I stared out the window into the darkness as we flew out over the Atlantic Ocean. I could see millions of stars. It is surreal at times, crossing the ocean at night in an airplane; looking out the window there is no real sense of time, distance, or speed, just blackness. At times, when I looked out, I wondered if I was dreaming, instead of flying along at 600 miles per hour. Even the distance the airplane had traveled was unclear. Looking at a map it appeared we had traveled far, but the mind really cannot grasp such scale. If I had walked it, or driven it, or sailed across it over the course of many days, or months, or years, then I would have a reference.

Somehow, though, it always felt a long way from home when I traveled halfway around the world. I felt much the same with each of the lives I have lived. It was all so ethereal. It was supposed to be impossible, but for me, my mind knew it happened. I had woken up many mornings, just like any other human being. But, instead of greeting myself in the morning and saying to myself, "I am so and so," I had to question myself and look in the mirror to see who I had become. I have always felt like Frank Freiberg; it is who I identify with, but he has taken many forms. I thought a moment. I wonder if people would really do this if they had the opportunity and if they understood the consequences of exchanging with other bodies. I wondered if avoiding death and prolonging life was really a recipe for happiness, understanding, and fulfillment. Maybe there was something better after death? Or if everyone had the opportunity to do this, would it simply bring greater chaos to the world? Possibly that is why the government did not want to release this technology to the masses. They understood that would be a huge fight to gain access to the technology. Who would decide who got to use it and who didn't? There would have to be some sort of litmus test to ensure only the smartest minds would be exchanged, and that only those minds preserved so they could contribute something vital to the human race. It would be like taking the SAT or GRE, one would have to achieve a certain score in order to be considered for exchange. Of course, there would still the problem of who would be the new hosts, the young bodies needed for exchange from the old broken-down bodies. What was needed were human clones, bodies without minds for exchange. That would solve the body issue. But it seemed society was not ready for human clones. For the moment, I was just happy to be able to be me, whoever that was. "I think, therefore I am," as the saying goes. I knew I had a family, people I cared about: Miriam, Emma, Justin, and PJ. My family was important to me and I knew I must do what I had to in order to get back to them.

Some turbulence jolted me out of my contemplation. I realized I needed to start learning about my new identity. Emirates had wifi internet access. I needed to do research and read the information CD gave me on Zahi Hawass. I had only a few hours to prepare myself for this mission. How astounding, maybe life altering, the future could be.